WHAT HAVE YOU DONE?

BOOKS BY NICOLE TROPE

Standalone Novels

My Daughter's Secret

The Boy in the Photo

The Nowhere Girl

The Life She Left Behind

The Girl Who Never Came Home

Bring Him Home

The Family Across the Street

The Mother's Fault

The Stepchild

His Other Wife

The Foster Family

The Stay-at-Home Mother

The Truth about the Accident

The Day After the Party

His Double Life

Welcome to West Street

The Therapist

Grace Morton Series

Not a Good Enough Mother

A Mother Always Knows

NICOLE TROPE

WHAT HAVE YOU DONE?

bookouture

Published by Bookouture in 2025

An imprint of Storyfire Ltd.
Carmelite House
50 Victoria Embankment
London EC4Y 0DZ

www.bookouture.com

The authorised representative in the EEA is Hachette Ireland
8 Castlecourt Centre
Dublin 15 D15 XTP3
Ireland
(email: info@hbgi.ie)

ISBN: 978-1-80550-317-0
eBook ISBN: 978-1-80550-316-3

For D.M.I and J.

PROLOGUE
NOW

Neighbours are drawn out of their large gated homes by the sound of police sirens. Not one but two ambulances gather in the street. The small crowd whisper to each other as the sun sets on another warm day.

'Is that...?' asks a woman dressed in tight black leggings and an iridescent pink T-shirt.

'Goodness, look at the state of her,' says a man, his grey tie loose around his neck, his crumpled white business shirt untucked. He has parked his car at the bottom of the street, unable to get into his garage because a police car is parked across his driveway.

'Did you know she was capable of this? Did anyone know?' asks the woman, and those standing around shake their heads.

'Wasn't she sent away after she... tried to... you know?' says the man.

'Yes, but then she came home, they said she was better,' replies the woman. 'I talked to her mother when she came home and she said that she was doing well, that's what she told me.'

'Obviously not,' the man replies with a snort. 'I haven't seen much of them since she came back. I only saw them out once or twice and they just waved. Usually, they would stop for a quick chat.'

'That's true,' says the woman. 'I haven't spoken to them for weeks.'

They watch the girl writhe and attempt to kick the police officer who is dragging her down the front path.

As she gets closer to where they are all standing, the fury on her face, the wildness in her eyes and the way she is struggling with the stone-faced policeman make each of them instinctively take a step back, cautious in case she breaks free and attacks.

'Her parents are such nice people,' says the woman.

'Well,' says the man, scratching his jaw, 'you just never know, do you.'

'Let go of me, let go of me,' the girl shrieks. 'Where's Adam?' she shouts. 'Where is he? He said he would... come get me... he...'

The woman lifts her phone. 'No one will believe this,' she murmurs and then the man lifts his as well and the others standing in the group do the same.

'Hard to believe it happened in this suburb... I mean, we don't like that sort of thing here,' another man with a small dog standing by his side says. The dog yaps, bouncing with excitement at all the activity. 'Shush, Winston.'

The policeman shoves the girl towards a police car and the woman with the pink T-shirt winces as she sees that the girl is barefoot, that her feet flinch and curl as she walks over the sharp white stones of the front path. The grey silk dress she is wearing is stained and torn and she has make-up smeared across her face.

'Please calm down,' the policeman says as he pushes her into the back of a car with silent, whirling blue and red lights.

'Oh no,' exclaims the woman and everyone turns to where she is now pointing her phone. A stretcher is wheeled out and on it there is a body, lying still, a face covered with an oxygen mask.

It's followed by another stretcher, another face covered with an oxygen mask.

'What on earth went on in that house? What has she done?' says the man with the grey tie, shaking his head as a police-woman steps towards them. 'Please step back so the ambulances can get out, folks,' she says, raising her hands, and the neighbours all do as they are told.

The girl is in the car now but everyone hears her yell, 'Are those my parents? Are those my parents?'

The policeman doesn't reply.

'What happened to them? What happened?' she cries.

And those standing close enough to the car watch the policeman turn around to face the girl and, through his open window, they hear him speak.

'Why don't you tell me?' he says to the now sobbing girl and then as he starts the car, he repeats, 'Why don't you tell me?'

ONE

SIX WEEKS AGO

Juliet

'And you know that Mary comes to clean on a Wednesday and she arrives at eight, so it would be good if you could get up early. Then the gardeners come every two weeks because if we don't have them out all the time, the whole back garden is just a mess and...' Her mother trails off into silence, having run out of things to tell her, things she already knows. Juliet rubs a hand over the plush tan leather seats of her father's Mercedes and then stares out of the window at houses flashing by. Narrowing her eyes makes everything blur into zipping mixed colours and induces a sickly wooziness inside her, helped along by the drugs she is taking. Her stomach churns. She hates the way they make her feel, hates this detached giddiness.

'I always woke up early at the hospital,' she says as she remembers the sounds of the private psychiatric hospital crashing and banging into life as voices filled the corridor. She remembers the squeaky wheels of Martha's tea trolley coming with strong pots of tea, bitter coffee and homemade shortbread biscuits, and she remembers Martha's cheerful greeting, the same every day. 'Morning, love, good night? I slept like a baby.' At first, Juliet had enjoyed the shortbread biscuits Martha served up, savouring the thick buttery squares covered in sugar. But eventually, they started to turn her stomach. It was always the same biscuit, the same selection of milks, the same tea and coffee.

In the first few days she was at the hospital, she was shocked awake at 6 a.m., her heart racing, by the tea trolley, the nurses calling to one another, doors slamming and people shouting. But after a couple of weeks, her body woke her at 5.55 a.m. every day, bracing itself for the noise. Perhaps she will never sleep past 5.55 a.m. again.

'Well, it's always nice to get up early when it's warm like this,' her mother responds. 'You could take a walk in the morning or join a gym or...' She stops speaking again and Juliet turns away from the window, watches her father reach across to touch her mother's arm gently and then return his hand to the steering wheel. Such a kind gesture from such a kind man.

'Ha,' says Juliet aloud and then she coughs to cover the sound.

You could be normal again. That's what her mother would like to say, would like to beg for. *Please, Juliet, just be normal again.*

'Here we are,' sings her mother unnecessarily as they pull into the spacious double garage.

Juliet sighs, stifles a yawn and moves to get out of the car.

'I'll bring your case,' says her father. 'Why don't you go up and lie down?' His tone conveys this idea as a suggestion and Juliet would love to stubbornly refuse but she's exhausted.

'Okay,' she answers and then after a beat, 'thanks.'

'No trouble, on the double,' her father murmurs, a phrase from her childhood that she giggled at every time he said it.

Or did I? Is that memory really true?

In her mind, there is the before and the after. Not just

before she went into the hospital, but before she knew the truth. The painful, buried truth about her own parents.

Now it is the after. After she discovered the truth, after she learned not to trust her own narrative of the supposedly wonderful childhood she'd had. And after she stopped believing a word her parents said.

But still, there is a piece of her heart clinging to what she used to know about her childhood and her parents. She wishes it would let go but its hold is tight, determined, saying, *You were loved and cared for. They love you and they always have. Liar, liar, liar.*

The garage leads into the kitchen, picture-perfect and neat. The white marble countertop is free of detritus, and even the stainless-steel sink gleams as though guests are expected. But Juliet is not a guest. She is a reluctant returning resident.

'Are you hungry?' asks her mother, pushing a piece of perfectly dyed blonde hair back into its neat bob. Juliet turns to look at her, comparing the sagging grey tracksuit bottoms and oversized T-shirt she is wearing to her mother's neat black jeans and tucked in floral blouse, teamed with strappy sandals and rose-pink painted toenails. 'You look just like your mother,' her high school friends used to tell her, meaning it as a compliment. Now Juliet's hair is too long and the ends are split and her blue eyes are dull. But her mother still looks the same. *How can she still look the same after everything she did, everything I now know she did?*

'I could make you a sandwich or perhaps you'd like a slice of cake? I baked your favourite, lemon sponge with cream cheese icing, or I could—'

'No,' says Juliet, turning away and leaving the kitchen. The sheer absurdity of her mother offering her something to eat after everything Juliet has accused her of bewilders her. How can her parents even want to be in the same room with her after everything she has accused them of? *They don't believe you or they just don't want to believe you remember it.*

She and her parents are engaged in a game of pretend. *Let's pretend our only daughter didn't try to hurt herself. Let's pretend she didn't accuse us of terrible things. Let's pretend we're a perfect family.*

By being here, Juliet is playing as well but she can't quite make the game work. She was never very good at pretending.

Pretending is hard, tiring, and Juliet needs to sleep, to disappear. She makes her way to the staircase in the entrance hall, standing, for a moment, in the hot beam of sunlight coming in through a side window, shining on the parquet floor. And then she takes the staircase, absentmindedly running her hand along the smooth banister, the way she always did as a child, as she climbs the stairs. Along the way she passes framed photographs of Juliet in the before. There she is at birth, then two, then five in a school uniform. She stops in front of before Juliet in her first ballet costume, a pink tutu with matching satin pink shoes, a huge grin on her face showing that she has two front teeth missing. Lifting her hand, she strokes the glass and then moves on to Juliet at ten, twelve, fourteen and sixteen. And then she turns away from all the Juliets who were burying pain deep inside them, pain that she has only just found again. Pain that will never leave.

Her childhood bedroom has a decorative ceiling rose in the centre and pale blue silk curtains that are moving gently in the slight breeze from the window that has been left open just a crack. The familiar smell of summer jasmine drifts through the air and Juliet takes a deep breath. It's a luxury to be able to open a window, to not breathe the stale, slightly warm fug of manufactured air that she grew used to over her months in the hospital. It was such a short amount of time, only three months, but it has changed everything, rewritten her past and cast a shadowy gloom over her future.

She sinks down onto the double bed made from white painted timber, running her hands across the soft cotton duvet in a rich navy blue. Moving and lying down so her head is on the pillow, she listens to the sounds she grew up with. Sounds are softer here – different to her apartment where she lived before the hospital. There, an open window let in the noise of trucks changing gears as they struggled up the hill, sending a waft of diesel her way, a rushing train in the distance, irate drivers on their way to work, leaning on their horns to express frustration. Here, there is the slight whisper of a car driving past and then the squawking call of cockatoos as they fly over the house. And then nothing.

Closing her eyes, she turns on her side. She doesn't want to be back here with these people.

These people. Her parents. *They love you. No, they don't.*

She felt she had no choice but to come here. She is twenty-one years old. But she has no degree and no real qualifications. She wanted to leave the hospital and return to her old job but, in her absence, that job has been filled. And she's not sure she's ready to work just yet. She wants to be. But even simple everyday tasks feel difficult right now. Her parents are still supporting her and they wanted her to come home, to live with them again. They pay for her car, for her health insurance, for her therapy, for her existence. It's a privilege to have that support. But it doesn't feel that way. Instead, she feels trapped.

The hospital offered to set her up in a group home with other adults struggling to fit into the world, or to even help her get her own cheap place and government assistance. But she couldn't bear the thought of living with other people who are figuring out how to exist just like she is.

And she is also afraid of being alone. Afraid of what happened on the long dark night of the soul in the silence of her apartment when there seemed to be no way out of the pain, when she had her 'moment'. That's what her mother calls it when they speak of it – 'your bad moment'. Juliet likes the euphemism. It makes it sound like it was something she dealt with quickly and moved on. But that's not what happened.

She doesn't want to be here but cannot be completely alone.

She thought about finding a roommate, imagined a girl her age that she could bond with. But she needed money for that and then she was back to needing a job, something she wasn't ready for.

When she called her father from the hospital, after taking more than an hour to work up the courage to do so, and asked him for help paying rent, he said no.

'You need to come home so we can... help you get back on your feet,' he said. 'I'm not paying rent.'

'I don't have to come home,' she replied. 'I'm an adult.'

'You do what suits you.' His voice on the phone was clipped, harsh. She had never thought of him as harsh before she went into the hospital. In the before, she loved him, trusted him, felt safe with him. These feelings humiliate her now because she knows that they were a mistake.

According to the wider world, her parents are nice people, outgoing and well liked in the community. Her father is a respected accountant and her mother is a retired pre-school teacher, still remembered fondly by the children and parents alike. But she knows now that those façades are concealing ugliness and evil deeds. A truth that no one, apart from Juliet, can accept or believe.

Opening her eyes again, she sits up on her bed, taking in the bedroom where she grew up. It looks like the bedroom of an adored, happy child. But sometimes, now in the after, when she closes her eyes, she sees not this princess canopy bed or the plush blue carpet but something else, something awful, dirty and smelly, a room where there is pain and suffering, marks on the walls, dirty clothes piled everywhere and the stale smell of unwashed sheets. The image lives inside her, pulls at her heart and stomach, makes her feel sick.

Her memory is tangled up in the weeds of her mind so she cannot be sure how old the recollection is. Only that it's definitely there, and definitely real. Is it from when she was three or four or five?

She turns her head to see her bookcase, covered in ribbons and trophies from every dance competition she has ever won. At seven, she walked into a ballet studio, holding her mother's hand, wearing a pale pink leotard. She remembers it was a good day and that her mother was happy.

She loved ballet from the first step, the first plié – the bend, the first relevé – the rise and the first sauté – the jump. For eleven years, it was her everything. But then at eighteen, it was taken from her, and now, at twenty-one, she has... nothing. She is nothing but a muddled collection of memories, good and bad melding together, neither of which she can trust.

She had a life to look forward to and now she doesn't. She had a life to look back on fondly and now she doesn't. She is in the after now, the terrible after.

The walls of her bedroom are the palest of blue and are covered in pictures, happy family snaps on holiday and at birthdays, her and her parents with their arms around each other.

The pictures are a lie. The room is a lie. There was no happiness in that childhood, no love. She knows that now.

It was all a lie. Her whole life is a lie.

TWO

Juliet doesn't go down to dinner. Her mother sends her a text: *Dinner is ready. Would you like to come down or I can bring a tray up to you?*

She can imagine her mother in the kitchen, writing and rewriting the message so that she only says the right things. Her mother is afraid of her, of the things she has said and accused her of. She is afraid of the truth that Juliet has told. Juliet can imagine her mother's fear at the neighbours, the community, their friends finding out exactly what went on in her daughter's childhood.

She hasn't said that to her face. Instead, she has said, 'I'm worried about you, Juliet,' and, 'None of the things you're saying are true – how can you imagine that they are?' and, 'I am here for you to help you until you are able to understand that these are not memories, they are stories.'

A tray would be good, but you don't have to bring it. I can get it from the kitchen myself.

She doesn't know if she will have the energy to get off the bed but she doesn't have to because five minutes later there is a soft knock at her bedroom door.

'Yeah.'

'I thought I would bring it to you, sweetheart. I made chicken casserole and I've put a slice of cake on as well.'

Juliet nods and sits up and her mother places the tray on the bed in front of her. She leans forward and pushes a piece of hair behind Juliet's ear. 'We're so glad you're home, sweetheart.' Juliet flinches and her mother moves back, away from her, a look of such profound hurt crossing her face that Juliet feels an ache inside her.

Who are you pretending to be? I know what you did. I remember it. Juliet needs to keep this belief sharp at all times. Part of her longs to hug her mother, to just let go of all the memories she has unlocked, and the truth she has discovered. It would be easier in some ways to just trust her, to allow her mother to care for her.

'You can leave the tray outside your door,' her mother says, standing up.

Juliet nods and her mother leaves, closing the door behind her. Once she's alone, Juliet feels her shoulders drop and her body relax. How on earth is this going to work? How will she live here with everything she has remembered and everything she has said?

If she closes her eyes, she can see the stricken looks her parents gave her in that first family session at the hospital. 'What?' both her mother and father repeated each time Juliet made an accusation. 'What?'

Leaning forward, she picks up the cake and takes a bite, the sweetness filling her mouth, but as she chews, the cake sticks to her cheeks and tongue and she has to swallow twice to get the one bite down. She can't eat anything else. Getting off the bed, she picks up the tray and places it outside her bedroom door, feeling bad about the waste of food but unable to stand the smell. She closes the door, notes that the lock has been removed. *Of course it has.*

In her pocket, her phone chimes with a reminder to take her medication and she pulls it out, silences the notification and goes to her en-suite bathroom, running her hands over the caramel-coloured mosaic that is used in all the bathrooms in the house. 'Home,' she says, but this is not home. Nowhere is home anymore.

The shower is a luxury she has missed. In her apartment, the hot water came and went and she never thought to complain to the landlord, and in the hospital, it ran out after five minutes. Juliet stands under the powerful spray, letting the water loosen her muscles.

'You have made good progress, Juliet,' she hears Dr Choudry say. 'You need to continue to work on yourself, to examine critically things that you think are memories. Take your medication, meet with your new psychiatrist, get out in the world and find your joy.'

In her head Dr Choudry, in the brown corduroy pants and black button-down shirt he liked to wear, is always dancing, shuffling his feet from one side of his square, light-filled office to the other, the same way he shuffled his belief in her from one way to another. He believed her at first, believed everything she told him. And then he met her parents and changed his tune, changed the dance, decided that Juliet was the problem.

And that's when he began expressing that she needed to think critically, to examine her thoughts, to question herself.

'Your parents deny that any of the things you accuse them of have happened,' Dr Choudry said. 'Why do you think that is?'

'Because they're liars,' Juliet replied. 'I know what happened.'

'Do you?' she says aloud now, her voice echoing in the

shower, as she picks up a new bottle of the citrus shower gel she has always used. Grabbing a pink sponge that looks exactly the same as the one she has always used, she can see that her mother has tried to replicate everything that was in the bathroom when she last lived here two years ago. But there is no trace left of the Juliet from two years ago. There is only this shell of a person, beset by terrible memories that she has no proof of.

Her hands have begun to prune and she turns off the water, grabbing a soft chocolate-brown towel, obviously new. Her father has not brought up her suitcase although perhaps he has just left it outside the bedroom door. She doesn't want to open the door again.

But as she starts opening drawers in her walk-in wardrobe, searching for something to wear, she realises that she doesn't need anything in the suitcase because everything she owns is here, unpacked and put away neatly.

While she was locked away, fighting demons and memories, her parents resigned her from the job she had selling tiny T-shirts to teenage girls, ended her apartment lease for her, packed up her life and dragged it home for her.

She is twenty-one but she is still a child to them.

'That's what you get for having a bad moment, Juliet,' she mutters as she puts on a summer nightshirt and clean underwear.

Back in bed, she closes her eyes and breathes in and out, counting, just the way Dr Choudry advised her to do. He was big on breathing exercises to relax, to allow the body to loosen up and the mind to open. He wasn't as interested in all the secrets that spilled out of Juliet when that happened though. Then he was more inclined to believe that she was, as her parents told him, suffering from a vivid imagination.

'Goodnight, Juliet,' she hears her mother call but she doesn't answer, sinking into sleep as her body lets go of her time in the hospital, of the day, of everything.

On the very edge of sleep, she admits to herself why she has come back here at all. She has no money, that's true, but she is also back here for the truth.

That's what she wants, what she needs. That's why she's really here.

THREE

She wakes with a start at 5.55 a.m., her ears straining for the sound of the tea trolley. But she is no longer in the hospital. The mattress is soft underneath her body, the bed large so she has spread out. She is in her bedroom at home.

Closing her eyes again, she wishes to return to sleep, which took a long time to come last night, but any hope she has of sinking back into the blank, dreamless space she longs for is destroyed by the sound of a leaf blower and lawnmower, starting up at the same time. Of course, it's Wednesday and the gardeners are here to make sure everything is shipshape. They start very early in summer, hoping to beat the scorching heat of the middle of the day. Juliet stretches in bed, imagining a leaf blower going through her brain, blasting out all the bad memories.

Instead of staying in bed, she moves quietly, pulling on black running shorts and a soft worn grey T-shirt. Her suitcase is sitting outside her bedroom door and she takes it in, opening it and searching for her medication, shoving the bottles in a top drawer of the whitewashed dressing table that matches her bed.

Making her way downstairs on tiptoe, so as not to alert anyone that she's awake, she's relieved when she's at the front door and the house is still silent. Her phone chimes to remind her to take her morning medication and she silences the notification. There's no one to check she's taken it here, to hand her a little plastic cup containing her pills and a little paper cup of water and watch her swallow.

She couldn't bear to stay at the hospital and at the same time she didn't want to leave. It felt like outside, life was moving forward, the world turning, and she was standing still. She was suffocating. But she was also terrified. She had no idea how to be in the world after everything that happened.

She hasn't met her new doctor yet and she is still hopeful that Dr Janet Kelly will be someone she can talk to and, more importantly, someone who will listen and believe her. Unlike Dr Choudry, who listened and thought she was a liar. In every session she had with him, he nodded his head as she talked, occasionally stroked his dark beard and took notes all the time, so many notes. *Juliet has an overactive imagination. Juliet is a liar*, she thinks those notes must say.

She steps outside into the warm air, taking a deep breath. The February humidity in Sydney is heavy and thick and she immediately feels damp.

She could leave right now, just walk away and not come back, but she is afraid to. She has no job, no money and no other place to live.

Perhaps she could ask a friend for help but she hasn't spoken to her friends in months. They took her phone away when she arrived at the hospital, and when they finally gave it back, the thought of responding to all the messages and calls was overwhelming, exhausting. She told a few people, knowing that where she was would get around. And she responded to the kind messages letting her know that they were thinking of her and there for her. But those messages stopped after a few weeks as everyone went back to their lives. On Instagram she can see that the girls she was close to, Riley and Lia and Joanne, are all getting on with their perfect lives. They are all at university, all have boyfriends and regularly meet up at clubs and restaurants. The job in the clothing store selling tiny T-shirts was temporary and part time for them because they had big lives to live and things to do. Juliet was working there full time. There is no way she would be able to slot back into their lives.

She and some of the girls from the ballet company kept in touch for a while after her accident but then it just got too hard to be with them and know that they were deliberately stopping themselves from mentioning anything to do with dancing.

They are all moving forward and she is stuck, trapped and filled with despair despite all the therapy and the medication that makes her sleepy. How long until it's out of her system and she can think clearly? Surely, no more than a few days.

The sun hits her arms as she walks down the garden path, and she glances down at her wrists, at the angry, rumpled scars. She was not meant to be here anymore, not meant to be dealing with any of this.

'People experience disappointments all the time. What is important is that you find a way to move on from that and establish a life for yourself,' Dr Choudry told her when they discussed her former dancing career. She had been unable to stop herself from biting down hard on her lip when he said that, when he reduced what had happened to her to merely a 'disappointment'. He had been alarmed by the blood as her tooth pierced the skin, had handed her a tissue and given his head a shake. She hated him for his words, for his cavalier attitude. The end of her career was not just a 'disappointment'. It was the end of her life.

He didn't understand what it felt like to rise up onto her

toes, to twirl with a stiff black tutu around her body, to feel the muscles in her calves and thighs contract, to leap and know that she would be caught by another dancer. He couldn't imagine the feeling of bliss as the music filled her body and each part of her responded. It seemed to her that she spent a lot of time not quite taking a deep enough breath to fill her lungs, not until she laced up her shoes and admired her perfectly pointed toes. Only then could she take in enough air to fill her lungs. She hadn't just lost a career. She had lost a way of breathing, of living, of being.

He had no idea what she had lost. And instead of finding solace at the hospital with Dr Choudry, she found the terrible truth about her childhood.

The memories had obviously been waiting, skulking deep inside her. A collection of monsters ready to tear her apart.

Everything feels worse now, so much worse. She rubs at the scar on one wrist, contemplating how hard it would be to reopen the wounds, to reopen them and not get caught.

Once she hits the road, she puts her earbuds in, pulling out her phone and cranking the music up so she stops that thought right there. She's not going to let *them* win.

Who are you talking about?

Them. My parents, the memories, Dr Choudry, everyone who has ever hurt me.

She walks fast, even as pain starts to radiate from her knee. She will never not feel that pain.

'You'll be lucky to be able to pick up your child,' the physiotherapist told her when she began rehab, a slight smirk on his face. An imaginary child, as if that was the main purpose of her future.

'Screw you,' she spat and then he ended the session early, telling her that she needed to be more respectful. Juliet wanted to scream and scream at him. He had no idea either. No one understood what she had lost.

Let it go and breathe, just let it go and breathe. She repeats the mantra that one of the nurses, Lacy, gave her when she couldn't sleep. The nurses at the hospital were lovely, kind and gentle and obviously used to dealing with people who had reached a crisis point in their lives.

Juliet gets to the bottom of the road and sees a new coffee shop has opened while she has been... 'away', as her mother optimistically and sensitively calls it. A grey and white striped awning shades people sitting at small round tables and chairs, even this early in the morning.

The pleasant burning smell of roasting coffee perfumes the air and Juliet feels her mouth water at the idea of a really good cup of coffee.

She joins a queue of people, mostly dressed in Lycra cycling gear, and studies the menu, deciding she will order a strong latte when she gets to the counter. Checking her bank balance quickly, she sees she has a few hundred dollars, enough for coffee every morning for some time, if that's what she wants.

She needs to get a job. And she will. She just needs some time, just some time to figure this out, to find the truth, to get back on an even keel. Something that feels impossible right now. *One thing at a time.*

Looking around her, she spots two inside tables with loved-up couples, sharing pastry and coffee, unable to keep their hands off each other. *Not for you,* she thinks and then she hates herself for the thought. Her life is not over, it's not. It just feels like it is.

As she gets closer to the counter, she studies the array of business cards there, reading about gardening services and computer services and a mobile hairdresser.

For a minute, she allows herself to indulge in the fantasy that instead of living with her parents, she is out getting coffee for her and her boyfriend. Who would he be? A tall man with kind eyes who is waiting at home for her.

'What can I get you?' a young woman whose hands are busy plating up a pastry asks her and Juliet abandons her fantasy.

With her coffee in her hands, she makes her way to the nearby park. It's getting hotter now and there are lots of people around. She sits on a bench and studies mothers with young children in the playground and then turns her attention to a group of people practising tai chi, their slow movements peaceful and filled with purpose.

Be here now and appreciate this blue sky, this warmth, this comforting smell of coffee, she tells herself.

'Damn, missed it again,' she hears and she looks up at a man standing near the bench. He's tall with messy brown curls and he sits down, shaking his head.

'Sorry?' says Juliet, unsure if he's talking to her.

'Oh,' he says, turning to look at her and then gesturing to the tai chi class, 'didn't realise I'd spoken aloud. I always mean to get up early enough to catch the start of the class but I've only made it a few times.'

'I'm sure they'd let you join now,' says Juliet.

'Nah, I'd never get into the rhythm,' he replies with a smile, a dimple appearing on one cheek. 'I'll just sit here next to the pretty girl and that will be the best way to start my Wednesday.'

Juliet looks around for who he is talking about and he laughs.

'I'm Adam,' he says and he holds out a hand for her to shake, which she does.

'Juliet,' she replies. His hand is large, slightly damp in the heat.

'Ah, a beautiful name for a beautiful woman.'

And that does make Juliet laugh, really laugh for the first time in a very long time. Because even though she knows it's a line, it makes her feel something other than the despair that she is always weighed down by. No one has said anything nice about her or to her for years.

Instead, they have said: *Pick yourself up, get on with things, stop moping, it's not the end of the world, you'll find something else to do, why did you do that, what's wrong with you? Where are you getting this from? Why are you making things up? We don't understand you, Juliet, we just don't understand.*

'Good coffee?' asks Adam.

'Yes, very, it's a new place – well, new for me.'

'Just moved here?'

'No... I've been... away but I'm back living with my parents for a bit.' She likes the way that sounds, as though she has returned from travelling the world.

'Right. I just moved to the neighbourhood so I'm always on the lookout for a good coffee shop. What's it called?'

'I can show you,' says Juliet, knowing she's being impulsive but not caring. 'I wouldn't mind another coffee myself.'

'I'll buy if you do,' he says with a smile and she notices his deep brown eyes, kind brown eyes.

'Deal,' she says and she stands and they walk back to the coffee shop together.

'So, what do you do? I mean, like, for work?' she asks.

'Me, oh... computers, cybersecurity, like every other computer geek around.' His voice is deep and smooth and something inside Juliet yearns to listen to him talk a lot more.

'How about you?'

'I'm um... kind of between things at the moment, taking some time to figure out what I want to do,' answers Juliet, liking that idea. It feels... hopeful.

'That's a good plan. I sometimes wonder if I want to do what I'm doing for the rest of my life. Maybe there's something else I would be good at? I don't know. You should take your time; choose something you'll love forever.'

'I will,' she says with a nod.

As they join the queue for coffee, Adam begins patting his pockets. 'Damn, forgot my wallet and my phone. I was supposed to be having an hour without them.' He flushes slightly, the tips of his ears turning red, and Juliet can't help smiling.

'I can buy, don't worry.'

'I feel bad, are you sure?'

'It's just coffee.' Juliet shrugs. She wants to keep talking to him.

'Okay, a flat white for me, I'll grab us an outside table?'

Juliet nods.

Her heart lifts when she emerges from the coffee shop with two coffees to see him sitting there, waiting for her, just for her.

'I didn't know if you take sugar or sweetener,' she says as she sits down and places some packets on the table for him to choose from.

'Nah, just like this.' He lifts his cup and takes a sip. 'Perfect, thank you so much.'

'My pleasure and I agree. I always think sugar ruins the taste of coffee and this is really good.'

'It is and it's always nice to find a new place. I hope it lasts. Coffee shops seem to open and close so quickly.' He shakes his head.

'It's hard to run a business. I would never be brave enough to take the chance.' Juliet takes another sip of her coffee as she studies his face, liking the way he keeps pushing his curls off his forehead.

'Me neither. I prefer to do my work and go home and know someone else is in charge.'

'Oh, I agree,' Juliet says with a laugh. She sits back in her chair, studying the people around them.

'Ah, you're a people-watcher,' says Adam and he leans forward so he's closer to her.

'I always have been.'

'Me too.' He points at a couple at the next table. 'First date or have they been together a long time?'

Juliet studies the couple who have their hands entwined. 'A month or two, I think.'

'Definitely still at the beginning stage,' says Adam and then he points at the next table and they discuss a mother and child. Juliet feels herself relaxing in the sun as they chat. It doesn't feel like she's just met Adam. There's something easy and casual about the way he talks that makes her feel like they have known each other for longer.

Half an hour later, when Adam has to go to work, he says, 'Maybe we can get a coffee tomorrow at around this time?'

'I would like that.'

'This is where we exchange numbers,' he says with a smile and her cheeks burn with embarrassment. She has forgotten how to do this.

'Till tomorrow,' he says with a wave and another beautiful smile and Juliet nods.

It is only as she walks back into her house that she realises that for the first time in years, she has spent more than an hour not thinking about what she lost or what was done to her or how awful her life is.

'Adam,' she says as she opens the front door, enjoying the way his name sounds. 'Adam,' she repeats as she dashes up the stairs for the comfort of a cool shower and thoughts of a new friend.

FOUR

In a nice suburb, there is a pretty house with a wall rendered in rich cream and contrasting blue gates. The garden is well tended and flowers line the front path, blooming pink and red and yellow in the spring. Large trees shade neatly cut grass and rainbow lorikeets come every day for the seed in the bird feeder.

Every room inside the house is neat and tidy, everything in its place. The living room is filled with family pictures, of those alive and those long gone. Pictures of holidays and special days, pictures of those who are loved and those who were loved.

Upstairs are three bedrooms, a space large enough for a family. The main bedroom is well decorated with heavy grey curtains and a matching upholstered grey headboard. The other bedroom has versatile white furniture and the bed is permanently made but never used.

And then there is the third bedroom, the child's room. There is no beauty here, only mess and chaos.

No one cleans in here.

'It's your job to keep it clean,' her mother says.

The child doesn't understand. She is only four. How do you clean a room? Her mother showed her once, brought in the heavy *vacuum cleaner and the cloth and spray. 'Like this,' she huffed as she made her way around the room, 'and this, and this.' The child watched carefully, trying to remember. 'You will be obedient and disciplined. This will teach you to be independent,' her mother said. The child remembers the words but not what they mean.*

The mess infuriates her mother and she will routinely come into the room and deliver a quick, hard slap across the cheek. 'Clean it up now.' The slap stings but not as much as being ignored and forgotten does. She spends a lot of time alone in the dark, smelly room. Her mother is always busy with other things and doesn't want to be bothered. She thinks her mother must hate her very much. She is a bad little girl who won't clean and tidy, who makes her mother angry. Of course she hates her.

Outside the house, when they are in public, it seems to her that she is mistaken and that her mother loves her very much. On very occasional trips to the shops, she holds her hand and strokes her hair and tells her she is 'a good girl'. Her mother is happier outside the house.

'But you said I am bad and you hit me,' she said once, confused by the difference in behaviour.

'Nonsense,' said her mother. 'You're making that up. Little girls shouldn't make up stories. We love you. We've always loved you.'

'You've always loved me,' the girl repeated and for that moment, it was true.

When she is six, her mother, angry at her over her dropping a plate, twists her wrist, snapping the delicate bone, and then rushes her to the hospital. 'Tell them you fell at the playground,' her mother instructs her.

'But I didn't. You were angry and—'

'Nonsense,' interrupts her mother. 'Don't make up stories. You fell. I would never hurt you. I love you and I have always loved you.'

And in the hospital, as her mother holds her hand and hugs her and cries a little in front of the doctors, the child thinks it must be true. Her mother loves her and always has and whatever she remembers, whatever she thinks has happened, has not.

She prefers the story of the fall at the playground. If she thinks really hard, she can see herself at the top of the climbing frame, shouting, 'Look at me, Mum,' the way she has seen other children do. She can see how she holds her body and then how a small movement causes her balance to shift and she falls, putting out her arm to stop her face from hitting the ground. She stores the image inside her. That's what happened.

She prefers to think that her mother and father love her and that they always have. That thought gives her a warm feeling inside so she clings to it.

It makes her happy and sometimes, at night, when she is very sad, she will repeat over and again, 'They love me and they always have.' And then she will feel better and her tears will stop and she will embrace sleep, even though some part of her knows, despite how young she is, that it's not true. It's not true at all.

FIVE

Juliet

She thinks about Adam all day as she does a load of washing and tidies her room. She imagines what will happen on their planned date tomorrow, feeling her heart flutter at the idea of seeing him again. Will he be there? *Please be there.*

She is in a good mood, even finding herself humming until her mother messages her, *Dinner is on the table,* and she is reminded of where she is and why she is here. The terrible memories stab at her, letting her know that she cannot just let this go. She needs the truth. Dinner will be an opportunity to talk to her parents, to ask them, to find a way to make them admit what they did. Maybe they will be ready to talk, ready to tell her the whole truth. Maybe if she can approach them as an adult, if they can all have a mature discussion, things can be resolved in some way.

The moment she walks into the dining room, where a large glass chandelier hangs over the long, beautifully carved timber table, she knows she's made a mistake. Her parents don't look happy that she has joined them.

Juliet wants to leave but decides to stay even as her good mood dips and she feels a heavy black cloud surrounding her.

The three of them sit silently, only their chewing and the scrape of cutlery providing sound until a flash of a memory rears its head and Juliet says, 'This is my favourite meal,' as she forces down a mouthful of her mother's lasagne. She is finding it hard to swallow because of where she is. The game of pretend has destroyed her appetite.

Her mother nods and offers Juliet a wary smile.

'I know. I added extra cheese, just the way you've always asked,' she replies.

Juliet takes a sip of her water. Her parents are drinking wine but it wasn't offered to her. She isn't allowed alcohol because of her medication, the medication she isn't taking anymore.

She watches her father cut his food into neat squares and feels her jaw clench. She gave her mother an opening, an opportunity. She was waiting for her mother to say something about this meal, about what it meant in the past. It would have been a chance for a discussion but Juliet can see that's not going to happen. Her parents are still pretending, still lying, still concealing everything. She will have to push, to goad, to force them into the revelation.

'You used to give it to me after you didn't feed me for a day. Do you remember that?' She says the words casually, her tone neutral as though she is just discussing the weather.

'Oh... God,' her mother says, dropping her fork onto her plate with a clank and lifting her serviette to her eyes.

Her father stands up, shoving back his chair and throwing his own serviette onto his still full plate, the heavy white linen covering his portion of lasagne, the red sauce creeping into the white, staining a corner.

'That's right, walk away.' Juliet sneers as he turns to go. It doesn't feel like the voice is hers, like the cruelty belongs to who she knows herself to be, and yet she cannot stop it.

Her father stops and looks down at her, his brown eyes dark with anguish.

'I want you to know, Juliet,' he says, and she watches him clench a fist, controlling himself, 'that we love you. We have always loved and cared for you.' He shakes his head sadly. 'These stories are just that, stories. We have pointed this out to you again and again. Dr Choudry pointed it out to you and I am sure that your new psychiatrist will tell you the same thing. We wanted you home because we are afraid... because we want to help you. But you are torturing us, my darling. In every session we had with you at the hospital, you told us something else, something dreadful, something unthinkable, and it's killing us. You are killing us with these terrible lies.' He waves a hand as his shoulders sink in defeat. 'And I do wonder,' he says softly, 'if that is the plan, if you are hoping that one or both of us will die.'

He folds his arms when he is done speaking and Juliet stares at her mother sobbing quietly into her serviette.

Inside Juliet, emotions crash into each other, her stomach churning. She hates her parents, and yet, as she looks at her father, there is also an overwhelming pull towards him as a memory surfaces of him holding her hand while she twirled on the kitchen floor, small, soft ballet shoes on her feet.

That's a lie, it must be false. It's something they told you happened in order to conceal the truth. She knows it is the same with all the happy photos everywhere. They are all lies. Her mother's weeping makes her angry. How dare she cry now? How dare she?

'I know what I know,' she says. She stands and leaves her still full plate on the table, desperate to get away because once again, she is questioning her memory, questioning her own thoughts. Were they all just stories? Is it possible that she is making it up? She pushes her hands against her eyes, a headache thumping through her brain, and then she leaves the dining room, standing just outside, leaning against a wall.

'I can't take much more of this,' she hears her mother say.

'We need to get her to leave as soon as possible,' her father replies. She hears him sit down again. 'I am sorry about your lovely meal.'

'She's not strong enough, George,' her mother says, her voice thick with tears. 'She'll do it again. I won't be able to live with myself if she does it again.'

'I don't know,' her father murmurs, 'I simply don't know what to do anymore.'

Juliet remembers her mother's tears as she sat by her hospital bed after the dark night of the soul. 'Why didn't you tell us?' she said. 'We would have helped you.' Her father had spent the night, angled uncomfortably into a chair, waking each time Juliet moved and patting her hand, telling her, 'You'll be fine, you'll be fine. We'll work this out.' And then they sent her to St Augustine. But instead of getting better, everything got worse.

Juliet creeps away from the dining room, anguish inside her. She closes herself in her bedroom and falls into a deep, dreamless sleep that only lasts an hour, her eyes springing open and her heart racing.

Picking up her phone, she is shocked to see that she has a message. And even more surprised to see that it's from Adam. Surprised and delighted because she would never have had the courage to text him first.

Looking forward to meeting up tomorrow.

Me too.

Did you have a good day?

Juliet thinks about how to respond to this question. As far as Adam is concerned, she's a pretty girl he met this morning. Did he see her scars? He must have done but he didn't say anything about them.

It was okay. It's hard living with my parents again.

I get that. When I go home, it feels like I instantly turn back into a kid, like I'm powerless again and have no control over anything. And then a whole lot of stuff comes up because my dad and I don't have the best relationship.

That's exactly how I feel. Things between me and my parents are not good. Maybe if they saw me as an adult, they would be able to apologise for some of the stuff they did when I was a kid.

Totally. When I have kids, if I screw up, I'm going to say sorry. I don't know what's so hard about that for parents to get. All we want is someone to acknowledge what happened and apologise.

Juliet feels like Adam has tapped directly into her head. Does everyone feel this way? Perhaps. But not everyone had a childhood like she did.

When she first arrived at St Augustine, Juliet had been certain that she knew why her life was such a mess. The 'accident' had changed everything. She would never dance again and her life was over. She knew that for sure.

But only a few weeks into her stay, something happened. From deep inside herself, memories began to emerge. They were dark and twisted, shocking her in the day and waking her with nightmares at night.

She cannot share this with Adam – not yet and maybe not ever.

Yes, yes, yes. That's exactly how I feel.

Last time I went home, I eventually sat them both down and told them that I had some things I wanted to discuss and then I just... I guess said what I had to say. Mum didn't talk to me for two days and my dad was so incredibly angry. They thought I was ungrateful and awful. But a few weeks later my mum called and said, 'I'm sorry, we did our best.'

That's not really an excuse though, is it?

No, but it's better than nothing. I'm going to try and get to sleep early. Have a good night. See you in the morning. X

See you in the morning x

Juliet clutches her phone to her chest, her heart racing at the thought that she has a reason to wake up tomorrow, a reason to get out of bed and a reason to exist.

Just over a day ago, she was still in the hospital, and now she has met this man, this lovely man. It amazes her how quickly life can change. But then she knows that. Her life turned one hideous way in an instant so why shouldn't it turn a wonderful way as well? This thought cheers her and she grins. Tomorrow she will see Adam again.

A soft knock at her door irritates her and she doesn't respond.

She thought she wanted the truth but that's actually just one part of it. Adam is right: what she wants is an apology, an acknowledgement of what happened, and then maybe she could work on forgiving her parents. But until she gets that, she cannot let go of everything that happened to her. She doesn't want to.

And no one can make her do something she doesn't want to do. Not anymore.

SIX

Juliet

Juliet gets to the coffee shop first as she always does. The queue is short today and she's glad because less time in the queue means more time with Adam.

Every morning for the past two weeks, they have met here at the coffee shop. Every morning, she has been scared he won't actually turn up, but he always arrives – a little after her, with a huge grin on his handsome face, like seeing her is all he wants.

Sometimes, they sit and have coffee outside, where the air is warm and fragrant with coffee and summer flowers, and other times, they walk to the park, where they can feel like they are completely alone, even surrounded by people.

After the first few times they met, Adam took her hand as they walked, bumped his fingers against hers and then held on and she felt her whole body respond. He hugs her when they leave each other and a few days ago, he added in a kiss, sweet and gentle.

She wants to spend every moment with him but at the same time, the more they get to know each other, the more worried she is that he will find out everything she's hiding from him. She wants to tell him everything but what if it scares him away? Her life has had too many terrible complications.

'The usual?' the young woman behind the counter asks her for the first time this morning. Her name is Lou and she has red hair and freckles. Juliet nods, delighted to be recognised.

'The flat white is for my... boyfriend,' she says, knowing she shouldn't but unable to resist testing out the word, 'and the latte is for me.'

'Right,' replies Lou with a smile and then she looks around, as though seeking the boyfriend Juliet is buying coffee for.

'He's getting a table,' says Juliet and she hopes he is.

Outside she searches the street, holding two cups of coffee.

'Hey,' she hears and there he is, running towards her.

'Sorry, sorry, I am going to get here before you one day.'

'That's okay,' she says, handing him a coffee.

Together, they walk towards the park. Adam takes her hand as he usually does and Juliet doesn't want to be anywhere but where she is, anyone but this woman holding this man's hand.

They sit on their usual bench and Juliet closes her eyes, faces up towards the sun. There has been no rain and it feels like summer will go on forever.

'Perhaps you would like to come to dinner at my apartment,' he says after taking a sip of his coffee. Her heart quickens at the idea that they are moving forward with their relationship.

'I would like that.' She looks up at him and he leans down and places a soft kiss on her lips. Her body moves towards his, yearning for more.

'I'm so glad,' he says as he moves his fingers against hers and then lifts her hand, kisses the palm, and then he moves up to her wrist and kisses the raised scar there.

Juliet pulls away, the shock of his lips on her scar dancing through her body.

'Don't do that,' he says, grasping her hand again. 'It's part of you.'

'It makes me feel... embarrassed,' she says. If it weren't so hot, she would permanently be in long sleeves.

'We all have scars, Juliet. Some are on the inside but it's okay to wear yours on the outside. Life is not easy.'

'No,' agrees Juliet and she feels her eyes fill, blinks quickly.

'Can you tell me why?' he asks. 'I mean what were you thinking at the time? I know you must have been sad, depressed, but what were you actually thinking?'

A hundred images float through her head, a hundred reasons.

'I just couldn't see a way to feel better. Life was impossible to live. That's what I thought. I thought, "This is impossible. I can't do it anymore."'

'And you didn't have therapy, someone to help you? Like after the accident?'

She has told him she had an accident but little more than that.

'I did but... it seemed to me that the woman, the psychologist, I was seeing thought I was overly dramatic.' She had only seen Anne, the sweet, young psychologist, a few times, and then she told her parents that more visits weren't necessary and she was able to see her mother breathe a sigh of relief at the idea that Juliet was fine with everything now, just fine.

'She told me that a lot of people have their lives derailed by an accident and that I was still young enough to do whatever I wanted with my life.' Juliet hates how many people have told her this, how many times she has heard this phrase as though her youth was the only thing that mattered.

'You are young, but that doesn't invalidate your pain,' he says as he clasps her hand tighter.

She nods her head. She never wanted to talk about this with him, but she can see that she has to. Relationships are built on trust and she wants him to know that she trusts him. 'The thing is… I understood that I should just let it go but I couldn't seem to. And even now…'

The moment her future came crashing down, literally, assaults her as it always does when she thinks about it. It is a punch in the stomach and she cannot help seeing herself on the day it happened.

She is dancing, her ballet shoes a delicate pearl pink and the black tutu stiff around her body. She feels her legs, the muscles in her calves and thighs, feels their strength as she spins her body. She can see the graceful curve of her arms, the line of her back and the smile on her face. It was a dress rehearsal so she was in full make-up, her long blonde hair tamed into a tight perfect bun, red lipstick on her lips and her cheeks heavily rouged so she didn't look pale under the stage lights. She watches herself step forward, twist, spin and then she leaps.

'He didn't catch me,' she says, almost to herself. 'The lead dancer was supposed to catch me when I jumped and he didn't and I fell and landed at an odd angle, and I felt my knee pop and then the pain. He just didn't catch me.'

'I'm so sorry, that's, wow, that must have been really painful.' He winces and frowns, as though he can feel the pain she experienced.

'It was. At first, they thought I hadn't really hurt myself that badly. The X-ray showed no breaks but my leg swelled up, and after three days, I couldn't walk and we went for another opinion and an MRI.'

'Always good to get a second opinion.' He nods his head as his thumb massages her palm. Even though she is explaining one of the worst times of her life, one of the worst moments, she still feels calm. She always feels calm when she is with him.

'Yes, and it turned out I had torn the tendon off the bone. And there were bits of bone floating around. I had an operation but the doctor said I would never dance again and the physio-therapist said I might never walk properly.'

'But surely something could have been done to help you?'

A child stands at the top of the slide in the playground, screaming, 'Mummy, Mummy, look, catch me, catch me.'

'My parents told me they did everything they could. I never danced again. I will never dance again. And that's what kept going around in my head on that night when I... you know.' Saying the words out loud takes her breath away and she knows that if she was not sitting here with him, she would grab the packet of sleeping pills she has at home, more pills that she is not taking, and use them to end this pain. Ballet was her breath, her life. She still cannot believe it's gone.

Adam shakes his head as his gaze sweeps across the park. An old couple walk hand in hand towards the lake.

'Did he get into trouble, the guy who didn't catch you? Do you know why he did it? Was it just an accident?'

'No,' she says. 'He said it was but I never believed him. We'd been dating and we had just broken up. He was angry but he wouldn't admit it.'

'He should pay for that.' Adam's brown eyes darken and she realises that this is the first time she's ever seen him look angry.

'There was nothing that they could charge him with or anything. He said that it was an accident, and he even... cried because he was so sorry. Accidents happen all the time and no one could prove it wasn't one. And in the end, he got angry at me because they took away his lead role. The lead male dancer needs to be able to catch his female partner when she leaps. He came to visit me after my operation and told me that I needed to tell them that the accident was my fault. I wouldn't, obviously.'

'Well, obviously, what an arsehole. What was his name?'

'Benji,' she says, seeing him again with his slicked-back blond hair and green eyes. After her operation, when she returned home, he had arrived with flowers and chocolates, profusely apologetic in front of her mother, who was taking care of her. 'I am so sorry,' he kept saying until her mother left the room to make tea and then he said, 'You need to tell everyone that it was an accident. You need to stop telling people that I did it on purpose. Tell them you were in the wrong. It wasn't my fault. You're making it up.'

'I'm not, you did it on purpose,' she had said, the chocolate she'd been eating coating her mouth in thick sweetness so she felt sick. 'I know you were angry.'

'It was your fault, your jump was off,' he replied, and she could see his growing anger.

'It was your fault,' she retorted.

'You've ruined my career,' he spat at her. 'You and your lies.' His face was puce with anger.

'You ruined mine,' she replied, equally angry as she lay on the sofa, her knee in a cast, the throbbing pain filling her whole body.

She hated him with every fibre of her being as she looked at him slouched in a chair, whining about losing a lead role with his healthy strong body and years of dancing ahead of him. When her mother returned with the tea, his polite demeanour returned as well and he wished her a quick recovery. 'We're all waiting for you to come back,' he said, a fake smile plastered on his face, knowing that she would never return. And then he left.

She never saw him again.

'Have you... spoken to him since your... I mean does he know?' asks Adam, dragging her back to the bench where they are sitting, back to the park where the air is warm. 'No,' she says. She cannot imagine what she would do if she did see him now. Or she can imagine it but only in the long hours of a sleepless night. Then she can imagine exactly what she would do.

In the distance, there are children shrieking with joy as they play in the playground and a dog running after a ball his owner has just thrown.

'I don't think he would care, anyway.'

'He shouldn't get away with it,' says Adam, shaking his head. 'He really should pay for what he's done. People should pay if they hurt someone.'

'I know,' says Juliet and she shrugs. 'But what can I do about it?'

Adam is quiet and then he kisses her palm again.

'The worst thing is that he got to move on and establish himself somewhere else and I'm supposed to dope myself up with pills so that I don't think about what he did anymore.'

'I understand why it felt impossible, and why it's still hard to move on now.'

'I'm not taking them anymore, the pills,' she confesses because this feels like the time for confession.

Adam sighs. 'Honestly,' he says, 'I would do the same thing. I hate the feeling of not being able to think straight. When I got my wisdom teeth out when I was twenty, they gave me stuff to stop the pain and I hated the feeling so much, I just stopped taking it. It feels like something else has control of your thoughts.'

'Exactly,' agrees Juliet. 'And now I have to go and see another psychiatrist and I know she's going to tell me I have to go back on the medication.'

'Just don't tell her you've stopped then. Doctors don't know everything. They don't have all the answers. They just act like they do.'

'You're right about that. After I... you know' – she waves her hand – 'I had some time in a place where the doctor was just... he was just awful.'

'In what way?' Adam looks around, watching a toddler on a tricycle being followed by his father.

'I don't... Not today, okay.'

'But you will tell me one day?'

'Yes, if you like.'

He moves towards her, pushes a loose piece of hair behind her ear and strokes her face. 'I want to know everything about you, Juliet, everything, the good and the bad. I just want to know you.'

'I feel the same way.' Juliet cannot hide her smile, cannot stop the fizzing joy she feels when she's with him. Right now, sitting on a bench in the park in the early-morning sunshine, she is the happiest she has ever been and she can't believe that she was lucky enough to meet this wonderful man.

'And now, I need to go,' says Adam, standing up. 'Work calls even though I wish I could stay here with you.'

'That's okay, you have a good day.'

He leans down and kisses her lightly on the lips, warmth spreading through her whole body. 'And you don't worry about what some quack doctor thinks,' he says. 'You know yourself better than anyone.'

Juliet nods her head and then she too stands, walking slowly back to her house.

Back at home, she opens the front door cautiously, not wanting to see her mother, who seems to be waiting for her every time she leaves her room so she can ask what Juliet is doing.

But the kitchen is empty and Juliet takes the stairs two at a time to get to her room quickly, where she will enjoy thoughts of Adam alone.

Her bedroom door is open and she's sure she closed it when she left. When she walks in, her mother is standing in front of the chest of drawers, the top drawer, where Juliet stashed her medication, open.

'What are you doing?' snaps Juliet, stamping towards her mother, who whirls around, her face pale.

'Oh, I... I was just, I was putting away washing,' she stammers.

Juliet looks around the room. 'That would be easier to believe if you had the laundry basket with you.'

Her mother sighs. 'I'm... I just wanted to check...'

'If I was taking my medication. I can see that. Can you just leave this up to me? Can you just give me a little privacy? After everything you did, you could at least give me that.'

'What did I do, Juliet?' her mother explodes, her face growing red with fury. 'What did I really do? Everything you said at the hospital was rubbish, just rubbish you made up and I... All I do is worry about you, all day that's what I do.'

'Well, maybe you won't have to worry about me for much longer,' Juliet spits.

'What does that mean? What does it mean?' her mother yells, panic making her voice high and squeaky.

'Nothing, get out of my room, get out, get out.' Juliet grabs her mother's arm and shoves her out the door.

'You can't behave like this, you can't do this,' her mother cries but Juliet doesn't care to listen. She slams the door in her mother's face.

'I don't know who you are anymore, Juliet,' her mother calls through the door and it's easy to hear she's crying.

Juliet dives onto her bed, burying her head in her pillow, and she opens her mouth and screams until she runs out of air. *I don't know who I am anymore either.*

Her phone pings with a message and she sees it's from Adam.

At work but missing you, can't wait to see you again xxx

Me too xxx

Her heart slows down and she takes a gentle breath, wiping away her tears.

She's with Adam. That's who she is right now and who she wants to be, Adam's girlfriend, the woman in Adam's life.

That's the only thing she needs right now, to be with him. The only thing.

SEVEN

Juliet

'Janet Kelly,' says the psychiatrist, holding out her hand for Juliet to shake. Juliet had not wanted to attend the late afternoon appointment, not after the argument with her mother this morning but she understood that it was something she had to face.

She nods and lets the woman grip her own limp hand tightly. The psychiatrist's hand is warm, her handshake firm, and Juliet understands that the message being conveyed by the older woman with short grey hair and black-rimmed glasses is, 'It's okay, I know what I'm doing.'

'Please,' she says, gesturing to a pale blue sofa, where three deep blue scatter pillows are sitting at perfect angles.

Juliet sits, instinctively grabbing a pillow and holding it in front of her. Dr Kelly sits down in a matching pale blue tub chair and immediately makes a note on the writing pad she has picked up from a small round side table next to her chair. Juliet feels like she's already messed up this session by seeming defensive but she doesn't want to put the pillow down.

Dr Kelly crosses her legs and smooths her black skirt. 'So, Juliet,' she says, her voice carrying the practised soothing tone that Juliet has learned to expect from the profession, 'I know you were referred here by Dr Choudry and I do have basic information on what happened to you but I would prefer to hear your version of events.'

Juliet scoffs at the word 'events'.

'This is a difficult time for you and I want to help you.'

An unusual flare of anger makes Juliet clench her fists. 'Everyone wants to help me but no one believes me.'

'Why do you think that?' Dr Kelly holds her pen poised on the notepad, ready to write down everything.

Juliet sighs and looks around the office, her gaze lands on a large vase of carnations in orange and white. 'I know that I ended up at St Augustine,' she says, the words coming slowly because it feels exhausting to have to do this again, 'because I had… a bad moment, and I know why that happened. And I also know that if I had never gone there, I would never have discovered exactly what went on in my childhood.'

'Meaning?' Dr Kelly's brow wrinkles.

'Didn't Dr Choudry tell you everything?'

'No, as I said, just the basics. I like to make my own judgements. He will send me his notes but I always find it better to let my patients tell me where they are before I factor in anyone else's opinion.'

Juliet's heart quickens. Is a fresh start possible? Dr. Kelly has not read the endless notes from Dr Choudry and simply accepted them as true.

Maybe she will believe you. Maybe she's different.

'What I mean is that I discovered in a session with Dr Choudry, I mean not just in one session but it happened during a breathing exercise, that I began to see images of the things my parents had done to me when I was a child, things that hurt me.

Abuse, physical abuse and neglect,' she says as she remembers the dirty room and the days without food.

Dr Kelly nods, watching her, concern on her face.

'Dr Choudry believed me at first but then he met my parents when we had one of those family sessions and suddenly, he didn't believe me. He thought I was making it all up.' Juliet can hear the childish petulance in her own voice.

'Why do you think that was the case?'

'Well... my parents told him I had a vivid imagination. They, like, they used something so stupid, something that happened when I was eight, as proof that I make stuff up and Dr Choudry just accepted it.'

'Tell me about that,' says Dr Kelly and she looks like she is listening, not just writing notes but actually listening.

'At the first family session with my parents, I told them all these things that I had remembered, and my parents just freaked out and denied everything. My mother said that my report cards always said that I had a vivid imagination and she told Dr Choudry that I had once made up a story about my father drowning in a fishing boat accident. And I know that was made up because my dad has never even been out on that type of boat and he's obviously still alive, but I was eight and kids make things up, and anyway, I couldn't even remember telling the story so my parents could easily have been lying.'

'Why do you think they would lie?'

'Because they are liars!' explodes Juliet, dropping the pillow. 'I kept trying to tell Dr Choudry about the things they had done and he just... wouldn't believe me.'

Dr Kelly nods her head like she understands. 'The problem with memory is that it can be a funny thing. It's always subjective and influenced by emotions and social context.'

'I know that.' *There is no problem with my memory,* she thinks but doesn't say aloud.

'Do you think it's possible that if you did make up that story when you were eight, that somehow, you have made up other stories as well? Could you have read something in a book or seen something on television and that's what you now feel may be a memory?'

'Are you saying that I'm lying about what happened to me?' demands Juliet. *She's the same. They're all the same. No one is ever going to believe you.*

'No, no, not at all. Not at all, Juliet.' Dr Kelly raises a hand. 'It's important that you know that I will always tell you the truth. And I really want you to be able to get to the truth about your life and childhood so that you can move on and live your life in the healthiest way possible.'

'It sounds like you just want me to accept that none of the stuff they did ever happened.'

'Not at all. I want you to examine these memories with me. It doesn't mean that none of the things you have suddenly uncovered didn't happen, but it does mean that we need to investigate where the memories come from, why they have been buried and what brought them out now.'

'What brought them out was losing everything and trying to kill myself,' snaps Juliet.

'Why don't we start there? Can you explain what you thought about on the night of your' – the psychiatrist looks down at her writing pad – 'bad moment?'

'I just didn't want to be here anymore,' says Juliet without thinking about the words. She is not talking about that terrible night but rather here and now. She doesn't want to be here anymore and she turns away from the psychiatrist, looks at the digital clock counting down this interminable session, and then she picks up the pillow again, holds it close to her.

That terrible time in her apartment, nearly four months ago – when she picked up the blade and touched it against her skin as she lay in warm water in the cracked tub and thought about everything that she had lost, about the future that would never be hers – is not something she wants to discuss again. And anyway, in the hospital, she realised that she would have been able to withstand the cruel blow of fate that led to the end of her career if she had been raised the way her parents said she had been: surrounded by love. Her depression over never being able to dance again opened something up inside her, let squashed-down secrets into the world, and it was then that she understood. Everything was their fault.

'Can you tell me more?'

'No,' says Juliet, unwilling to discuss that night.

'All right, perhaps you would like to share one of the memories that came up in the hospital. Let's really examine it. Can you do that?'

'You won't believe me,' says Juliet, hugging the pillow closer to her.

'Well' – the psychiatrist taps her pen on her writing pad – 'I am here to listen to you and I want to help you but I can't unless you speak to me.'

Juliet stares at the flowers again. It's very hot outside and this morning, on the news, there were lots of warnings to pregnant women and the elderly: 'Keep yourself hydrated, stay out of the sun, protect yourself.' It would be so easy if you could protect yourself from horrible memories the same way you could do from the sun, just stick on a hat and rub in some cream and you'll be fine.

'Why do you think your parents deny abusing you?' Dr Kelly asks, her tone measured and her voice soft as though the question isn't able to provoke a storm of violence inside Juliet.

'Surely that's something you should ask them? They should be in therapy for what they did, or jail even.'

'And what did they do, Juliet? Can you give me an example? Just one?'

Juliet knows this could be a trap because she has already

fallen into it with Dr Choudry but she then feels a flare of hope that this doctor will be different. *Maybe she is different.*

'They hurt me.' A thousand images flash through her mind, everything that she is keeping inside her, all the terror on repeat. They come and go so fast, it's difficult to really understand them.

'Yes.' The doctor nods as though she agrees.

Juliet closes her eyes, seeks out one single memory, a memory that is more fleshed out than the others.

'My father hit me so hard one day he broke my tooth,' she says and she feels a brief moment of happiness that she has found this memory, that it hasn't flitted away. The image of this in her head is suddenly clear. She sees her father's large hand coming towards her small face, winces as she feels the sharp pain as it connects with her cheek and she can almost taste the metal feeling of blood in her mouth.

'Why did he hit you?' The doctor cocks her head to one side, genuinely interested, and Juliet feels herself relax.

She is not sure of the reason but she wills the answer to come. What had she done to make him hit her? What could she have done and did she even have to do anything at all for them to hurt her?

'I... Just because, it was a Tuesday... No, it was a Wednesday and he was home from work. Maybe I said something or did something... I don't know.' The memory is fading as she speaks, as though giving it air has stolen it away. What was clear only moments ago is now fuzzy. It was so long ago.

'I can't remember everything,' she snaps.

'Please try, Juliet.'

Juliet leans her head back against the sofa, puffs out her cheeks and blows the air out as she thinks.

'Where was your mother when this happened?'

'She was...' And with that question, the memory changes, the hand coming towards her face changes, and she knows the answer. 'Actually, she was the one who hit me.' In her mind, Juliet can see her mother's hand swing towards her face. The image with her father disappears because suddenly she understands that her father never hurt her. He let her be hurt. He stood by and did nothing. Why? This is a new revelation and Juliet would like to examine it but the doctor seems fixed on this one single memory, prodding Juliet to keep going.

'Okay and do you remember why your mother hit you?' The air conditioner in the office is on high and Juliet feels goosebumps ripple along her arms.

'She... didn't like me,' Juliet mumbles because the memory is fading, drifting away. 'I don't know.' She lifts her head and looks at the doctor, frustrated. 'I just don't remember.'

'All right, can you perhaps tell me how old you were when this happened?'

'I was seven or eight. I was small. I think I was small.'

'Do you remember which tooth it was? Did they take you to a dentist to have it repaired? Or was it a baby tooth?'

'It wasn't a baby tooth and they didn't take me to the dentist.' She runs her tongue around her mouth, touching each tooth, searching for the crack, the break that is surely there, but she can't find it. She can't remember being in the dentist chair and having a tooth repaired. She's had the same dentist her whole life and after each visit Dr Stevens says, 'You have a beautiful mouth, Juliet, make sure you keep taking care of your teeth.'

She can't remember Dr Stevens even giving her a filling, let alone repairing a broken tooth.

'Maybe it was a baby tooth,' she says, her gaze roaming around the office.

'Did you tell anyone about the incident? You would have had a bruise on your face after being hit like that I imagine. Did anyone ask you about it – a teacher perhaps?'

Juliet shrugs as she thinks hard about her teacher at school when she was five or six or seven but she can't remember any of them. She thinks about her ballet teacher who used to push her hands against her back and say, 'Stand tall, Juliet, a dancer always stands tall.' Surely Lizette would have said something if she'd had a bruise on her face? Had she already been in Lizette's class then? Was she seven or eight or even nine? She can't remember – why can't she remember?

Dropping the pillow and sitting forward on the sofa, she bangs on the side of her head, once, twice. 'I can't... It's all disappearing again,' she tells the doctor as tears threaten to fall.

'Take your time, just relax and stay calm, and maybe it will come to you. Breathe deeply,' she says and Juliet does this, sniffing as she grabs a tissue from the box in front of her, and wiping her eyes.

'It was a baby tooth,' she says. 'I was four, not yet in school.' She focuses on the grey carpet on the floor because she doesn't want to look at Dr Kelly. She's lying. The memory is there but the specifics aren't.

Dr Kelly nods her head and writes on her pad, her hands moving slowly. Juliet watches her eyes move across the page as she reads through her notes and then the doctor clears her throat.

'From what I understand, Juliet, you had a "bad moment" because you were extremely depressed over the end of your career, which is understandable. I know that it would have been devastating to you. But until you entered St Augustine, you had never remembered any abuse from your parents. Why do you think that is?'

'I realised... that there's stuff I haven't wanted to think about, stuff that I've suppressed.' The images came at her all day long when she was at the hospital and they infiltrated her dreams as well, forcing her to wake sweating and crying. But they were never completely clear, and overlaying each fuzzy image was her mother's voice telling her that she loved her. It doesn't make sense but she knows that her parents are liars. That's one thing she is completely certain of.

The doctor nods and then there is more writing.

'I don't want to talk about this anymore,' says Juliet. She is sick of this, of being here, of doing the same thing over and again and expecting different results.

'All right, can I ask you how you are responding to the medication? Are you feeling okay and getting enough sleep?'

'Yes, it's fine,' lies Juliet. Every morning and every night the notification on her phone goes off, reminding her that she needs to take the awful medication, and she instantly silences it, does nothing. Since she caught her mother snooping this morning, she knows she needs to start throwing away or at least hiding the pills.

At night she looks at the box of sleeping pills that would allow her to rest and turns away from them.

Without the pills, everything feels clearer, sharper, brighter. And she has fewer nightmares. There's an edge to her thoughts, something sharp, and she understands that, perhaps, this sharpness might be damaging but she's not going back to the pills. The terrible dreams that woke her in the hospital have faded but perhaps that's because she sleeps so little.

She is tempted by the sleeping pills when her heart races and her eyes seem frozen open but then she remembers the nightmares and accepts that she will not sleep, scrolling her phone instead as the night hours pass slowly. She is awake most of the night, sleeping for an hour or two at the most before she wakes again, her brain whirring with thoughts.

'It's all fine,' she repeats and Dr Kelly nods.

There is a long silence, broken only by the sound of a ringing telephone somewhere outside the doctor's office.

'Okay, and have you been getting out, perhaps getting some exercise? The weather is so beautiful now.'

'I have been getting out,' says Juliet, her mind settling on

Adam as everything else drifts away. She smiles, unable to stop herself.

'Perhaps you have a new friend?' the psychiatrist asks, uncannily guessing what Juliet is hiding.

'Oh, no,' she lies again, 'I just like being outside.'

Juliet has no desire to tell Dr Kelly about Adam because she has a feeling that the psychiatrist will warn her off a relationship so soon after she has gotten out of the hospital and she doesn't want to hear that at all.

'That's good,' says the doctor and Juliet nods, feeling a warm glow inside her. Soon she will spend the night with him and she knows how wonderful it will be.

'And have you thought about what you might do now, as you get stronger?'

Juliet shrugs. 'Get a job, move out, be independent again.'

'That's good. I'm glad you have that focus and I hope I can help you achieve that,' says Dr Kelly.

There is a low buzzing sound and Juliet knows that means the end of the session. She stands. 'Do you believe me at all? About the things my parents did? Do you think I'm telling the truth?'

'I think we're going to work together, Juliet, and we're going to figure it out,' she says and Juliet feels another flicker of hope. Maybe Dr Kelly will be on her side.

As she leaves the office, she feels her phone vibrate with a message.

How did it go?

Even though the session was emotionally draining, Juliet smiles. He remembered and he cares.

It was okay. I think she might be better than my other doctor.

*That's so great. I've never really trusted psychiatrists but if it
works for you, I'm happy. I hate the idea of people poking about
in my brain, telling me what to think.*

Juliet bites her lip as she thinks about this text. Can she
trust Dr Kelly? She thought she could trust Dr Choudry but she
was wrong. What if Dr Kelly is just saying she can help her but
all she's going to do is tell her that she's made up all the awful
things her parents did? She didn't actually say she believed her.
She said, 'We're going to figure it out.'

In the lift to get to the ground floor, Juliet shakes her head.
Dr Kelly will be the same as Dr Choudry. She wants Juliet to
believe she made up these stories. Adam is right. The psychiatrist wants to tell her what to think and believe. She can't trust
this psychiatrist either. And now she knows, without thinking
too much about it, that she will not be back. Next week she'll
have a cold and the week after that a job interview and she'll
have to think of other things for the weeks after that but she is
never coming back here.

Adam is right, doctors don't know everything and Dr Kelly
is just another quack who won't believe anything Juliet says.

When she's outside she takes a deep breath, feeling free and
light because she will never do this again. No more doctors, no
more pills, just Adam and a different life.

'Good session?' asks her mother as Juliet gets into the car,
because her mother insisted she drive her here.

She looks at her mother and just for a second, her face
morphs and melts and Juliet gasps, moving away, but then she
blinks and it's her mother again.

It must be the lack of sleep but she'll get better at going
without sleep. She's sure of it. A body can get used to anything.

'Yes,' says Juliet. 'She's really nice and we had a good chat
and I can get myself here next week.'

'That's good, darling. I am so happy you like her.' Juliet can hear relief in her mother's voice because maybe Dr Kelly will be the solution to her troubled daughter and then maybe everything can go back to the way it was.

Juliet nods. There's no reason she can't lie to her mother. No reason to tell the truth to the woman who denies everything she ever did. Juliet can lie with the best of them.

At home she goes straight to her room, where she texts Adam.

You're right, I've thought about it and my new psych is a quack and I'm never going back.

Good for you. You don't need a doctor. You're fine.

I am.

Everything is going to be fine, better than fine. But now I have to get back to work. Can't wait to see you tomorrow xxx

Juliet lies on her bed with her phone on her chest, willing the hours to pass until she can see Adam again. He is the only good thing in her life.

It would be different if Benji had caught her. She would be at rehearsal right now, complaining about how sore her feet were. But Benji didn't catch her and then she tried to end her life and then she went to St Augustine and discovered these dark memories.

Adam says Benji should have paid for what he did and he's right. But he's not the only one who needs to pay because he's not the only one who hurt her.

EIGHT

When she is ten, on a dark winter's day when the wind howls through bare-branched trees in the garden, her mother pushes her down the stairs. She had broken the rule of silence that governs the house. Earlier in the day, she told a teacher that her mother refused to allow her to take lunch to school that day.

The teacher called her mother and her mother arrived, in a hurried flush of smiles and explanations. She watched her mother speak as she sat at a desk in the classroom and she understood that she had made a mistake, but the teacher is kind, an older plump woman who refers to all her students as 'little darlings', and so she had made the confession without thinking.

Her mother spoke quickly, telling the teacher that she would never, ever do something like that. 'She just forgot, silly thing, but here it is. It was ready and waiting for her on the kitchen counter. I'm trying to help her become more independent. It's what children need; don't you agree?'

The lunchbox was produced, brimming with fruit and sandwiches and even a treat of a small chocolate bar. The girl's stomach rumbled and she wondered if she would be allowed to eat the food or only look at it as the bell for the end of the lunch break rang.

The teacher nodded and smiled because of course mothers don't send their children to school without lunch.

She was starving because breakfast wasn't allowed either. Her mother handed her the lunchbox and stroked her head. 'Silly sausage,' she said. The child ate gratefully, quickly stuffing the food in her mouth, as her mother and the teacher spoke about how funny young children could be and other students began to enter the classroom, their cheeks ruddy from the wind, their chatter filled with energetic joy.

Halfway through the maths lesson, the girl needed to go to the bathroom and throw up all the food that she had eaten because she knew what was coming. She spent the rest of the day churning with anxiety and when she got into the car after school, her mother didn't speak to her or look at her.

At home, when the front door closed, her mother sent her to her room with a silent pointed finger.

Then her mother waited for her father to come home so she could report to him, so she could tell him what a bad child his daughter was. And she knew that her father would nod, would agree that she is awful. He would not hurt her because he never hurts her but he knows what happens and he approves. The child knows he approves.

In her room, she does her homework, trying to concentrate on her spelling words and her reading, but mostly, just waiting for the sound of the door opening and closing at exactly 6 p.m. She finds herself hungry again but doesn't dare leave her room.

When she hears the sound of the door, her heart sinks and she stands, readying herself with a deep breath. How bad will it be this time? Will it be so bad that others can see, that others will know, and what will the excuse have to be? She will have to miss her after-school activities if it's bad enough, and she will have to have a suitable, agreed upon explanation. Bruises need to be explained to teachers and other students.

A minute later, her mother bursts in and demands she come downstairs to explain to her father why she lied about the lunchbox to the teacher.

As the girl moves towards the stairs, her mother shoves her and she tumbles down, lying in a shocked heap at the bottom, one foot at an odd angle. She yelps in pain as she understands that this means many weeks of afternoons stuck in her room, in this house, with her mother just waiting for her to make a mistake she can be punished for.

Her mother crouches over her, a smile on her face. 'What happened?'

Sudden fury rises up inside her at what she will lose because of this new injury and she shouts, 'You pushed me.' She struggles to stand but can't put weight on her foot. Hot tears fill her eyes and spill over onto her cheeks and her mother puts an arm around her as she laughs. 'Don't be ridiculous. Why would I do that? I love you. I've only ever loved you.'

'You... don't,' she protests but she speaks softly, weakly. The pain is taking over her whole body.

'Come on, my love, we need to get you to a doctor,' says her mother. 'I think that ankle may be broken.'

Her mother practically carries her to the car and her father drives them to the hospital. Her mother tells the doctor she fell down the stairs. 'She's always been a bit of a clumsy child, silly sausage,' says her mother as she strokes her hair adoringly. The doctor gives her pain medication and she feels lightheaded, woozy, out of pain and happy as her mother touches her so gently.

The child wonders if her mother did push her, or if she did make a mistake because why would her mother lie? She loves her and she has always loved her.

And if she made a mistake about being pushed, then perhaps she made one about the lunchbox, and about being slapped for *leaving a glass in the sink only two days ago, about being starved for forgetting to take out the garbage, about any number of things that she knows happen to her but sometimes seem like things that have not actually happened.*

Her parents love her and they always have.

'Not all memories can be trusted,' her mother says as she comforts her when they return from the hospital and she has her foot in a cast and a pair of crutches to help her walk.

And the girl nods because this must be right. She must be the one at fault, the one with the bad memory. Her brain is making things up. Her parents love her and they always have.

NINE

Juliet

Taking a seat at the café, she orders a coffee from the waitress while she waits for Adam. They are meeting for breakfast today instead of a quick coffee and a walk. In fact, they are spending the whole day together. A glorious gift of a day off from work for Adam and a day he wants to spend with her. He seems to always be at work, even on the weekend. He is, he has told her, 'in the middle of a big project.' A redesign of a security system, he has explained.

A week ago, she was meant to have dinner at his place but then he texted her midway through the day and told her that there had been a huge problem at work.

So sorry, I have to stay late.

She had replied, eager and desperate to see him:

I could come to your office and wait. We can have dinner when you're done.

No, I'm going to be really late, and the first time we have dinner, I want to be alone with you, not in some restaurant. It will happen soon, don't worry.

She wanted to push him to meet her because seeing him for a quick coffee in the morning was not enough for her anymore. She wanted more of him, much more, but she counselled herself to be patient.

She cancelled her appointment with Dr Kelly for last week and she has just cancelled her one for this week. She is off the pills, not sleeping much, but she feels like she's more in control of her life. In fact, she feels a kind of bubbly electric energy now. She doesn't eat much but that's fine because she's fine. She is, as Adam says, doing really well without the help of doctors and drugs.

'Here you go,' says the waitress, drawing her back into the noisy café, where a toddler is banging his spoon against the side of a cup and a man is talking loudly on his phone. She thinks about the idea of getting a job and moving out and just being in the world away from her parents. It's an idea that goes around in her head all day long as she thinks about what she might like to do with her life, what she can do. But something is stopping her from taking this step, from moving on. It's the reason she came home, what she needs to do before she can leave this all behind her. She needs the truth and an apology. Picking up her coffee, she takes a deep, too-hot sip and feels the liquid burn her throat as it goes down.

She doesn't want to spoil this day, this wonderful day, by thinking about her parents but she can't seem to help herself.

Now that her body is completely free of the medicine, she is taking the time to think about the things they did, to try and find enough details. If she finds something she can hold on to, like an image of her mother putting a padlock on the fridge as she stands in the kitchen, she holds on to it, repeating it, filling in details and writing it down if she can. She is polishing up the horror of her childhood so that it shines too brightly to dismiss and hide away. She will get them to admit what they did. She needs them to. That and being with Adam are her only goals right now.

'Lost in thought,' she hears and she looks up and there he is and her heart flips, just like it does every time she sees him. He is dressed casually in jeans and a black T-shirt.

She smiles. 'Oh, you know.'

He leans down and kisses her gently on the cheek, his hand squeezing her shoulder, and she is surrounded by his ocean smell, fresh from the shower. And then he sits down and picks up the menu.

'I'm going to get the avocado toast,' he says after a moment.

'Sounds good, I'll have the same but with a couple of poached eggs on the side.'

In the bag she is carrying, she has stashed a toothbrush and some of her sexiest lingerie, despite feeling ridiculous when she did it. But now looking at him, she can't wait to go back to his place later and slip on the lacy black bra and thong.

'You're smiling, I like that,' he says. 'What's making you so happy this morning?'

Juliet feels her smile grow wider. 'Just, you know... a whole day with you. I might finally get to see that bachelor pad of yours.' Her face flushes. She feels like a teenage girl but Adam is not a teenage boy.

'Maybe...' He laughs. 'But we have the whole day, so you never know.' He winks, making her giggle.

'What can I get you?' asks a waitress that Juliet has never seen before and Juliet quickly recites their orders.

Adam leans across the table and holds both her hands when the waitress is gone, stroking the skin. Her whole body warms up and she looks around the café and sees the mother of the toddler looking at her with something like envy on her face and that makes her giggle.

'Something funny?' Adam asks, sitting back.

'I was just thinking that the mother over there, the one with the kid, that she's looking at me like she's jealous and it's... silly' – she shakes her head – 'but I can't believe anyone could ever be jealous of me. I mean, I thought that before I met you.' She feels her face flush as their food arrives. She's embarrassing herself.

'Can I say something?' says Adam as he picks up his cutlery, and Juliet nods her head.

'I know that what happened to you was terrible, like the accident, that you felt like everything was lost, but sometimes when I talk to you, I feel like there's something more, something you're not telling me.'

Juliet has taken a mouthful of her food and she feels a sharp corner of toast lodge in her throat. For a moment she thinks she might actually choke to death but then she picks up her coffee and drinks it down, grateful that it's now lukewarm and the toast moves.

'Are you okay?'

'Yes, it was just, just got caught,' she says, lifting her serviette to wipe her mouth. Why is he saying this now? Where did this come from? Is it that obvious that she is keeping secrets from him?

'You can tell me anything, you know,' says Adam as he takes a bite of his toast. Juliet nods because she knows that this is true.

She doesn't want to talk about her childhood and ruin this perfect day. But now that she thinks about it, perhaps this is the final step they need to take as a couple before they do anything else. She knows all about his family life with his alcoholic father and passive mother who are still together. She knows that he was bullied at school until he got taller than everyone else, that he was singled out for being so smart and that he was lonely as a teenage boy. She knows his favourite foods and what his dreams for the future are, like seeing the Northern Lights in Alaska and the mountains of Peru. He knows a lot about her as well but he doesn't know this, this one thing that is keeping her trapped in her parents' house.

'It's hard to talk about.'

'Why?'

'Because when I was in the hospital, I tried to talk about it to my doctor, and he thought I was lying.' Saying the words out loud to him makes her feel strange.

'But you're not the kind of person that lies. It's just not in you. Surely, he could see that.' Adam waves around the knife he is using. 'I mean, how ridiculous.'

Juliet feels her heart fill with love for this man who doesn't just seem to understand her but who believes her, believes in her.

'Tell me, Juliet. Tell me everything.' He leans closer to her so that everyone else in the café is blocked out and it feels like they are alone.

Juliet cuts a piece of toast with her knife and fork and then cuts it in half and half again. She doesn't want to eat anymore. 'My parents hurt me,' she says, looking away from Adam, at a couple walking down the street outside.

When she turns back to look at him, he is quiet, his gaze focused on her. And she knows that he will sit here and wait for her to speak for however long she wants. He is so patient with her.

'My parents hurt me. When I was younger, my mother abused me. She pushed me down the stairs, hit me, left me alone in my room with no food. And then she stopped. I think she stopped when I was about eleven or twelve. And for some reason, I just suppressed it all. I didn't remember any of it until I began speaking to Dr Choudry in the hospital. And then it all came back. And he didn't...' She shakes her head and stares down at the slightly sticky wood tabletop, biting down on her lip because she doesn't want to cry.

'He believed me at first, like he understood and he wanted to help and then he met my parents and they told him that I make things up and from then on, he didn't believe me at all. Instead, he kept making me question myself and it's only since I've left that I've realised that he did the same thing my parents did. I know they hurt me but they always made me question what had happened. They just deny it.'

'You can tell me,' Adam whispers, so softly that she almost doesn't hear it. 'You can tell me, Juliet. I'll believe you. You can tell me everything.' He has stopped eating now as well and she's glad. This is not a breakfast conversation.

'Perhaps we can walk?' she says and he nods.

'I'll just go pay and meet you outside,' he says. Neither of them has finished their food but that doesn't matter.

'I might just head to the bathroom first,' she says, her stomach churning with what she's about to tell him.

When she's done in the bathroom, she is walking past the café counter when the waitress calls out, 'Excuse me, miss, miss.' Juliet stops and turns around although she's certain that the waitress is not talking to her.

'Me?' she questions.

'Yes, you forgot to pay.'

'Oh no, my... Adam paid,' says Juliet, walking back to the counter.

'Um, no, no one paid,' says the waitress and she flushes as though this is a difficult situation she does not want to be dealing with.

Juliet peers outside the large framed windows of the café, hoping to spot Adam, but she can't see him and then she pulls out her phone and sends him a quick text: *Did you pay for breakfast?* But he doesn't respond.

'Can I just go and get him? I'm sure...' Juliet starts to say but then a heavy sigh from someone behind her makes her turn and she realises that there's a queue forming and everyone is irritated.

'No problem,' she says, 'I'll just pay.'

'That'll be twenty-two fifty,' says the waitress, grabbing her machine so that Juliet can tap and pay.

'Gosh,' says Juliet, 'that's well priced for two breakfasts and two coffees.'

The waitress smiles uncertainly at her. 'Just one breakfast – it was just you,' she says.

'No, I was with my boyfriend,' says Juliet.

'Um... you were at table twelve, right? It was just you.'

'No,' Juliet tries but the person behind her cannot contain his irritation any longer.

'Look, can you just have this conversation later? I have to get to work.'

'Sorry, sorry,' says Juliet, feeling her cheeks warm with humiliation. She taps and pays and walks out of the café as quickly as she can. She's probably just paid for someone else's breakfast but whatever.

Outside she still can't see Adam but she walks a few steps and there he is, staring into the window of a store selling clothing. A male and female mannequin stand together, both dressed in matching leather jackets that seem incongruous in the warm sunshine.

'There you are. The weirdest thing just happened.'

'Really, what?'

Juliet explains about the waitress and Adam nods his head thoughtfully. 'Well, that's rubbish. I paid for both of us. She made a mistake. I'll go back and explain it to her.' He looks angry and she doesn't want him to be angry on the one full day they have together.

'No.' Juliet shakes her head, wanting to avoid any kind of

confrontation in the busy café. 'I'll just chalk it up to someone getting a nice surprise.'

'Are you sure?'

'Yes, let's go.' She shakes off the encounter, hoping that, somehow, her paying for a stranger's breakfast means that some good will come her way, that karma is real. Because if it is, then the people who damaged her will get what's coming to them. *My mother, my father, Benji. Let it go.*

Adam grabs her hand as they make their way to the park that they know so well now. They walk around the man-made lake where ducks happily swim, occasionally diving under the water to find something to eat. She is quiet for a long time but Adam doesn't push her. He just waits.

Finally, she begins to speak. And somehow, the memories that have seemed elusive, misty, impossible to pin down are stronger as she speaks. She knows that she has filled in a lot of the details by thinking about them. There are times when a few elements do seem made up, as though she has read them or heard about them from somewhere, but once she slots them into the story of the incident, they fit so well, she knows that's where they belong.

She tells him about her mother breaking her wrist and hitting her hard enough to break a tooth and pushing her down the stairs and starving her as a punishment and always, always telling her that she was wrong about what she experienced. She feels like she talks for hours and when she is done, her head is pounding.

'That's called gaslighting,' says Adam when she has finally run out of words. He leads her to a bench and they sit down. He holds her hand but she can't look at him. She worries that he will not want to be with her anymore, that she is too damaged, that she is a broken person not worthy of love. She worries he will find her ugly and unlovable.

'None of it was your fault,' he says quietly. 'They hurt you and then they gaslit you and it wasn't your fault and you aren't the damaged person; they are damaged people because they hurt you.'

Juliet feels her eyes fill with tears at how Adam has understood her and she has to scrabble in her bag for a tissue. She cries softly, her breath shuddering inside her as she tries to get a hold of herself.

Finally, she calms down and she drops her head onto his shoulder. He strokes her hair.

'Isn't gaslighting what happens between people in a relationship, like a romantic relationship?'

'No, not just that. It's any relationship and you were gaslit by your parents and they are probably still doing it. I don't know how you are managing to live there. That's not a criticism, especially since I understand now, it's just... I didn't know how hard it was for you to be there.'

'I want them to admit it,' she says. 'I feel like I can't move on until they do. I hate them but I still... kind of love them, if that makes sense. I wish I felt nothing for them but I have good memories as well and I don't know, I just don't know if the bad ones are true, if the good ones are true or if all of it is.'

'They don't deserve to be parents,' says Adam, his voice low and menacing.

Juliet knows that this is the one real truth in her life and anger suddenly sweeps away her despair. 'No, they don't and I wish... I wish they were just dead... It would just be so much easier if they were,' she says, the words a shocking explosion of hate.

'Well' – Adam shrugs – 'you don't mean that.'

'I do,' she spits. 'I really do.'

TEN

Juliet

Juliet regrets the words as soon as they are in the air. Adam looks at her, concern on his face. Does she wish that? Really? And how would it help?

'Shall we walk some more?' he asks and Juliet nods, standing up from the park bench. The bag with sexy lingerie seems really silly now. Her confession has cast a shadow over the sunny day, and now, she would really like to go home and go to sleep, wipe away the things she has told Adam.

'You don't mean that. I know you're angry but you don't mean it,' he says as he holds her hand and she's grateful for the chance to back away from the terrible words.

'No,' she admits. 'Not really. I need... closure, I guess. I just want them to admit that they lied to me, that they hurt me.'

They exit the park, walking back past the café where they abandoned their breakfast and she unwittingly made someone's day.

'It's less busy now,' says Adam, 'should I go and explain it to her?'

'No, no,' says Juliet, not wanting to revisit the situation.

'Okay, how about another coffee, from somewhere else?' says Adam as they walk past a bakery and she nods. Inside the air is scented with chocolate and sugar and Juliet's mouth waters as she stares at all the pastries in the cabinet.

'Have one,' encourages Adam and Juliet nods, points at a croissant, round and pillowy with thick chocolate oozing out of the sides. 'I'll get it,' says Juliet, 'you paid for breakfast. You go grab us a table.'

Juliet waits patiently for the coffees and then takes them outside with her croissant, where Adam is waiting at one of the small metal outdoor tables on the pavement. Juliet bites into the croissant and closes her eyes, savouring the thick, rich chocolate and buttery pastry.

'Good?' Adam laughs and she nods, offering him a bite, which he takes. 'Very good,' he says as he chews.

'Sorry for being weird.' She swallows a sip of coffee, not quite looking at him.

'You're not weird, Juliet, you're hurting.'

She nods because this is the truth. Moments of pain have pancaked on top of each other for the last three years and she doesn't know if it will be possible to move on from what Benji did, from what happened to her life as a result and from the things she discovered when she went into the hospital.

'Tell me what would help?'

Juliet finishes the croissant and smooths the paper bag, and then her hands begin folding it into smaller and smaller squares as she thinks about this. 'The truth and an apology.'

'Well,' he sighs, 'you may not be able to get that and you have to figure out if you're okay with that.'

'I don't know if I can be. Isn't what I remember and what I feel enough of a reason for them to believe me and to try and make it right?' She stops folding and looks up at him and he nods.

'I think,' says Adam, his gaze moving over the people walking past the bakery, 'I think that in order for them to admit what they did, you would need some kind of proof. Unfortunately, a child's memories are not proof. Aren't there any X-rays in your house, anything that could at least show a history of the broken ankle and the broken wrist? That may help.'

'Nothing – my mother said I never had those because none of that happened and she's sure to have chucked away any old X-rays.' She had asked about visits to the doctor and the hospital in the first family session she had with her parents after the memories returned. 'What are you talking about?' her mother kept saying. 'You never broke your wrist; you never hurt your ankle. Why would we have taken you to the doctor? You hurt your knee, Juliet, remember?' she explained as though Juliet had lost the ability to form intelligent thought.

Adam sighs. They sit in silence for a moment as Juliet unfurls the paper bag and then folds it up again. She has ruined their whole day and she is filled with regret.

'Well... it's not like you couldn't get your own proof. Old breaks show up on an X-ray forever.'

'That's true,' says Juliet and her hands stop moving, 'but how would I... I mean... like, how would I do that?'

She feels very young as Adam reaches across the table and takes her hand, like she is a child who has no idea about anything.

'Well, it would be possible. Basically, we can go to any medical centre and tell them you hurt your wrist and ankle, one or both, and we can ask to get sent for X-rays. And you get that done and then you'll know, you'll actually know. You'll have the proof you need to finally show them so they can't deny it.'

Juliet thinks about this as she begins to fold the paper bag into triangles. 'Do you think that would... I mean, how easy would it be to convince a doctor? I would need to have a reason for why I hurt both my wrist and my ankle.'

'Maybe,' he says, finishing his coffee. 'Maybe, you could say that you went for a run and fell over.'

'That would work,' Juliet says. 'Of course it would work. I can try that tomorrow.'

'Well, why not go today? I have the day off and I did some acting in my university days. I can come with as the supportive boyfriend.' He laughs at this idea and Juliet feels her face flush with heat at him calling himself her boyfriend. She has a momentary vision of the future, of her and Adam together and a sparkling diamond ring on her finger. *Don't get ahead of yourself, Juliet.*

'We could get it done. It would be easy.' Adam stands and holds out his hand as though everything is just that simple.

Juliet nods, standing up and taking his hand. If she knows for sure, then maybe that will be enough. Maybe she can stop doubting herself and just move out of her parents' house and get on with her life. She will know and that's all that matters. He pulls her into a tight hug, her head resting just below his chin.

'I just want you to be able to move on,' says Adam. 'I mean I want to... build a life with you...'

She looks up and is astonished to see him blushing.

'Okay,' she says, a sudden excitement brewing inside her at the idea that one day she will be someone else entirely, that if she can put this behind her and find a way to move on, she could live the kind of life that other people actually get to live.

'Let's go today... right now.'

Adam smiles. 'Okay then, let's do this,' he says, letting her go and taking her hand again.

It is shocking to her that the solution to the huge black cloud hanging over her life is so simple and she wonders why no one has thought of doing it before. Why didn't Dr Choudry suggest X-rays? It would have been so quick to do and then she would have had the evidence she needed or he would have had the proof that she was making it up. It was because he didn't believe her after talking to her parents; he saw no reason to distrust them and every reason to distrust Juliet.

Part of Juliet is excited to get this done, to know the truth, but she is also terrified. There was some bizarre comfort in her parents denying the abuse. It allowed her to have moments of convincing herself that she had made it all up, that somewhere between her suicide attempt, her hospitalisation, her insomnia and all the meds she was taking, her mind had played an awful trick on her. Now she will know for sure.

Thirty minutes later they are walking into a medical centre. She fills out a form as a new patient, hobbling as Adam holds her hand to help her. While they wait, she rests her head on his shoulder, looking around the full waiting room, where a mother is trying to calm a fussy toddler who keeps whining, 'I wanna go home.' A good number of the chairs are taken up by older people scrolling through their phones as though they have all the time in the world, and in the corner, two teenage girls are hunched over their phones too, whispering and giggling.

'It may take a couple of days to get the results,' says Adam. 'I'd like to be with you when you get them. I think...it may be upsetting. I want to be there for you.'

Juliet looks up at him and then she nods, imagining being alone in her room as she finds out all the things that have happened to her body. She shudders at the thought of it.

'Juliet Cordell,' she hears and she sits up to see the doctor, a young woman with bobbed dark hair, dressed in a navy skirt and pale pink blouse.

'Careful,' instructs Adam as she stands and he helps her. She leans heavily on him, enjoying the physical contact with his body.

'Now,' says the doctor, as they sit down in her office, 'tell me what happened.'

'I fell over while I was running,' Juliet says and she concentrates hard as the doctor touches her ankle and her wrist, wincing in the right way as she remembers the pain of her knee, of those first few moments as she lay on the floor after she flew through the air and Benji did not catch her. She had tried to move her leg as the other dancers crowded around her.

'Don't move a muscle,' the director, Boyd, instructed her and so she remained still, even letting Benji hold her hand for support. Juliet pushes all thoughts of Benji out of her mind as the doctor gently manipulates her wrist.

'We need some X-rays and then I'll let you know where to go from there. I may have to send you to the fracture clinic at the hospital but let's take this one step at a time,' says the doctor now as the phone on her desk begins to ring. They have only been in the office for ten minutes but Juliet can see that the woman is keen to get to her next patient.

'I think X-rays will be good. My ribs hurt as well,' Juliet says, wanting to have as much evidence as possible. Does she remember her parents ever breaking a rib? She has no idea but then there is probably a lot that she has forgotten.

'Right,' says the doctor and she taps at her keyboard and a referral instantly emerges from the printer next to her computer.

'How long after the scan until we get images?' asks Adam.

'Could be this afternoon but no more than a couple of days, and I'll call you when I get the report.'

Adam leans towards her, whispers in her ear, 'You'll know everything soon. I hope I'm with you when the results come in.'

'Can you call Adam? I have um... I can't answer my phone at work,' says Juliet, suddenly fearful of what is going to be found, of the idea that she will probably be alone when she receives the news that confirms her parents' abuse.

'Are you sure?' Adam says and she nods her head, knowing

that she will want to be with him when the truth is finally revealed.

'Okay, call me,' says Adam, giving the doctor his number. The doctor doesn't even question him and Juliet is grateful for the level of anonymity in the walk-in clinic. The doctor didn't even ask if they were a couple or how they knew each other.

She pays for the consultation and then limps out of the waiting room, holding on to Adam's hand until they are out of sight of the clinic and she can take a relieved breath and walk properly.

At the imaging place they have been referred to, they wait together until Juliet is taken to the back. By then she has perfected her 'running' story and she is able to chat with the technician while images are taken.

'You okay?' asks Adam when they have walked away and are sitting in a bar, sharing a bottle of wine. It's after 3 p.m. and Juliet has seven missed calls from her mother on her phone. She has not stayed out the whole day since she left the hospital and she knows that her mother is panicked and worried but she doesn't care. There is no place in the world she would rather be than with Adam. She nods in response to his question.

'Are you sure you want me to get the results?' Adam asks as he picks up the bottle. Juliet watches the ruby-coloured wine fill her glass as she considers this.

'I'm sure.'

'And what if...?'

'If?'

'What if it shows that your parents are telling the truth?'

Juliet takes a sip of wine, letting the acidic taste fill her mouth. She hasn't had alcohol for a long time. Swallowing the wine, she stares down at her hands, her mind twisting at the wild possibility that her parents are not lying, that she is actually making a mistake and that she has been mistaken all along.

She is surprised by the tears that appear. 'That will change everything,' she says, swiping her hand across her face.

Adam leans forward and puts his hand over her arm, warming the skin there.

'It won't change how I feel about you, Juliet. We'll figure this out together. I promise.'

'Okay,' she says with a nod, 'okay.'

'I think we should leave it for tonight,' he says.

'You mean you don't want me to come back to your place?' she asks, feeling sick at the idea.

'I think I want you there more than anything but it's been a long day and I can see that your phone is vibrating with calls from your mother.'

Juliet looks down at her phone, where the word 'Mum' is popping up over and again. 'She's worried but I don't care. I want to come home with you.'

'Juliet, I want that too, believe me, but it's been a long day and she will keep calling. I don't want you to be distracted and I know you must be tired. I'm tired as well. I want you to be relaxed. I want us both to be in the best space possible.'

Juliet is exhausted. Adam is right. She nods her agreement.

Picking up her phone, she sends her mother a quick text. *Coming home now, stop calling me.*

'You're probably right. Another night would be better,' she says as Adam pours the last of the wine into their glasses. He has drunk a lot more than she has but she's fine with that. She doesn't want to feel weird and spacey when she's with him.

'Another night, I promise,' he says, his smile warming her all over.

'I wonder why the doctor hasn't contacted us,' she says.

'Maybe we went too late in the afternoon? They'll come soon, I'm sure of it.'

They take a slow walk back to her house as the air grows cooler and the sun drops low in the sky. They don't speak much, each wrapped in their own thoughts, but for once, Juliet doesn't think about all the things that are bothering her, all the things that make her unhappy. Instead, when her mind wanders, it is with thoughts of what a night with Adam will be like. She thinks about what his apartment will look like and what it will feel like to lie next to him, to feel his naked skin next to hers, and she finds that thought is the only thing she wants to concentrate on.

'I'll see you tomorrow,' says Adam when they stop, two houses away from her home, and Juliet nods. He encloses her in a hug and she holds on tight, even as her mind betrays her, straying to the X-rays and what they will show her about her life and who her parents really are.

ELEVEN

When the child is eleven, she tells her mother she needs new clothes because she has grown out of her old ones.

'Ungrateful brat,' her mother mutters and the child gets angry, even though she knows that she shouldn't, even though she knows what happens when she does.

'I'm not ungrateful,' she shrieks, 'you're a terrible mother. You have more than enough money and I look like a poor person.'

'You look fine,' her mother responds.

'I look like I have no one taking care of me and people at school are beginning to talk about my clothes,' says the child, triumphantly, knowing that this is all that matters to her mother, this and nothing else. She is telling a lie but she figures that her mother lies all the time. There is no reason she shouldn't as well.

'Fine,' her mother hisses, standing up from the kitchen table where she is doing a crossword puzzle, 'let's go shopping. Let's spend hundreds of dollars on new clothes for the princess.'

The child follows her mother to the car, even as she realises that she thinks she has won something but that there will be a price to pay because there is always a price to pay.

Once they are at the car, she opens her door and her mother

says, 'Wait a moment,' and the child turns to see why she must wait, not realising that her hand is on the door frame.

Her mother moves so quickly, she doesn't have time to react and the door is slammed, trapping her hand. The pain doesn't start right away and all she can do is gasp. 'Please, please, open the door,' she says because she can't make her other hand function to do it herself. Shock is rippling through her body.

'Oh dear, oh dear, what have you done?' Her mother clucks and steps forward to open the door. The child's hand is bruising and puffing, and now the pain begins, radiating all through her body, making her shiver with the force of it.

'Oh dear, oh dear,' her mother mutters again. 'What have you done? I'm sure your fingers are broken, silly sausage, what did you do that for? We were going shopping.'

'I didn't... I didn't...' The girl gasps, cradling her hand, the pain searing itself into every part of her. She looks at her mother and sees something flicker across her face, something dark, something evil, and she knows that if she protests, something even worse may happen.

'We need to get you to a hospital.'

Her mother runs back inside and grabs an ice pack and all the way to the emergency room she repeats, 'Why would you do something like that? Why would you hurt yourself when we love you so much?'

In the emergency room of a different hospital to one she has been to before; she is whisked through as soon as the triage nurse looks at her hand and she is placed on a bed for a doctor to see. A second nurse comes into the room to take her temperature.

'What happened, you poor thing?' she asks.

'The silly sausage had her hand on the door jamb when she was already in the car. I didn't see it when I went to close the door. I've told her not to do that,' says her mother, dabbing at her eyes with a tissue. 'I just hate it so much when she gets hurt.'

'It will be fine,' says the nurse, 'we'll send her up for an X-ray as soon as the doctor has seen her.' The nurse hands the girl some liquid in a small cup. 'For the pain,' she says, and the girl drinks it down eagerly, not worrying about the strange taste. The pain begins to dissipate almost immediately and the girl looks at the nurse, who is young and has her blonde hair tied up in a ponytail, and she thinks how wonderful it must be to be the person who can take away pain.

She would like to live in a world where she doesn't have to worry about pain.

All the fingers on her hand are broken and she knows that this will mean more time at home, more time in her room, more time with her mother.

But while she is at home, her mother goes out every day and comes home with bags full of new clothes, delighting in showing them to her. 'I told all the shop assistants that my darling daughter was at home with an injured hand but that she needed new clothes.'

'Thank you,' says the girl as she watches her mother take beautiful blouses and soft pairs of pants out of her bags.

'Of course, darling, anything for you. I love you and I always have. You know that, don't you?'

'I do,' says the girl. 'I really do.'

TWELVE

Juliet

She opens the front door then slumps against a wall, steeling herself for her mother's questions as her fatigue grows.

She can feel that she is on the precipice of something, that the test results will change everything. Thinking about Adam cannot keep that truth at bay when she is in her parents' house. She is uncomfortable, uneasy. Everything feels wrong.

If the broken bones are there, she will know that the terrible memories are certainly the truth, and if they are not, she will know that she is mad, certifiably mad.

Bed is all she can think about but as she goes to climb the stairs to her bedroom, she can see her parents sitting together at the round kitchen table. They have had the table for Juliet's whole life and she can remember sitting there after school, doing her homework, eating a snack, talking to her mother as she prepared dinner. Now it looks odd and out of place because a few years ago, her mother had the kitchen redone, and the sleek white cabinets and white marble countertop don't go with the scarred timber table but her parents have held on to it.

She contemplates just ignoring them but can see from the way her father is sitting, with his arms folded, his face grim, that they won't let her just walk away.

'Where have you been?' her mother asks her, blowing her nose, and Juliet can see that she's been crying. 'You didn't answer your phone. I thought, we thought... Where have you been?'

Juliet goes to the fridge and takes out a small bottle of sparkling water and then she goes to leave the kitchen. They don't deserve an answer or an explanation. She owes these people nothing.

'Your mother asked you a question,' her father says, his voice low, threatening.

Juliet stops, turning back, squeezing the bottle in her hand. 'And if I don't answer, what will happen?' she snarls. 'Will you hit me?'

Leaping out of his chair so that it falls backwards on the ground with a clatter, her father moves right up to her, looks down and points a finger at her face. 'We are sick of this, Juliet. Your lies are going to kill your mother and I won't have it. I won't have it anymore, do you understand me?' he yells.

Juliet steps back, fear spreading through her body. Her father has never hurt her. In all her memories it is only her mother, but she can feel, in this moment, that he wants to hit her, to hurt her. His need to lash out vibrates off him like heat.

'I'm not lying,' she says, taking another step away from him. 'And if you just admitted it, and said sorry, everything would be better.'

Her father sighs and turns around, picks up the chair and sits down again, and then he drops his head into his hands. 'You need to go back to the hospital, Juliet.'

'I don't need a hospital!' yells Juliet, furious. 'I need you to admit the truth!'

'Oh, Juliet,' says her mother and she bursts into tears.

Juliet runs from the kitchen, taking the stairs two at a time, the bottle of water in her hand. Inside her bedroom she slams the door and throws herself on her bed, dropping the bottle on the floor.

Willing tears to come because at least tears bring relief, she closes her eyes. But she cannot cry. There are no tears inside her left for this situation.

Turning over on her bed, she sits up and grabs the bottle, opening it and drinking down all of it. *I'll know the truth soon enough and then everyone will know it too.*

She shakes away the picture of her mother sitting at the kitchen table, tears running down her face.

Making her mother cry stabs at her in a way that she cannot explain. Are they real tears or just for show?

A niggling part of her is worried that they may actually just force her back into hospital. She can see it's possible in the way her father looks at her. If she returns to the hospital, she will not be in their house and will not be their problem anymore and that's what they really want, for their problem to go away. Her mother looks older than she did when Juliet came home from the hospital nearly a month ago and that bothers Juliet for some reason. Her thoughts and emotions bounce around inside her with no clear way to go and no clear understanding of the truth and she hates feeling this way, hates it.

Opening up her computer, she thinks about when she did move out, a year after her accident. Her parents begged her not to. 'Stay until you have figured out what you want to do,' said her mother. 'You can go to university or you can open a dance studio and teach, but stay and let us help you until you are ready to stand on your own.'

But Juliet needed to get out of the house, away from all the pictures of her in perfect poses and all the trophies and ribbons she had won over the years in ballet competitions. Even the programmes from every single dance season she had participated in were framed on the walls of the living room. The house was a shrine to her ballet career and even if everything was taken down and locked away, she would still know it was there. Now she realises that something else was driving her out of the house, something she only accessed in the hospital.

Scrolling idly through Instagram, she thinks, as she has done millions of times, about how different her life would have been if not for the accident.

Impulsively, she clicks on Benji's profile and lets the pictures there make her feel sick. In one, he is holding another dancer above his head, the muscles in his arms and legs standing out. The female dancer is in a gossamer skirt, a smile on her beautiful face, and she looks light and free. That was exactly what should have happened when she leapt. Benji should have caught her and he didn't.

Her rage at him is always there, always brewing, and yet there is nothing she can do. Why is there nothing she can do about anything that has happened to her?

Adam said that Benji should be punished for missing the catch, especially since Juliet thinks he missed it on purpose.

It happened three weeks after she had taken him aside one day at rehearsal and told him that she wanted to end their relationship. 'But we're perfect for each other,' he had protested. 'I don't understand. We've been together forever and we just fit. What did I do wrong? Tell me what I did wrong.'

'Nothing, it's not you, it's me,' she told him. 'I just... I'm only eighteen and I just want to be single for a bit.'

'You want to screw other men? Is that what you need to do?' He was red with rage and humiliation.

'No, no,' she replied. 'I just want to... I can't explain it, Benji, I just need some space.'

And that was the truth. All she had wanted was some space to breathe. Between rehearsals and being with him and living at home, she felt like she had no time alone, ever, like she was always with someone who expected her to talk and engage and she just wanted some time off. She was eighteen and it was fine for her to make that decision but she hadn't thought about the consequences. Benji tried, for a week, to get her to change her mind. He came to her house, sent her gifts, messaged her all night long, begging her to reconsider. But when she wouldn't, he eventually seemed to accept it. He sent her a text message: *Hey, I've been thinking about this a lot. I didn't want the break-up but I also don't want to be in a relationship with someone who doesn't love and appreciate me. So, I wish you well. I hope you get the space you want and figure yourself out so you don't break someone else's heart the way you have mine.*

Juliet hadn't liked the tone of the message but had been happy to have him let go.

I wish you well too and I hope you find happiness with someone else, she had responded. And she had breathed a sigh of relief at the idea that it was done and the drama of the break-up was over.

In the days that followed, Benji kept his distance and she even noticed him flirting with some of the other girls. A good-looking male ballet dancer has his choice of women and Juliet knew he wouldn't be alone for long. But then there was the dress rehearsal and he didn't catch her and her life was over while his continued.

Without actually thinking about why she is doing it, she sends him a message through Instagram.

Hey, how are you? It's been a long time. I know that you were angry at me after everything but I thought that you might want to catch up? Maybe we could both use some closure?

Her heart thrums with anxiety after she sends the message. She hopes he does respond but also hopes he doesn't. What will she say to him?

The salty smell of roast chicken drifts up to her room and she knows that her parents have sat down to dinner. She's hungry but there's no way she's going down there. They don't want her here as much as she doesn't want to be here.

So why can't she leave?

The night she made the decision to end her life circles in her mind. She can remember the oppressive, heavy feeling of loneliness that felt like it was holding her down on her bed. She had picked up her phone and looked through her contacts, wondering who she could call, who would answer and find a way to say something to her that would help. But not one name stood out to her. She nearly touched on her mother's number, knowing she would answer, but then she didn't. Instead, she made a bet with herself: *If no one reaches out with a text or a call or a message in the next half an hour, I shouldn't be here anymore and I don't have to be.*

It was a desperate act on her part, even more desperate than doing the deed. She had watched the time pass on her phone screen, willing something to come in, waiting for any sound, even a message on her Instagram from a stranger, hinging her life on fate. Fate had taken away her dancing career after all. Fate or an angry ex-boyfriend, but she could have landed differently, could have only inflicted a minimum amount of damage on herself. Fate sent her flying to the floor knee first. No ping on her phone indicated anyone was thinking of her. The only sound in her small apartment was her own breathing. As the time ticked away towards the thirty-minute mark, she convinced herself that she was completely alone in the world and that if she got off her bed and opened her front door, it would be to find an empty hallway. If she went downstairs in the lift, it would be to find an empty lobby, and if she walked outside, it would be to find an empty street. And she thought, *This is impossible.*

She waited for one minute past her deadline and then, a

calm descended over her and she got off her bed and ran a bath and got in with the blade for a razor.

After that it was easy.

Five minutes after she had done it, her phone rang, and instead of ignoring it, as she wanted to do, she answered. It was her mother.

'Hello, darling, just checking in.'

'Mum... Muuuum, I'm so sorry, so sorry,' she said, her voice soft and the words coming out slowly.

'What do you mean, you're sorry? Juliet, what are you talking about?'

'I'm so...' she said and then she was sleepy and closed her eyes.

The last thing she heard was her mother screaming for her father. They had a key to the apartment because Juliet had lost hers once and so had given them a spare. They came rushing over. And saved her.

Knowing what she does know about the reality of her childhood, she doesn't know why they bothered.

Juliet pushes thoughts of that night away and goes back to scrolling through Instagram when a bleep sound alerts her to a message. Benji has replied.

Heey! How are you? I heard you were in the hospital. Are you okay?

Juliet lets out a snort laugh at how public her whole life is, even without having any actual friends she feels like she can call now.

She has no one now. No one except Adam. And yet everyone knows what she did.

I was, yeah, but I'm out now. I'm fine.

I'm so glad.

So do you think we can get together? I would really like to talk about everything that happened.

I mean, I think it would be better if we just left it, you know.

'Yeah, I bet you would,' says Juliet aloud. 'Your life is just fine but you don't get to hurt me and get away with it.' The anger inside her makes her restless and the need to see Benji face to face is overwhelming. She would like to see him and tell him what he did to her and what it has led to. He shouldn't get to just pretend that this has nothing to do with him. But if she gets rude and nasty, he will just block her and now she wants to meet him. Maybe she can even meet him with Adam by her side. She would like him to see Adam, to see how good-looking he is and how successful.

Well, it would really help me, like with my recovery. But if you don't want to, that's fine.

Ten slow minutes pass and she knows that Benji is talking to other people, asking them what he should do. Finally, he replies.

No, of course I want to help. Whatever you need. Just tell me a time and a place.

How about Saturday night?

I have a performance so it would have to be really late. Maybe another night?

Late is fine. Do you remember the park near my house? I can meet you there by the entrance at 11 p.m. I know performances usually end at 10.

She knows because once it was her life and it was supposed to be her life forever or until she got too old.

Yes, sure, fine. I'll meet you there. It's close to where I live so I can just walk over.

She sends him a thumbs-up emoji and closes down her computer and then she picks up her phone and texts Adam.

You know the guy who hurt me, the one who you said should pay for what he did?

Adam responds immediately. He always responds immediately, which is one of the many things she loves about him.

Yeah.

I'm meeting him on Saturday night. At the park where we walk.

Why?

Closure, I guess. Will you come with me?

I don't think that's a good idea.

Why?

Just because I don't. We're still waiting for the results of your X-rays and I know that you're feeling kind of weird. Now is not the time to be talking to the guy who ruined your career. What time are you meeting him?

11 p.m. and I'm meeting him no matter what anyone says. I need to start getting some closure. Too many people in my life have hurt me and I've had enough. I understand if you don't get it.

Please don't get angry with me, Juliet.

She is angry with him. For the very first time since she met him, she is angry with him.

I need to do this. I can't explain why exactly but it feels like a lot of stuff has happened to me and I have just let it happen. I have to fight back. I want to be the kind of person who can move forward from the accident and what my parents did.

Okay, I understand. I can't come with you but I hope you get what you need. Will you call me after so we can talk?

Why can't you come with me?

I have a work dinner and they usually end late. I can't miss it.

His response upsets her so much she throws the phone across the room and then she lies on her bed staring up at the ceiling for a minute before she sighs and gets up, picks up the phone and replies, **OK.**

Maybe this is something she should do herself. Maybe the things she wants to say to Benji are not the things she wants Adam to hear. He knows she's angry with Benji and with her parents but he has no idea how deep that anger is, how it's like a thick black sludge inside her that only stops bothering her when she's with him.

She can walk to the park but she won't. She'll drive so she has her car. It will be dark and she hates walking in the dark. She hasn't driven much since she got out of the hospital but it will be fine. She's sure it will be fine.

This is the first step to a new life. First, she will get the news about her X-rays and then she will meet with Benji and then she will deal with her parents and then, hopefully, she can move forward into her dream life with Adam. That's all she wants now. Being clear about this makes her feel better. She has a way forward now, just one step at a time and then her life will be something she is controlling, rather than something controlling her.

It's all going to come together. Things are going to get better. She can feel it.

THIRTEEN

Juliet

On Saturday morning, she wakes up filled with anticipation of the night ahead. Thoughts of her meeting with Benji make her restless but she lies in bed until it's light outside.

She has been doing everything she can to avoid her parents but she's hungry for something sweet so she gets out of her bed and goes down to the kitchen, where her mother is sitting with the Saturday paper, a large cup of coffee and a freshly baked chocolate muffin. For as long as Juliet can remember, she has found her mother like this on a Saturday morning.

Her father wakes up early and walks to the local bakery, buying a batch of their freshly made muffins as they come out of the oven, the chocolate chips melted and oozing inside. And then he stops and gets the paper and puts everything in the kitchen before heading off to his golf game. Her mother will spend hours over the paper, reading everything, and if Juliet is in the kitchen, she will comment on politics, explaining what she thinks about what's going on in the world.

When she walks into the kitchen and finds her mother just

as she knew she would be, Juliet has a moment of dizziness at the idea that this is the woman who hurt her so badly and then lied about it. But before she can even begin to question herself, she pushes the thought away. The results should come in today.

By the time she goes to meet Benji, she will know what her X-rays say.

'There are muffins,' says her mother when she sees her and Juliet nods, taking one from a plate and sitting down. Biting into it, she is unable to stop a sigh of pleasure at the rich chocolate taste. She has been home about a month now, which is a long time, but she has never made it to the kitchen on Saturday morning for a fresh, still-warm muffin. Instead, she has let them go stale and be thrown away. She is losing weight because she doesn't want to eat with her parents, doesn't want to see them in the kitchen, so she just stays away from food. Her parents like to see her eating, view it as a sign of a healthy attitude, so she is eating as little as possible, enjoying the way her hip bones are beginning to protrude.

'You've always loved those,' says her mother, looking over the top of her reading glasses at Juliet, who shrugs. Her mother watches each bite she takes and Juliet resents the pleasure she is giving her but she can't help stuffing the muffin in her mouth.

'Listen, Juliet,' says her mother and then she clears her throat.

Juliet is quiet.

'Dad and I have been talking and we feel that it would be best if you began attending your sessions with Dr Kelly. She called to tell me that she's worried about you. You need to attend them, Juliet, if you want to get better.'

'No,' says Juliet. Because why bother lying anymore?

'Please, Juliet,' her mother says.

'No,' she replies, 'I'm not going.' She finishes her muffin and crumples the paper in her hand, feeling the waxy softness against her palm.

'But Dr Choudry highly recommended her and she's supposed to be very good. And you didn't even give her a chance.'

'Dr Choudry was useless as well.'

Her mother shakes her head and Juliet knows it's time to leave, even though she would really like another muffin. She grabs one from the plate and stands up, turning around and walking away from her mother.

'Juliet,' says her mother, and Juliet stops and turns around.

'What?'

Her mother sighs, clears her throat again. 'Are you taking your medication?'

'I'm doing what's best for me,' says Juliet, knowing that her mother has been going through her things and counting her pills. Instead of throwing them away, she's been stuffing them in her mattress, in case she needs them. In case. She's obviously missed a few.

'Well...' her mother says softly.

'Well, what?'

Her mother meets her gaze, her blue eyes shining with the tears that she always seems to have ready when she speaks to her daughter. 'Your father and I are finding this very... very hard. We don't think we... I mean, you don't seem to want to try and... we think it would be best if... You need more help than we can give you...'

'So you're kicking me out!' Juliet explodes, knowing exactly where her mother is going with this. They want her to go back to the hospital, to get locked away in a room, nice and safe and not be here to bother them at all.

Her mother seems to sag at the table as she shakes her head. She looks thinner than she did a few weeks ago, as though she has also stopped eating.

'Everything would be fine if you just admitted it,' hisses Juliet. 'If you just told the truth.'

She watches as tears drip from her mother's face onto the paper. 'There is no truth, Juliet. We have only ever loved and cared for you.'

Juliet cannot bear to hear the words again and she leaves the kitchen, stomping up the stairs. Screw them if they want to kick her out. She'll leave right now, that's what she'll do. Maybe she can stay with Adam? They haven't even spent the night together but he supports her, he would help her, she's sure. She drops the muffin into her bedroom garbage bin.

And then she begins throwing things into a bag, clothes and make-up, even grabbing a soft, caramel-coloured teddy bear from her bookshelf that she has had since she was a baby.

Holding the bear against her for a moment, she has a vision of her and her mother walking around a store holding hands, her mother talking to her, and then her own small hand holding up the bear for her mother to kiss. She shakes her head; that's not true, it probably never happened.

As she finishes packing her bag, her phone pings with a text message and she grabs it.

Got the results.

What do they say?

I think we should meet.

A shiver runs through her. If there was nothing to see, he would tell her. And even if it was just the wrist and the ankle, surely he would tell her. It's what she's been expecting.

Just tell me.

She waits an agonising few minutes for a reply.

It's worse than we thought.

Staring at the text, she sinks down onto the bed, her packing forgotten. Here it is, the confirmation she has been waiting for. She imagined she would feel relieved, almost happy to not be crazy. She imagined showing her parents the results, throwing the truth in their faces. But now, she is just sad, so deeply, deeply sad.

Tell me.

No. We should meet. I'll go to the park and wait by our bench.

Please just tell me. I can handle it. I'm not a child, you know.

Juliet, just come to the park. I'll be waiting.

Just how badly has her body been damaged? How many more terrible memories are buried inside her mind, shuttered away because they are too painful?

Okay, I'm coming.

Dressing quickly in jeans and a T-shirt, she sneaks down the stairs, peeking into the kitchen, which she is grateful to see is empty. She has no desire for another confrontation with her mother, not until she has all the information, not until she cannot be questioned.

She leaves the house, walking quickly in the fresh autumn air.

She enters the park, making for the bench Adam will be at as she watches the joggers run around the track by the lake.

When she gets there, the bench is empty and she sits down,

glancing around, suddenly fearful that Adam will not turn up, that he has seen what is wrong with her and now he will just disappear.

Two girls about her age jog past, light on their feet and giggling about something. Juliet wraps her arms around herself, feeling stupid and ugly.

'Sorry, sorry,' she hears and she looks left to see Adam, panting. 'I had a call from work, something stupid and it was a whole thing. They don't care what day of the week it is; it's always something that needs to be fixed now. It was something so simple that they didn't need me but I still had to talk them through it.' He waves his hand, dismissing the incident, and then he leans down and kisses her on the cheek. He's usually working on a Saturday so she's grateful he has been able to see her now. But he looks so worried, so sad.

'Just tell me.' She folds her arms more tightly across her chest.

'Okay.' He sits down next to her. 'The images came in yesterday and I looked through them and... well, I'm not a doctor but I could see places where the bones were broken. I mean, I thought I could but then I didn't want to call you because maybe I was wrong. And then the doctor called and she...' He looks out over the lake and she watches as he bites down on his lip.

'Adam, please, I can't take this waiting anymore. What did she say?'

He sighs. 'She said that she'd never actually seen so many old fractures before. Not just the wrist and the ankle but all the ribs and your fingers on one hand. She said that all of your fingers had been broken and then healed.'

'My fingers?' Juliet rubs her hands together and then pulls slightly on her fingers, manipulating each joint, searching for the pain that surely should be there if they had been broken.

'Can I see?' she asks him and he opens his phone and shows

her X-rays on which the fractures are easy to see because it's obvious where bones have parted and cracked. Juliet stares at the images, scrolling through them twice, and then she can't look anymore. She hands the phone back to Adam.

'She also said that there were no new fractures but she was kind of... like she felt sorry for you but you're twenty-one and she's not your real doctor so she didn't want to... you know... have too much of a conversation. She said she'll send through the report on Monday. There was something weird with her email or something.'

'They don't deserve to live,' she whispers and Adam lets out a bark of nervous laughter but when she turns to look at him, he is instantly serious.

'You don't mean that.'

'I do,' she says, knowing that she has said something like this to him before.

But this time, he doesn't dismiss her or change the subject. Instead he says, 'Well, I'll help you do whatever you want.' And then he takes her hand in his, lightly massaging the skin, soothing the old pain that she can't actually feel but she is sure must be there.

FOURTEEN

When she is twelve, the abuse simply stops.

Or, at least, something happens to stop it. Her mother is a small woman, neatly made with long, fine hair, and at twelve, the child is taller than her. Taller and stronger.

One Sunday morning, in the middle of winter, when frost is thick on the neatly mowed grass outside, her mother comes into her room and pulls the covers off of her, shrieking, 'Get up, get up. I need you to help me clean this house.' Her mother hates dirt, almost as much as she seems to hate her child.

Her room is no longer messy or dirty. She is good at cleaning it now, at doing her washing, at keeping everything neat and tidy.

'I'll come down soon,' she says, sitting up and pulling the warm duvet over her body again. Incensed, her mother leans in to hit her, but the girl moves quickly and is out of bed and across the room in seconds. 'Don't you touch me,' she hisses.

'You monster,' her mother growls, and she comes for her but, again, the girl is quicker and she darts to the side and out of the room. Her mother follows her out and moves in close. 'Don't you dare run,' she says but the girl will not listen and she turns to run

down the stairs, not caring how cold she is, just needing to get away. She feels a hand on her back and her foot twists and she slips, falling down the steps and hitting her head on a chunk of the timber banister that sticks out at an angle. And she instantly blacks out.

When she opens her eyes again, she is lying on the sofa in the living room. Her mother is sitting next to her, holding her hand. 'What happened?' she asks and her mother shakes her head.

'I don't know, darling. I was out and I came home to find you lying on the stairs. You must have fallen. You hit your head on the bottom of the banister. There's a cut but it's stopped bleeding now. I would like to take you to a doctor, just to check you out.'

'You weren't out,' says the girl. 'You were here and you wanted me to help you clean the house.'

Her mother pats her hand and smiles sadly. 'I wasn't here, my darling. I met Vivian for breakfast and a walk; remember I told you that I was doing that? I told you last night before you went to bed.'

The girl thinks about this as she gazes at her mother and she can see that her mother is dressed for being out in a nice pair of black pants and a warm grey jumper.

'No,' she says, sitting up and wincing at the pain in her head. 'You came into my room and pulled off my duvet and screamed at me to clean the house.'

Her mother shakes her head and her eyes shine with tears. 'That never happened, darling. I wasn't here. Dad wasn't here either. He popped out to the shops. He said you were still asleep when he left. I got home before he did and you were just lying there. I nearly had a heart attack. I probably shouldn't have moved you but I panicked and tried to lift you up, and then Dad came in and carried you to the sofa. We were just about to call an ambulance. I've told you not to walk around in socks.'

The girl closes her eyes as the room seems to spin. 'No... no,' she begins but even now the memory is fading and being replaced by another. She just got out of bed and tripped going down the stairs, her socks slipping on the polished timber.

'Let's get you to a doctor, my love, and... Dad and I have been thinking that, I mean this may not be the best time to discuss it, but maybe you need to see someone about these... well, some of the things you say...'

The girl gets off the sofa slowly. Her head is sore and she has a headache but otherwise she feels fine. 'I don't need a doctor. I'm fine. There's nothing wrong with me.' She touches her head where she can feel pain and dried blood. 'And I don't need a doctor now.'

Her mother looks down as if afraid to have the conversation with her. 'You always seem so angry, my love, and I don't know why.'

'It's because...' She stops speaking. Why is she so angry? Her mother is so kind and she loves her and always has. Why is she so angry? Her mother didn't push her down the stairs, she fell.

'I don't know,' she says to her mother and she leaves the room and goes to her bedroom.

When she walks into the room, she can see that her mother has made the bed, her thick warm lilac-coloured duvet pulled straight and matching lilac pillows piled on top. Looking around the room, she can see that everything is neat and tidy, her book-case filled with books and things she has won through the years. It's a pretty room with pale blue curtains and pictures of her and her parents everywhere.

In her mind she has a memory of another room, a terrible room, but she has no idea where that memory comes from. Her head throbs with pain and she lies down on her bed, curls up small. Where do the terrible memories come from, and are they memories or just things she is making up?

She falls asleep and only wakes up when her mother comes to

get her for lunch. 'Darling,' she says, shaking her, 'you shouldn't have slept, you may have a concussion.'

The girl sits up and finds that she is feeling much better. 'I'm okay,' she says.

And she is okay. And from that moment on, she only knows that her parents love her and they always have.

FIFTEEN

It is only when Adam nudges her that she realises she has been sitting in silence for a long time.

'Please speak to me,' he says and Juliet shakes her head.

'I don't know what to say.'

'What do you want to do?'

She turns her head and looks at him, seeing the concern in his beautiful eyes. 'I think I need some time.' She stands up.

'Okay and are you still meeting Benji tonight?'

'Definitely,' she replies. 'I'm tired of feeling this way. I hate the idea that all these things have been done to me, that my parents hurt me and Benji ruined my career, and I'm going to deal with that now. I'm not going to let everyone get away with the things they've done.'

'You shouldn't meet him,' says Adam forcefully, and while Juliet would love to agree with him, to say she will listen to him, she won't do that now.

'I'll call you tomorrow and let you know how it went, okay?'

she says and then without waiting for Adam to answer her, she walks away, her head down.

She walks fast, sweat forming quickly in the warming-up autumn day, and she is home in minutes. They hurt her and she has proof.

At her house, she sees that the kitchen is empty, and when she looks into the garage, her mother's car is missing. Her parents are out, probably grocery shopping together, and that suits her just fine. She's not ready for the confrontation, not yet.

Instead, she goes into the living room and opens the large black cabinet that contains all their photograph albums, yanking them out and starting with her baby photos. She is an only child and her whole life has been assiduously documented by her parents, except for the times they hurt her. Those have been hidden, ignored.

Paging through each album, she stares down at the pictures of her in diapers, walking, running, smiling, laughing, eating ice cream, sliding down a slide, blowing out candles on a Barbie birthday cake, on a beach. She looks like a happy child, like a really well looked after, happy child.

Moving from one album to the next, she searches through the pictures, looking for something. She's not even sure what it is but she thinks that she will know it when she finds it.

In the fourth album, she is paging through pictures of her first recitals when she sees it. It's a picture of her in a restaurant, a plate of sushi in front of her and a pair of chopsticks held triumphantly aloft in her hand. The memory of that moment returns. She had just figured out how to use the chopsticks to pick up sushi and she remembers her parents clapping and even a waitress standing nearby congratulating her.

But that's not what interests Juliet. What she focuses on is the fact that the hand not holding the chopsticks is encased in pink plaster from the hand to her elbow. She has no memory of it at all and yet there it is... a broken wrist or forearm in all its pink proof.

Ripping the picture out of the album, she takes it to her bedroom, where she lies down on the bed, holding it in her hand staring at it, trying to place herself in the picture and remember how she hurt her wrist. After a few minutes, her eyes are burning and she allows her emotional and physical exhaustion to pull her into a deep sleep.

She wakes when she hears a door bang. 'Juliet?' her mother calls and Juliet sees that she is still clutching the picture. Leaping off her bed, she runs downstairs, bursting into the kitchen, where the table is covered in grocery bags.

'How did this happen?' she demands of her mother, shoving the picture in her face.

Her mother steps back and her father shakes his head. 'What are you talking about?' he asks, a box of crackers in his hand.

'My wrist or arm is broken, and you never told me about it, so how did it happen? You told me I had never broken my wrist. You told me that in Dr Choudry's office, I remember. So how did it happen?'

Her mother peers at the picture and then gingerly takes it from Juliet's hand. 'That was... oh, I had completely forgotten about that. Remember, George, do you remember that?' She shows Juliet's father the picture.

Her father glances over at the picture, nods his head. 'Yes... right, yes, of course. Your friend, what was her name... she was your best friend, Emily, I think. She moved away when you were both still very young. She broke her arm and came to school with a cast and you insisted on having one as well.'

'So, you took me to get a cast put on an arm that wasn't broken,' Juliet sneers, furious at her father's lie. 'What kind of a parent does that?'

'It wasn't a cast, Juliet; it was a pink bandage that I wrapped around your arm carefully to look like a cast. You only wore it for a few days because we had to keep taking it off for bath time and you grew bored.'

'I don't remember that.'

'Well, you were about six or seven, I think. No one remembers everything from their childhood, Juliet.' The words are spoken quietly as her mother arranges some apples and bananas in a wooden fruit bowl. Juliet knows she is deliberately concentrating on the pile of fruit instead of looking at her daughter.

'Well, how come you didn't say anything about this when we were together talking to Dr Choudry?' Her fury is fading, as is her certainty. She vaguely remembers Emily, a bubbly, dark-haired little girl. She moved away when they were both eight and Juliet hasn't thought of her for more than a decade.

'I'm sure,' says her father, folding up grocery bags neatly, 'that we didn't think it meant much. We didn't tell him you thought you were Dorothy the Dinosaur when you were five either. It was make-believe, Juliet, and only when you started telling stories did we worry. But we still just decided you were a creative child and we let you be.'

Her mother nods in agreement at this statement.

Her parents look completely unconcerned.

'I think you're lying,' says Juliet and her mother looks up and shrugs.

'Think what you want, Juliet, it's the truth. It just slipped my mind because it was a game that went on for a few days, that's all.'

And then she turns away as though she cannot be bothered having the conversation.

Juliet wants to bring up the X-rays now but she needs the images and the doctor's report. They won't be able to argue with a doctor's report.

She waits a moment longer, hoping for something from

her parents, something... but she doesn't know what. And when nothing is forthcoming, she turns and leaves the kitchen.

Up in her bedroom she stares at the picture until she can't bear to look at it anymore. Did Emily have a cast? She thinks she remembers that. Emily's cast was blue. Are her parents telling the truth?

She picks up her phone and opens Instagram, scrolls until she can no longer think straight and then falls asleep again.

She doesn't go downstairs when her parents call her for dinner; instead, she creeps down when she is sure they are in the living room watching television, and stuffs cold leftover pasta in her mouth with the fridge open. She feels like an animal, like a crazy person.

And the only hope she can cling to is the hope that she will see Benji later and somehow find a way to move forward from what once felt like the worst thing to ever happen to her. *One step at a time*, she keeps repeating to herself. First Benji and then her parents.

At 10.30 p.m., warmly dressed because the nights are cooling down now, and with her heart racing with anxiety, she leaves the house, creeping down the stairs and opening the front door slowly so that she doesn't wake her sleeping parents.

Out in the street, she walks quickly, a cold wind at her back. She has left the car at home instead of taking it as she intended. Her knee complains at how fast she is walking, sending twinges of pain through her leg.

She stops at the entrance to the park and she waits, walking up and down to keep warm.

Looking around, she can see that she is the only person in the park; the air is chilly and the few lights only serve to emphasise how dark it is everywhere but directly under them. Juliet shivers. She is alone in a park late at night, a place no woman should be.

It's five minutes past eleven and then ten minutes past. Juliet messages Benji on Instagram: *Are you still coming?* At some point, she deleted his number from her phone and she can't remember when that happened. At twenty minutes past eleven, the cold is beginning to creep in under her jumper and she thinks longingly of her bed. At half past eleven, she knows he's not coming because he's a lying coward who can't bear to confront the truth of what he's done.

Juliet takes one last look around the park and then she starts walking home, absolute fury keeping her warm.

She's not going to let him get away with this. He didn't even think about the fact that she was alone in a park late at night. She pictures him, backstage, celebrating a wonderful performance with all the other dancers and probably laughing at her and how stupid she is, how much of a loser she is because she's still going on about an accident that happened three years ago.

She walks faster and faster, her heart thudding in her chest, unwanted tears running down her face as she mutters, 'Bastard, bastard, bastard.'

When she gets home, she stops at her front gate but she cannot make herself go inside. Her home is not a safe space, not a space where she can find comfort.

It's nearly midnight but she turns and walks away, back in the direction of the park. Maybe she can find an open bar somewhere and have a drink, get completely drunk, blot all this out, make everything go away.

Twenty minutes later, the sweat on her body has dried in the cool wind and her fingers are beginning to cramp up because she is clenching her fists so tightly. She has walked to a strip of shops she knows well where there used to be a pub but she's not sure if it's still there or if it will be open.

A warm yellow light tells her it is and she moves quickly to the nondescript glass door with faded gold writing declaring this the Butcher's Beer Garden. There's no garden although there might have been at one time. She pushes the door, walking gratefully into the warmth.

There is a man standing behind the bar, arranging glasses that steam even in the warm air. They have obviously just come out of the dishwasher.

Juliet pulls herself onto a stool and he walks towards her, immediate suspicion on his face. He's the only one in the pub. 'We close in twenty minutes,' he tells her.

'Can I just get a quick drink? A shot of vodka?'

'Do you have ID?' he asks, narrowing thick eyebrows at her.

A tiny bark of laughter escapes Juliet at the absurdity of this question. She feels way older than her twenty-one years but she dutifully shows the bartender her driver's licence on her phone. 'Make it a double, please,' she says as he peers down at the picture.

He nods and pours, sliding the glass over to her. 'That's it, then I'm closing up,' he says, bringing over a machine so she can tap and pay.

'I get it. Don't worry,' says Juliet.

She hasn't had vodka in a long time so she has no idea of her tolerance. But she picks up the drink and tips the whole thing back, swallowing quickly and then coughing, alarmingly and very embarrassingly.

The bartender silently hands her a serviette to wipe her streaming eyes as he shakes his head.

Juliet gets off the stool and leaves the pub, standing outside in the cold air, the alcohol churning in her stomach, her head spinning.

Where does she go now? What does she do?

Taking her phone out of her pocket, she does the only thing she wants to do.

She calls Adam, not caring if she wakes him.

'He didn't come,' she says when he answers the call, 'he just didn't turn up. And now he's laughing at me.' She bursts into tears.

'Slow down, slow down,' says Adam. 'Where are you?'

Juliet takes a deep breath and tells him where she is.

'Stay there, I'll be right with you.'

'Okay,' she says, her voice shuddering. She stands next to the pub door, comforted by the fact that the light is still on as the bartender finishes closing up.

And almost immediately, Adam is there.

'How did you get here so quickly?'

'Funny story,' he says. 'I was worried about you and waiting to hear from you and I couldn't sleep, so I went for a walk. I've been waiting for you to call. I'm sorry, babe, the guy's an arsehole.'

He opens his arms and she steps into them, resting her head against his chest and giving in to her despairing tears.

'Shh,' Adam soothes as he strokes her back, and when she manages to stop crying, he leans down and whispers, 'Why don't you come home with me?'

And it's the best offer Juliet has had in years.

SIXTEEN

Juliet

It's a twenty-minute walk from the pub to a large apartment block near the train station.

'You must have been walking for a while,' says Juliet, feeling warm and safe with her hand in his.

'Yeah, well, I was worried,' says Adam. 'Here we are.'

His apartment is on the tenth floor and they ride up in the lift in silence.

'Home sweet home,' he says as he slides the key into the lock and then they are inside and she looks around, absorbing every aspect of his space from the shaggy cream rug on the floor to the weird sprouting light fitting with ten globes.

'This is not what I imagined at all,' she says.

'Well,' he sighs, 'confession time, I guess. Sit down.'

Juliet sits down on the black leather sofa, feeling the cushion sink beneath her. 'Yes?' Immediately a parade of things crosses her mind. He's married or he's in a relationship, he's on the run from the law.

'This is actually not my apartment. I know I told you I was

from Melbourne but I didn't mention that I'm only supposed to be up here for a year and then I'm going back. The apartment is a kind of Airbnb situation my company have organised. I've been here for ten months already, so I'm going home soon.'

'Oh.' Juliet feels her heart sink. The future she has been planning disappears into wisps of nothingness and her nose starts to run. Using a tissue from her bag, she wipes her eyes and nose. Can things get any worse? How could she have only just found him and now he will be gone? She suddenly wants to be anywhere but here, in complete contrast to how she felt only moments ago.

'Why didn't you tell me?'

'Hey,' he says, sitting down next to her, wrapping an arm around her shoulders. 'Hey,' he says again, 'of course I was going to but I didn't think it was a big deal. I mean, I thought that you wouldn't mind.'

'Wouldn't mind?' she asks, incredulous, as she pulls away from him. 'Mind what, that I thought we were in a... a relationship and I thought you felt something for me but actually I'm just a casual screw while you're here in Sydney?' She spits the words out, venomous thoughts causing acid to rise in her throat. She hates him right now, hates him for making her love him, for lying. She stands.

'What? No. We haven't even slept together yet and I'm telling you this.' He stands as well, holding up his hands to stop her from leaving. 'How could you think that of me, Juliet? And we are in a relationship. I'll be here for another eight weeks and I thought that if we were still together, you wouldn't mind moving down to Melbourne. I thought it could be a fresh start for you. I'm old enough to know my own mind and I've known from the day I met you that we're meant to be together.'

'Oh... oh,' she says and she starts laughing at how silly she has been, relief flooding through her veins like water, 'a fresh start, yes, yes, I want that, I would like that.' And then he is kissing her and they are grabbing at each other's clothes and it feels so incredibly good and right and exactly what should happen.

They fall asleep afterwards and when they wake up, their bodies are entwined, their heads close together on the shaggy rug. It's nearly dawn.

'Hello, you,' says Adam and she smiles.

'Hello, you.'

'I think... I think I might love you.'

'I think I might love you too.'

'I want to give you everything, Juliet. I want you to come with me to Melbourne and I want us to buy a house and I want you to have the life that you deserve. I want kids and I want...'

She giggles. 'You want a lot, don't you? I'm only twenty-one and you're thirty – does the age gap bother you? I mean I won't be ready for kids for a while and I just... I'm still figuring things out, with my parents and everything.'

'Yes, I know that and I'm fine with whatever you decide.' He lifts one of her hands and kisses her palm. 'Mostly I want you to be happy, to find closure and to be able to put the past behind you.'

Juliet's heart sinks. 'I wish I could do that. I don't know if I will ever be able to and it makes me feel so... so damaged, like damaged goods. Do you really want to live the rest of your life with damaged goods?'

'You're not damaged; you've been hurt and the people who hurt you should pay.'

Juliet experiences a little shiver at the harshness of his tone. 'They'll never admit it, Adam, and I know that I've said that I want them to pay... but there's nothing I can do, not really.' She sits up, gathering her clothes and beginning to get dressed.

'But there's something I can do.'

'What can you do?' she asks, tugging on her jeans, upset now that the lovely mood has been ruined.

Adam stands as well and pulls on his jeans and his bright blue T-shirt.

'I can... Look, you don't have to do anything, you can just leave everything to me and I will make sure that they understand what they did, that they admit it and then maybe they... I don't know... They're really rich and you deserve some of that money, especially after everything they put you through as a kid. Maybe they will give you enough to say... I don't know as kind of a gesture to say that they're sorry. You wouldn't need to be involved. I would talk to them. I promise I will make sure that you get what you deserve. I'll show them the X-rays and threaten to go to the police, to help you go to the police.'

'My parents aren't going to listen to you, Adam. They won't listen to me and I'm their daughter.'

'They'll listen,' he says and she looks up at him, watches as a look crosses his face, a moment that changes his features, makes him look more dangerous, taller, stronger, someone to fear.

Juliet feels a sudden need to leave, to get out of here and away from him. She moves towards the door. 'Whatever they've done, I can't do anything to hurt them, Adam. It's just words but they are still human beings and I can't hurt anyone, not even them.' Is that the truth? Perhaps she could hurt them. She could certainly hurt Benji, but Benji never turned up.

He shrugs his shoulders. 'Up to you but you and I both know that they were awful people, that they still are. I've seen your X-rays and I've spoken to the doctor and no child should ever go through what you've been through. You can leave Sydney and come down to Melbourne but you will always have this hanging over you. You'll always carry this anger until you've dealt with it.'

'And I will. Leaving will help and maybe I can find a therapist in Melbourne and... everything will be better.' She nods her head as she speaks, certain that this is the truth.

But Adam frowns and she can read the concern on his face. 'Listen, Juliet... this may sound harsh but... I want to build a life with you.' His hands move to her face, cupping it gently as he kisses her. She can see, in his eyes, that he is struggling to say what he needs to say. He steps back, away from her, and she suddenly feels cold. 'You could even be the mother of my children someday, if that's what you want. And...' He moves further away from her, towards the window in the apartment where the morning sunshine is streaming in. 'I've always thought it's so important to be ready for parenthood. I want to do better than my parents did. I would like that for my partner as well. I want her to be as mentally healthy as possible. And... all the therapy you've had, it hasn't worked, has it? All those doctors have just made things worse.'

Juliet finds herself nodding because he's right. In fact, things are a lot worse since she started interacting with mental health professionals.

'I think that's because it's not just that you need therapy. You need real closure. Someone needs to pay for what they did to you. Otherwise, you'll always be angry. You'll never be able to let go and move on. It's your decision but... it will be hard for us to be together if you don't deal with this, really deal with it.'

He moves back to the door of the apartment and she is horrified to see that a tear is trickling down his face.

He opens the front door and Juliet can see that she will never come here again unless she agrees to what he's asking. Maybe he can speak to her parents and get them to admit what they did. Maybe that will help her put all this behind her. She will never get that from Benji because he's always going to lie and say it was an accident but maybe she can get the truth from her parents. Maybe Adam is the one who can help her get it.

Juliet steps through the door and into the grey carpeted corridor. 'So, what are you saying?'

'You understand what I'm saying, Juliet. But I think we need some space, you need some space. I have a gym class in a few hours and I want to get some more sleep so I'll call you later, okay?'

Juliet understands they are on the cusp of something here, teetering between a life together and a life apart, but she doesn't know what to say to him, what answer to give him. She steps forward to kiss him goodbye but he closes the door in her face with a soft click.

And she is alone again.

In the elevator down to the ground floor, she is too stunned to cry. A few hours ago, she rode up with him with the promise of finally taking their relationship to the next level and there she found out that he loves her as much as she loves him... until they talked about her parents.

And now she may never see him again, she can feel that. He came to rescue her last night and now he is asking her to let him help her again. But does she want that? Does she really, really want the truth? And is she willing to give him up to allow her parents to maintain their lies?

A fierce ache spreads across her chest, so sharp she has to press down over her heart. She cannot bear for it to be over. He is the only good thing that has happened to her in three years. She has suffered alone, desperate and sad over the loss of her dream. She has been under a black cloud and finally, finally she thought she could see some sun and now it's gone again. How can the sun be gone again?

As she is leaving the building, an older woman is sorting through her mailbox, dressed bizarrely in a robe and slippers. When she sees Juliet, she confronts her.

'Who are you, how did you get in here?' the woman barks at her and Juliet jumps.

'I was visiting my... friend... my boyfriend.' Can she still call him that?

Only a few hours ago, she was so sure of him and now, she doesn't know.

'What's his name?' demands the woman, and Juliet edges towards the door, shocked and irritated to be accosted this early in the morning by a mad old woman.

'Adam,' she says.

'No Adam lives here. I know all the residents. No Adam lives here,' says the woman, pointing her finger at Juliet and scrunching up her face.

Juliet smacks the button to open the glass doors to get her out of the building and she darts out into the street, away from the woman who is standing, her post in her hand, staring at Juliet.

Using her phone, she calls an Uber, waiting around the corner from the building so that the old woman can't see her.

Creeping into the house, she is relieved that it's still early so her parents are asleep.

She closes herself in her bedroom, throws herself onto her bed and gives in to hours of tears before exhaustion finally claims her.

She wakes to afternoon sunlight streaming through her window and a text from Adam.

> *Sorry for being such a shit. I love you and I just want you to be happy, even if that means you never get to move on from what they did. I'm here for you.*

Her relief is so intense that she has to leap from her bed and run for the bathroom, throwing up the precious little that is in her stomach. *He loves me, he loves me, he loves me.* And because he loves her, she feels like it's possible that one day, at some point in the future, she can love herself as well, love her life, love her imaginary future children. But first she needs to put her past behind her.

After a hot shower that turns her skin red, she replies to him.

Just tell me what you want me to do. I'll do it.

SEVENTEEN

Juliet

'Got the report,' Adam tells her the day before his visit to her house and Juliet's skin prickles with dread. 'I've just sent it. Did you get it?'

'No,' she answers, studying the last text message she received from him, her heart racing as she waits to see the words written down.

'Okay, sending it again,' he says and she waits, staring at the phone, but it doesn't come.

'Nope, not here. Can you send it again, I really need to see it.'

'Okay, give me your email, I'll try that.'

Juliet repeats her email address twice so Adam gets it right. 'Sent,' he says and she checks but nothing has come in.

'No, not here.'

'That's so weird. This has been happening to me for the last few days. My phone is glitching and I need to get it looked at. I'm better with computers. Anyway, I'll see you soon enough and I'll show you on my phone.'

'Oh… but I…'

'It's one more day, Juliet.'

'Okay… okay.'

Adam's plan is not much of a plan at all but Juliet has gone along with the idea anyway. She cannot think of anything better.

In truth her mind is taken up with imagining her future, studying suburbs in Melbourne because Adam is renting now but is happy to buy an apartment or even a house where she wants to live. No matter what she texts him, he seems happy to let her lead the way.

Do you want to be close to the city when we buy?

I don't mind. I work in the city but I can also do a couple of days at home so it's fine. I would like to be close to a gym though.

Do you think our kids should go to private school?

Ha, ha, bit early to think about that and private school is expensive. But we can decide when you're pregnant.

How many kids do you want?

How many do you want?

2?

That's the perfect number. I'm an only child and always wanted a sibling.

Me too!!!

When she is talking to him, over the phone or text message, her whole life and future take on a rosy glow. Anticipation builds inside her every day and she wills the time away so that she can get on a plane to Melbourne and leave everything that happened in Sydney behind her.

But first, she knows she needs to deal with her parents, with what they did. Adam says he can make them admit what her childhood was like and Juliet believes him. He keeps talking about how important closure is and she knows that's true. She's never going to get closure with Benji, and even though that pales in comparison to getting closure with her parents, she has messaged him a few times since he was supposed to meet her.

I waited in the park for half an hour. Can you just tell me why you didn't come?

He didn't reply and a day later she messaged him again.

That was an arsehole move, Benji. Why say you're going to meet me unless you are? We've known each other for years. Even if there's some shit between us, you should at least be man enough to speak to me about everything that happened.

He still didn't reply.

You're a real dick. And I wish you nothing but pain and suffering.

After she sent the last message, she blocked his profile from her Instagram so she wouldn't ever have to see it again. As part of her fantasies about her move to Melbourne, she sees herself with a family and a big house, meeting Benji, who is alone and sad now that he's aged out of his career. She hopes that nothing good ever happens to him.

.   .   .

Late that night, Adam calls her to discuss the final details of his plan. 'I'll come over to your house, we'll get them a little drunk and then I'll ask questions until they slip up and confess. It will shock them to have me ask the questions and show them the report from the doctor, and if they've had some alcohol, they'll be off balance, not as easily able to keep the lies straight. Just tell them I'm coming over to meet them and leave the rest to me.'

'I'm still not really sure that will work,' Juliet says gently. 'They like a glass of wine or two but I don't think I've ever seen them drunk.'

'It will work. Trust me on this. And I'll record it and then you can play it to them the next day and threaten to go to the police unless they admit, sober this time, the truth of what they did.'

'But what if they don't want to drink?'

'They will, don't worry. It will be a nice occasion.'

To Juliet, the idea seems preposterous. 'And what will happen if you do get them on tape, if they do confess?'

'Well, then you decide what you want to do. You can go to the police but that may turn into a whole thing and I know that if you do have to go through a trial, it's almost retraumatising. You'll have to relive it all and I don't want that for you, but like I said, it's up to you. If you ask for some kind of... I guess, compensation, then we will have enough money to start a new life. They'll give you whatever you want to keep quiet.'

'But is money all I want?' She tries to imagine taking her accusations to the police, this time with proof, and the ensuing investigation and her parents being charged with abuse, but she can't come to grips with it. It doesn't seem possible and she keeps trying to work out why it doesn't seem possible while ignoring a little voice that keeps repeating, *They never hurt you. They've always loved you.* She dismisses the voice because the X-rays tell the truth. You can't argue with an X-ray.

Adam sighs. 'You'll have money and a confession. It may be the best you can hope for and then you can cut them out of your life forever. And then we get to start our own life.'

It's the first time he's said something that she thinks is wrong. It won't work. He has no idea how clever her parents are. There is no way they will drink enough to get drunk. The plan is ridiculous but it seems to her that he needs it more than she does almost. And she needs him more than anything.

On Tuesday morning, Juliet comes into the kitchen, where her parents are having breakfast, and sits down at the kitchen table.

'Juliet,' says her mother, absolute delight on her face, a look that makes Juliet's stomach turn with disgust. 'I'm so glad you're here. Can I make you something? What about scrambled eggs and toast, or wait, how about some French toast? You love... well, you used to love French toast.'

Juliet shakes her head, even as she has a flash of a memory of herself as a young child, old enough to feed herself, sitting on a special seat so that she is high enough to reach her plate on the kitchen table. She sees herself with her blonde hair falling over her shoulders. She is sitting in front of a plate on which two golden-brown pieces of French toast are dusted in cinnamon sugar.

'I can cut it myself,' she knows she said and then she knows that her mother sat patiently with her as she mangled the toast with her child-safe knife and fork. The memory doesn't gel with what she knows about her childhood so she shakes her head, pushing it away.

'No... no, I'm not hungry. I just wanted to tell you that I have someone coming over tonight for a... drink. He wants to meet you.'

Her father looks up from his plate, where he has been polishing off his usual fried egg and toast. 'He?' he asks with a smile.

'Yes,' Juliet says, nodding, 'he's my boyfriend and I think it's time you met him.'

'Oh, Juliet,' says her mother, 'that's wonderful. So that's where you've been going. Oh, I am so happy for you, sweetheart. Is he nice? Where does he live? What does he do? How long have you been together? How old is he?'

Inside her, instead of her usual anger, Juliet feels a swirl of sadness at how excited her mother is for her, at how happy she seems now that she believes that Juliet is happy. How can this be the same woman who pushed her down the stairs? And looking across the table at her beaming father, she wonders how he can be the same man who enabled the abuse for the first twelve years of her life by looking away.

'His name is Adam and he's thirty and he's in computers. I met him on a walk.'

Her mother bites down on her lip at the mention of Adam's age but she doesn't say anything and Juliet knows this is because there is no way she is going to risk the conversation when her daughter seems so happy. Large age gaps work in lots of relationships. Her own parents are six years apart and this is only a few more years than that.

'Well, we are really looking forward to meeting him,' says her mother, standing up. 'I'll get some nibbles, some nuts and chips and things.'

Juliet nods, unable to speak. This sounds like such a normal family conversation, something that goes on in thousands of houses each day, and yet nothing about it is normal. Everyone here is lying, pretending. But for the first time, Juliet is lying as well, pretending as well.

'He'll be over at six then, okay?'

'Absolutely, darling,' says her mother as she loads the dishwasher. 'We can't wait. We simply can't wait.' She can see that her parents have lots of questions for her but they will know the answers soon enough and they are aware of that. Being the one doing the manipulating instead of the one being manipulated makes Juliet feel more powerful, more in control, than she has in a long time and she likes the feeling. She likes it very much.

EIGHTEEN

Juliet

Adam rings the doorbell at 6 p.m. on the dot. Juliet and her parents are sitting in their living room. There is a platter of expensive cheese and crackers and a bowl of nuts on the coffee table and her parents are dressed up, as though they are heading to an upscale restaurant. Her father is even wearing a tie. Her mother is in a green skirt and a black and green matching top. Juliet has dressed up as well, feeling like she has to mark the occasion when she gets the truth from her parents in some way. She has seesawed between hope that she can get some truth from them and belief that it's impossible, all afternoon. But in the end, she decided that looking nice either way would be a good idea. She has put on a grey silk dress that falls beautifully around her body, disguising her recent weight loss.

'I like a man who's punctual,' her father says as the sound of the bell chimes through the house, and Juliet has to swallow a lump that appears in her throat at how vulnerable he sounds, how desperate he is to say the right thing. Again, she is struck by the juxtaposition of the parents who abused her until she was twelve and these two seemingly nice people waiting to meet her new boyfriend.

Juliet goes to the front door and opens it to find Adam there with a bag containing three bottles. Her father has already opened an expensive bottle of red wine that he said he had been 'saving for a special occasion'.

Adam is dressed in blue jeans and a green shirt and he smells as wonderful as he always does. She steps forward and lets him enclose her in a hug.

'Come in,' she tells him and he follows her to the living room, where there are a flurry of introductions and 'nice to meet yous'.

'I've brought some stuff…' Adam laughs. 'Truthfully, I'm taking a bartending course for fun and I was learning how to make negronis last week and I wondered if you would let me make you a couple… just for fun.' This is a complete lie but her parents nod enthusiastically.

Juliet looks at Adam, unsure where he's going with this. Her parents only ever drink wine. She cannot remember them ever mentioning having cocktails. Once again, she thinks that Adam's plan seems slightly ridiculous and she wishes that she had simply told him no.

He seems different tonight and she has no real idea why. It's hard to put her finger on exactly what it is. Perhaps his warmth is gone, or maybe it's that his smile doesn't seem genuine. Juliet doesn't know what it is, but there is a slight rumble of unease inside her and suddenly, she doesn't want to do this.

She wants to put her childhood behind her. It will be enough for her to move away. She doesn't need money from her parents. Adam is doing really well at work and she can get a job as well.

'My parents don't really—' she begins to say.

'That would be lovely,' her mother interrupts.

'Can I use the kitchen?' Adam asks. 'Sometimes I spill and I wouldn't want to do that here.'

'Of course, of course, Juliet will show you the way.'

Juliet leads Adam into the kitchen. 'Look,' she says when he is setting up the bottles to make the cocktails on the counter, 'I think… I think maybe I don't want to do this. I get… I understand the things they have done, but I just don't… I just want to leave with you. I promise, I don't need closure. I just want to be away from here. Once we get to Melbourne, I can ask them for money and I'm sure they'll give it to me, they'll give me anything.' As she says these words, she realises that they are true. Perhaps, somewhere along the way, they changed, realised what they had done and have, since then, been trying to be better people? They wouldn't pay rent for her when she left the hospital but that was because they were worried about her. If she's with Adam, they won't be worried and they'll be happy to help, she's sure of that.

Despite having the evidence of the X-rays, she can't help wondering exactly what it is that happened, exactly how true her memories are. Could the X-rays be wrong? Do doctors make mistakes like that? It's possible. Doctors are not gods. Dr Choudry was treated like a god by everyone at the hospital but Juliet found him awful and useless, arrogant and condescending. Of course doctors make mistakes. Or is that just what she hopes?

'Can I see the report on my X-rays?' she asks Adam, needing to silence the thoughts that she may be wrong.

'Oh, I'll have to call the doctor tomorrow and have it sent again. My phone did some weird update that I thought would solve the glitches but now it's lost a whole lot of my stored data.'

'Really?' asks Juliet. The slight unease inside her churns itself into a storm. 'But how will we show them the proof then?'

'I'll tell them. I've seen it and they'll know that tomorrow we'll have the proof.'

'But that's not...' Juliet takes out four glasses and puts them side by side as she speaks, her hands trembling.

'Look, Juliet, all you've talked about is wanting closure, about wanting the truth from people.'

Juliet can hear an edge of anger in his voice as he opens each of the bottles. Her heart pounds inside her chest and she wonders why she is feeling so anxious. This is Adam and he loves her and he just wants to help her.

'But now, you're happy to pretend nothing ever happened to you?' Adam continues without looking at her.

'No... I...'

'I mean, you didn't get closure from Benji because he just never turned up.'

'Yes, but...'

'But nothing, Juliet. You said you're tired of being a doormat.'

'I never said I was a doormat...'

Adam begins pouring Campari and sweet vermouth into the glasses. 'Look,' he says with a sigh and she feels like she is disappointing him, a feeling she really hates. He adds gin. 'We just want the truth. I mean you just want the truth. I'm doing a good thing; this is the right thing...' He sounds like he's talking to himself as he looks down at the kitchen counter.

'Adam, is something else going on?' she asks him, unable to shake the feeling that something is wrong here.

He shakes his head and smiles. 'No... no. Do you have any oranges?'

Juliet turns around, searches in the fruit bowl. 'No, sorry, I didn't know you would need them, but listen, Adam, I've been thinking—'

'No more now, Juliet. Take these drinks in to your parents and I will bring ours soon. Just go, please.' His voice is low and his tone clipped. Is he irritated or upset? She can't quite work it out. He is tired of discussing this and Juliet can hear that but she is liking this idea less and less as the minutes pass.

She opens her mouth to protest again but then she catches a look from him, the same look he gave her when he closed the door of his apartment on her, and she knows that she never wants to feel that way again and so she does as she's been told, taking two drinks and handing one each to her parents. Adam follows her with drinks for the two of them and then the four of them sit, somewhat awkwardly, making conversation. Her father asks Adam about his work and he tells him in great detail about his project for a company she's never heard him talk about. Although they don't usually discuss his work much.

Juliet sips the slightly bitter drink and her parents do the same. Adam gets himself some cheese from the platter and then finishes up his drink. 'That was okay, wasn't it?' he asks and for a moment he seems so young, like a boy asking to be accepted, that Juliet can't help her smile and she downs her drink. Her parents do the same. 'Yes, lovely,' says her mother, even as Juliet watches her wince at the bitterness.

'Can Juliet give me a tour of the house?' asks Adam. 'I've always loved these old houses and yours is really beautiful.'

'Of course,' says her mother, stifling a yawn. 'Oh dear, that drink has gone straight to my head. Excuse me, Adam. Show him around, love.'

'I think you should just say goodbye now,' says Juliet after they have walked slowly through the house and are on their way down the stairs. 'I don't care about a confession. I really don't.' Something about the whole situation is making her horribly uncomfortable. She feels like she is an actor in a movie where she doesn't have the script. And she wants to stop whatever is happening.

'Can we look in the basement?' he asks instead of replying to what she has said.

'Sure... I mean there's nothing in there but crap, but sure.' Juliet sighs. 'But then I think maybe you should go. They like you and they will give us whatever help we need. I promise they will.' She doesn't know how she knows this but she simply does.

As they are walking down the stairs, her phone pings with a message and she sees it's from her old friend Monica. Juliet is so shocked to hear from her she shows the screen to Adam. 'Look, I used to dance with her. I haven't spoken to her for at least two years.'

'Weird,' he says, his hand on the banister as he stares at a large framed family picture hung over the stairs. It's from a trip she took with her parents to the UK. They are standing in front of one of the guards outside Buckingham Palace, large smiles on all their faces.

'What does it say?'

Juliet opens the message and starts reading it aloud: '"Just wanted to let you know, in case you hadn't heard that Benji died. Everyone is completely devastated. I know things got complicated between you two but thought you might want to know. The funeral is next week Wednesday. I can send you details if you want to come. Hope you're okay."'

Disbelief ripples through Juliet's body. Benji is gone? Dead? When and how?

'I should reply to her. I don't know what happened. Maybe that's why he didn't meet me.' She holds her hand across her mouth, afraid she's going to be sick. 'Oh God,' she mutters. She sent him such awful messages. What if people look through his Instagram? They will think she's a monster.

'Well' – Adam shrugs, his brown eyes dark in his face – 'I guess he got what he deserved.' The casual way he says this, his tone flat and his face devoid of emotion, triggers something inside Juliet. Fear stabs at her but she doesn't know why she's afraid. This is Adam who loves her and he's just angry with Benji for hurting her. He never met him so why would he care if Benji is dead?

'I think I should text her back and ask her what happened to him,' she says.

'You can do that later. I want to see the rest of the house, and why do you care anyway? He ruined your career. Good riddance, I say.'

'That's not a nice thing to say.'

Adam turns to look at her and raises an eyebrow. 'Are we going to continue our tour or waste our time talking about a guy who ruined your life?' he says, his voice harsh.

She would like him to leave now but he seems determined to see the rest of the house. She'll finish showing him the house and then he can go. This was a mistake. She knows it was a mistake.

Nodding, she keeps walking, and Adam obviously picks up on her concern because he stops her with a touch on her shoulder so she turns around and suddenly, there he is again, the Adam she knows and loves with softness in his eyes this time.

'I know you're worried about doing this,' he says. 'But remember, they're terrible people and you want the confession, Juliet. Remember that. It's all about you. A few more drinks and you'll have everything on tape. I'm only doing this because I love you and I want you to be the best person you can be,' he says and then he kisses her on the cheek.

'I know,' she says, although doubt is swirling inside her. She turns around, continues on her way to the basement. If he truly loves her, he will understand why she doesn't want to go on with this.

When he's seen the basement, she will tell him to leave. She needs time alone to process Benji's death, to think about how she feels about that. Did she want him to die? Yes, yes, she really did. But also, only in theory. She's never hurt anyone and she never would.

In the basement, Adam looks around at the old furniture from her grandmother and the collection of suitcases and her old toys stored down here.

'Let's go,' says Juliet but Adam stops her, grabbing her by her shoulders. 'I want you to know I love you and I will come for you but I need to do this for you, for us. So, I'm going to ask you to stay here and let me get on with this. I will come for you. I promise I will come for you.'

'What? No, I'm not staying down here,' she says, pulling away from him, wild thoughts flying and terror building.

She steps forward but so does he and then he shoves her, making her step back again, almost tripping over in the stupid heeled black shoes she is wearing.

'What are you doing?' she yells, hoping she has been loud enough to attract her parents' attention.

'I'm doing this for us,' he hisses, 'and you don't understand that. You need to trust me.' In the dim light of the basement, his face is shadowed and odd-looking, as though someone else is here instead of Adam. He is frowning, angry, his body language threatening. He needs to leave now. She needs to get out of this basement now. He is bigger than she is, stronger too, and now she is trapped down here with him. What's going on? Why is he being like this? Instead of agreeing with him, she feels anger run through her.

'No.' She shoves him hard. 'You need to let me out of here and you need to go,' she yells. Her parents should be able to hear her. The basement door is open and they are only one floor above. Why haven't they come to see what's going on?

A terrifying thought pops into her head. What if this is what her parents want? What if Adam has been hired to get rid of her because she won't stop asking questions? Surely that's impossible.

Adam barely reacts to her shove because he is so much bigger and stronger than she is and then he smiles, a kind of lopsided creepy smile. 'This is what you wanted, Juliet,' he says and he pushes her hard, and as she stumbles backwards towards the basement wall, he pushes her again, her foot twists and she falls. 'I promise I will come for you. I will come back for you. I love you.' The words sound rehearsed, robotic.

She scrambles to her feet, kicking off her shoes. He turns to go and she pushes him again and then he turns and he swings. His hand is a fist and it connects with her jaw and everything goes black.

NINETEEN

Images roam through her mind as her body is suspended between wakefulness and sleep.

Her father holding a bicycle steady as she tries to ride, her mother cheering from the audience of her ballet recital, a hotel in Greece surrounded by deep blue water, her father laughing as he takes a picture. 'Smile, Juliet. Smile, sweetheart.'

A hand coming towards her face, her hand caught in a door, her body falling down the stairs. She can feel the cold basement floor beneath her but she can't move. She sinks.

Upstairs, the house is silent, the kitchen clean, except for three glasses drying next to the sink.

In the living room, the coffee table is clear, except for a book on exotic travel destinations and a picture of Juliet as a three-year-old in a princess dress, twirling for the camera.

Collapsed in two armchairs are Juliet's parents, their faces pale, their breathing laboured, their eyes closed.

All is quiet.

All is meant to stay quiet.

TWENTY

Juliet

When she wakes up, she is in the dark, lying on her back. She can feel the tiled floor of the basement beneath her and she moves slowly, her head pounding, her jaw aching.

She has no idea how long she's been out for. She is shivering in the thin dress.

Standing slowly, she touches her face, feeling a puffy bruise along her aching jawline. Her head is pounding but she can move and nothing seems to be broken. He hit her. Did he hit her? He must have. She takes a cautious step forward, waiting to see if she gets dizzy or falls over, and when she doesn't, she takes another step.

He hit me? How is that possible? Adam wouldn't hurt me... but he did. He hit me.

No, he didn't. You've made a mistake.

She knows the basement well enough, and even without any light, she knows how to find the stairs that she climbs slowly, turning on the light switch next to the door when she gets there.

The brightness of the light makes her squint and she blinks quickly, waiting for her eyes to adjust, and then she turns the handle of the door to open it. The handle twists but as she pushes the door to open it, it moves only slightly and then stops.

She twists it once, twice and then she pushes against the door in case it's just stuck. But it won't move. She steps back and then jumps against the door, shoving it with her shoulder, feeling the pain of the force she is using through her body, but it stays closed.

'What?' she says aloud.

Stepping down another stair, she lifts her leg and jumps towards the door awkwardly, trying to kick it open like she's seen people do on television, but the door is stuck fast and she falls backwards, catching herself on the banister before she falls down the stairs.

This must be a mistake. It has to be.

She rights herself, shakes her head and walks back up to the door. Banging on it with the flat of her hand, she shouts, 'Adam, Mum, Dad, let me out, I'm locked in here. Adam, Mum, Dad, Adam, Mum, Dad! Hello?'

When her hand starts to sting, she forms a fist and bangs on the door, changing hands when her arm is tired.

But no one comes.

Going back down the stairs, she looks around for something that can help her break out of the basement but her father's tools are all kept in the garage. There's nothing in the basement but old furniture and boxes of stuff that belonged to her, moments of her childhood, sealed up in case she ever wants to look through them again. She doesn't.

She returns to the door, banging again, using one hand and then the other, and only when she notices that the side of the hand she is using is beginning to bruise and her throat is growing scratchy does she stop and go back down the stairs.

She lifts a sheet off an armchair, sneezing twice as dust floats up into the air, and then she sits down.

Did the door just slam shut and they can't hear her or did Adam deliberately lock it? The basement door doesn't actually have a lock, just a loop to put a padlock in. It's a combination lock and it was only ever used because the house is on clay and moves with the weather, sinking slightly when there's been a lot of rain, and the door swings open randomly.

Adam watched her open the combination lock. She remembers that now. He wanted to see everything in the house... but he wouldn't have locked her in here, surely. Why on earth would he do something like that?

But he hit her. Maybe he would do anything.

And where is her phone? She checks her pockets and then looks around the basement floor in case it is lying there but it's gone. Was it in her hand? Yes, she got the message from Monica. But where is it now?

Her throat is sore and she goes over to the small basin that has always been here, turning on the tap. She lets the water run for a few minutes and then drinks deeply, feeling better afterwards. And then she returns to the basement door and bangs again, calling for help again.

They'll come for her. They can't hear her but they will wonder where she is in a few minutes and come for her. How long was she out? Surely her parents have asked Adam where she is? She goes back down the stairs, sinks into the chair again, her eyes on the basement door, knowing that it's going to open at any moment and then, if Adam is still here, she will tell him to go. He thinks he's helping but he's not and he needs to understand that.

Did he really hit her or did she fall and hit her jaw on a box or a piece of furniture? That must have been what happened. What was the last thing he said to her? That he loved her and would come for her, that's right. He said he would come for her but where is she supposed to be? In the basement? Surely not.

After a few minutes she decides she needs to search for something, anything, to get her out of here. She has no idea what would be of use but she has to try. She gets off the chair and opens a box.

But it's just her old things. It's hard not to start looking through those old toys, memories floating up at her as she unpacks Barbie dolls and her collection of tiny shoes and dresses for all of them. And she remembers sitting on the floor of the living room with her mother, telling elaborate stories about the dolls. She shakes the memory away. She has no idea where all these childhood memories are suddenly coming from. When she arrived home from the hospital, she could only find the hazy ones where she was hurt, damaged and sad but now, with each passing day in this house, more and more of the ones she imagined did not exist – the good memories, the happy times – are popping up.

The box is filled with craft supplies as well. Glitter and crayons, stickers and glue and a sketchbook.

She takes out the sketchbook and tears out a piece of paper. *I'm locked in the basement*, she scrawls with a bright green crayon and then she takes the note up the stairs.

She pounds on the door again, calling for Adam and her parents. She shouts and pounds until her voice is hoarse and her hands are stinging again. When no one comes, she slides the note under the door, hoping that they see it. They must be looking for her by now.

How long has she been in here?

She heads back down the stairs, looking hopefully over her shoulder on the way. Picking up the sketchbook, she sits down on the musty armchair again and turns the pages. There is drawing after drawing of her and her parents, stick figures in front of their house with yellow sunshine in the background.

Wobbly letters spell nothing but eventually later pages become clear: *I love my mum and dad.*

But this was when they were hurting her, when she was too young to explain things to the nurses in the emergency room. How could she have drawn pictures like this? Surely, they should be dark, filled with sadness, not these happy drawings of a normal childhood.

She is exhausted from yelling and pounding on the door and she curls up small in the chair as her mind moves through the images she has collected of her mother pushing her down the stairs, hitting her so hard a tooth broke, slamming her hand in the car door. She tries to examine the images, to see how her mother looked, what she was wearing, what her hair looked like, but she can't see anything. In the remembered incidents her mother's face is blank as though it doesn't belong to her at all.

What is going on upstairs in the house? Has Adam gotten a confession from her parents? Has he done something to them? Could he have hurt them in some way? Or have they thrown him out for suggesting they hurt their daughter and now they're angry enough to just leave her here?

Are all the memories actually true and now they will just leave her to die down here?

Wrapping her arms around her legs, Juliet sobs for all the things she can remember and for those that she can't.

Adam said he would come for her. Why hasn't he come?

It's the last thought she has before she falls into a deep sleep, even as she reassures herself that Adam will come for her because that's what he promised. He loves her and he will come for her.

TWENTY-ONE

Juliet

She wakes with a start, her body stiff and cramped in the armchair. How long has she been here? It must be days, she knows that. There are no windows here and she is keeping the light on so there is no darkness. Sometimes it flickers and her heart races with fear at the idea that the bulb might blow and she will be sitting here in complete darkness.

She unfolds her body, groaning as she moves and her muscles protest. Standing up, she walks over to the ancient basin that is in the corner of the basement. No one has ever known why it is here but she is overjoyed to be able to open the rusty tap and drink deeply of the metal-smelling water. It feels like it will make her sick but there's nothing she can do about it. Her mouth is desert-dry each time she wakes up, and each time she has woken up, she has gone to one corner of the basement to relieve herself. The smell is everywhere now, turning her stomach and humiliating her, even though she's alone.

She has gone through all her boxes of childhood toys and even some baby clothes her mother hung on to and there is nothing that can help her, just useless stuff that throws endless memories at her. She has walked around the basement what feels like a million times but she can't find anything to make the door open.

Once again, she drags herself up the stairs and pounds on the door, calls for Adam and her parents.

'Please, Mum, please, Dad, please let me out. I'm so sorry. I'm sorry, please let me out,' she begs. Her voice isn't loud enough and she is so weak. She has been without food for a long time now, and she thinks constantly and longingly of the full to bursting pantry that her mother was always telling her to take food from.

Why are they doing this? Her parents and Adam must be colluding against her. They are in this together. That's what's happening. Unless her parents have done something to Adam because they didn't like him accusing them of their crimes, and now, they want her to die alone in this basement. Closing her eyes, she sees her parents' faces, but they are ugly and distorted, monstrous.

Maybe her parents even hurt Benji... She hasn't thought about Benji in a while. Benji is... Monica said Benji was dead. How did he die? Did her parents kill him? She shakes her head. Her thoughts are muddled. Nothing makes sense.

Pushing her ear up against the basement door as she has done many times, she thinks, is sure, she can hear people talking. There are people in the house. Her parents are here and they can hear her but they won't let her out. If Adam was here, if he was okay, he would have freed her. They've done something to him.

Holding her breath so she can hear more clearly, she listens to try and make out what's being said. She thinks she can hear footsteps coming to the door and she starts pounding again. 'Hello, hello, help me, help me, please.' But there's no response. A tiny corner of the note she has written is under the door on her side and she sees it move. Someone is here. They are here. She pounds again with everything she has left but the door remains closed.

She closes her eyes and leans her head against the door, whispers, 'Please help me,' and then she hears someone whisper back.

'I'm sorry, Juliet.'

Energy surges through her and she twists the handle and pushes the door but it won't budge. She pounds on the door, even kicking it with her bare foot and hurting her toe but nothing changes. And finally, she gives up, acknowledging she must have imagined the whispered words. She is going mad. She must be going mad. There was no one there. She is all alone and she will die down here.

Sinking down onto the stairs, she drops her head onto her knees and roars her frustration and pain. She doesn't have the energy to drag herself back down the stairs and she knows there's no point in trying the door again.

She has not been wrong about the abuse and she can see her parents now, sitting in the kitchen, listening to her each time she pounds on the door, saying, 'She needs to learn not to accuse us. We'll show her.' She's not going to pound again. She won't give them the satisfaction.

Are they going to leave her here to die? Is that what they want, and what have they done to Adam? He said he would come for her but what if he can't, what if they've killed him?

Scrunching her eyes shut, she wills her mind to work properly, her thoughts to get into an orderly line, not buzz around her head the way they are doing.

She can't cry anymore. She has no tears left for Adam or for herself.

With her head buried in her knees she breathes slowly, willing herself to sleep, willing the hours to pass.

. . .

She wakes to the sound of footsteps, her back cramping from the awkward way she has fallen asleep. Did she hear that? Are they moving around the house?

She doesn't want to beg to be let out again but she can't give up trying.

Standing, her stomach cramping with desperate hunger and her head feeling too heavy on her neck, she goes to the door again. Sweating and shaking, she lifts her hand once more to beg to be let out.

'Mum, Dad, please, I'm sorry, please let me out, please, please, please.' She hits the door a few times, her bruised and bloody hands barely making a sound.

There's no one there. No one to help her. She will die soon. How long can a person live without food? How long has it been? Adam never came but there must be a reason for that. He loves her and she's grateful she got to love him but she's ready to die now. She's so tired, so sick and tired.

She turns to go back down the stairs, takes the steps one at a time, every muscle aching. It will be easy to die now.

Behind her, there is a gust of air, and holding tightly to the banister, unable to believe what she's felt, she turns around. There is a woman at the top of the stairs dressed in pants and a pale blue shirt, a badge on her chest and the lump of a gun on her hip. Juliet squints at her, unsure if she's seeing an apparition or not.

'What are you doing?' the woman demands. 'What's going on here?'

'Are you real?' Juliet asks, her voice a croak.

'Who are you? Why are you down here?'

'I was locked in. Adam locked me in but he said...' She feels her body sway as she struggles to hold on to the banister. 'Adam said he would come.'

Black spots appear in front of her eyes and she knows she's going to faint, the room tilts and the last thing she hears is, 'The door wasn't locked. It wasn't locked. Why didn't you just open it?'

When she wakes, her body is being lifted up and she starts to struggle. She kicks out and screams and shouts until they tie her hands with plastic and drag her outside, where her driveway is filled with police cars and ambulances and people, watching, looking.

Something bad has happened. Something very bad has happened.

TWENTY-TWO

NOW

Lacy

When the security door is buzzed open, she shuffles inside, a burly police officer on either side of her as though this slight, dishevelled young woman with her gaze fixed on the floor could be a threat. She has been accused of a terrible crime, but looking at her now, what they are saying she did seems impossible.

I am standing by the nurses' station, a half-moon cream melamine counter with shelves underneath and bookcases behind it. Kendra, who has buzzed the group in, is sitting behind the desk and she gives one of the officers, a young man with bulging tattooed biceps, a quick smile and then her eyes return to her computer. The new arrival is another patient whose file needs to be updated. But I know Kendra would love to be able to study her, to see what all the fuss has been about. Kendra is a qualified nurse but she also has a degree in business administration, which means she does paperwork in addition to treating patients. With quick fingers, she adds our new patient's name to our system. Again.

'Hello, Juliet,' I say softly, making sure to conceal my alarm at her appearance. She has been in hospital under police guard for two nights and obviously has not washed or brushed her hair in that time. Perhaps, given her fragile mental state, the nurses there did not want to force her into a shower. I can't imagine she's eaten much either and the green tracksuit they have dressed her in bags around her body. It doesn't look like she's eaten properly for weeks. I've seen pictures of her on the news, and on mobile phone videos taken by gawking neighbours that are all over the internet, and she doesn't look much different now to when they found her. She was wearing a stained grey silk dress and was barefoot, her blue eyes sunken and her hair matted.

According to news reports, she was starving but not dehydrated but then she had only been there for a couple of days and human beings can survive for a very long time without food as long as they have water. She was also incredibly aggressive, trying to kick and scratch and bite the police officers who found her.

'I can take it from here,' I tell the police officers, who nod, visibly relieved. Juliet's unwashed body odour fills the air.

'Your room is ready.' I hold out my hand.

She doesn't move to take it but I wait. I know to wait. It takes a minute for her to lift her head, for her to register who I am.

'Lacy.' Her blue eyes widen, tears appearing.

'Come on, let's get you to your room.' She sniffs and nods, takes my hand, letting me lead her to room three, her steps small and shuffling... hesitant in the generic white sneakers they have given her to wear, even though she knows the way. 'It's the same room you had last time,' I explain, unsure if this will be a comfort or something that she fears. She never wanted to return here but it's rare to find a patient who does want to be readmitted to a psychiatric hospital. I've known one or two who have become too addicted to the routine and care and safety of the place to want to leave but Juliet was only here for a short time. She should be out in the world, living her life.

'Would you like to have a shower?' I ask her when we are safely inside the room, the door closed behind us but not locked because there are no locks on the internal doors here. Outside the large, definitely locked window, the autumn sun is high in the bright blue sky and the grass a rich green. The grounds around the hospital are lovely but they haven't done as good a job inside. I hate the colour scheme of these rooms, where the walls are a pale grey and the laminate floor a dirty speckled cream, but at least this room has a window and a view of the outside, including the large gum trees that are now covered in patchy red and gold as the leaves change colour.

Juliet nods as her gaze bounces around the room from the bed to the simple desk and chair and then to the window. She makes no move to take off her clothes so I do it for her, moving slowly so that I don't startle her and telling her exactly what I'm doing as I go. Patients are more compliant if you explain what you are doing. They don't like to be surprised. I imagine just finding themselves here can be shocking enough. Juliet's ribs and hip bones protrude and I wonder how long she hasn't eaten any real food for.

'After you're clean, we can go and get some lunch.' She nods again, biddable as I move her towards the bathroom and start the shower. The small bathroom fills rapidly with steam. There's no mirror over the single basin because mirrors can be smashed and used to break the skin. There are only the grey tiled walls to look at.

'In you go.' I push her forward gently.

When the warm water hits her face she lifts her head, closing her eyes at the comfort of the spray.

I pick up the yellow sponge and add soap, moving around her body as I have been trained to do, quickly and efficiently.

When I stand to get the shampoo to wash her hair, she grabs at my uniform of pale blue scrubs, splashing water on me.

'Adam,' she says and then she lets go, and I feel the damp seep in through the scrunched material over one shoulder.

'Adam,' I repeat and she nods, her eyes filling with tears.

'Adam did it.'

TWENTY-THREE

She eats the lunch I place in front of her in small, birdlike mouthfuls, a small bite of the cheese sandwich, followed by a tiny bite of the apple slice and a sip of water. Her hands tremble and I focus on her nails, ragged and torn. I need to file them for her. Her hands are puffy and bruised.

It's noisy in the dining room but then it always is. The large open space is filled with tables that can hold either two, four or six people, simple square and rectangle timber tables with matching timber chairs, the kinds you see in many restaurants. Now, in the designated lunch hour, the room is filled with patients, most of them dressed in comfortable clothes like tracksuits but some of them still in pyjamas. Those are usually patients who have only been here for a short while and for whom the mere task of getting dressed feels like too much effort. People sit alone at the tables for two or in groups if they have made friends, talking about their lives outside the hospital. Next to me I can hear a discussion about childcare going on between four women sitting at a table, large bowls of salad in front of all of them. They all have complaints about their nannies or helpers and they chew over their troubles with their bowls of vegetables. They are all alarmingly thin and I can see that not much swallowing of food is going on. Serviettes go to mouths often. I make a mental note to suggest that these women are separated at lunch. They are here voluntarily, probably because a family member has begged them or demanded that they come. Or perhaps they have decided that they can no longer live a life tormented by every single bite of food. I know one of them, a woman in her fifties, has been here for many months and she is still no better.

We have very good psychiatrists and brilliant programmes to help people at St Augustine but a patient has to want to heal, to get better. Even the best psychiatrist, the strongest drugs and the most careful care cannot always achieve this if the patient doesn't have the desire.

Juliet doesn't speak. She too is very thin but I know she wasn't locked away for long, so perhaps she has also starved herself on purpose in the weeks since she left the hospital.

'Dr Choudry isn't here anymore,' I tell her as I pick up the sandwich she has just put down and hand it to her to encourage another small bite. 'You'll be seeing someone new.' She saw Dr Choudry three times a week the last time she was here but she never really connected with him. I imagine that when people start asking questions about why this happened, that will be one of the reasons that might come up. He never really helped her.

One morning, three weeks ago, I came into work and Dr Choudry was simply gone, just gone, his office empty and his many degrees and diplomas removed from the walls. The hospital rumour mill was in overdrive for a few days over where he might be but we have yet to have any official news. I don't believe he was a psychiatrist who had the best intentions for his patients but I would never be stupid enough to suggest that opinion to anyone. Even in a hospital, where suffering people are being cared for by medical professionals, the schoolyard is ever present. I know which members of staff are the biggest gossips and which ones are the best to tell your secrets to.

'Another bite,' I encourage Juliet softly and she complies, her gaze fixed on the blank wall at the back of the room.

She is here, but she is also very far away, lost somewhere, and perhaps is mentally still in the basement where she was found.

When she went home six weeks ago, she was, ostensibly, healed or at least able to function. On her last day here, as I was helping her pack up her things, she said, 'Can't I come and stay with you? I won't be any trouble.'

'I know you won't,' I said, 'but it's not allowed and I work all day. You would be alone and that's not a good idea. You need to look at going home as temporary, just until you feel stronger.' I squeezed her shoulder and was confronted by her big blue eyes and the despair on her face.

She is not the first patient who has asked to come and live with me and I'm sure she won't be the last. Returning to her family home did not make her stronger. Instead, it has resulted in terrible tragedy.

She was very far from healed when she left here and she is further away now. Perhaps she should have stayed here longer, had more time to fight her demons, both internal and external. But she was released back into the world and sent home to live with her parents. The weekly cost of staying here is enormous and I can't help but think that it may sometimes affect the decisions that are made by the doctors and those paying for the treatment.

After everything Juliet said about her parents, she was still sent home to live with them. Although perhaps it is more accurate to say that she chose to go and live with them, with a fair amount of encouraging from Dr Choudry.

She wasn't capable of being on her own, not then. At least,

that's what Dr Choudry said. 'She is still not separating fiction from reality as completely as I would like,' Dr Choudry told me when I expressed concern that she would be returning home, hoping that he would let her stay longer or, at least, encourage her parents to go on paying for her to stay. I felt she needed more time.

'She needs to stay on her medication and have extensive counselling. Her parents will do everything they can to help her get better,' he informed me, waving his hand to let me know he was done with the conversation. I don't think he liked Juliet very much. He is human after all, and despite his impartiality, he had patients he liked more than others. The more attractive patients seemed to be his favourites, and for a time, Juliet seemed to be one of them but then he met her parents and everything changed.

I would love to know what happened.

From the small amount of information I have been given, which is not much because I am only a nurse, Juliet only attended one therapy session with an outside psychiatrist and she did fill the prescription for her anti-anxiety medication and sleeping pills, although from blood tests taken at the hospital, there is no evidence of the anti-anxiety drug in her system. I'm not sure if she took any of the sleeping pills she was prescribed but I know she never liked those.

Her parents were supposed to be watching her, caring for her, but after everything she had been through, they couldn't even do that.

Juliet nods her head at the news that she will have a new psychiatrist, as she obediently takes another bite of her sandwich.

'Do you want to tell me what happened?'

She shakes her head. She has not spoken since the shower.

'Lacy,' I hear and I turn around. Abigail, the nurse unit

manager, is striding towards us. 'Dr Schaffer would like to have a word with you.'

'I'm just sitting with Juliet while she eats,' I say even though it's obvious that's what I'm doing.

Abigail purses her thin lips. I've irritated her because she prefers it when people jump up and do her bidding as soon as they are asked. Abigail and I are the same age, both thirty-six, but she has been deemed more capable of running the psychiatric unit than I am. I blame Dr Choudry for that. He and I did not get on. He believed that nurses should treat all patients as a number, as a diagnosis that needed to be dealt with. I believe our patients are people with broken hearts and damaged souls and I try to understand every single one of them. But the St Augustine private hospital is basically here to make money. I take too much time with my patients. A nurse manager needs to be on board with hospital policies and I admit that I stray from them if I really want to help someone.

'You are not here to save everyone,' Dr Choudry told me when he first began working here and I took the time to go to his office once or twice a week, arriving early for my night shift so I would catch him, to talk about the patients on the ward.

'I don't need to hear your opinion on every one of my patients,' he said, tapping himself on the chest just in case I was uncertain as to who he was talking about.

'Nurses spend more time with patients than anyone and they have instincts and information that many doctors find invaluable,' I replied.

'I prefer to be able to make an assessment without outside influence.'

At some point in his life, Dr Choudry decided he was the most intelligent person in every room. He must be insufferable at a dinner party. I am not unhappy that he is no longer with us.

Dr Choudry didn't like me and I know that's why Abigail got promoted over me but after a few days of being angry about it, I decided to let it go. It's more important to me that I form a connection with a struggling person than that I have the title and the pay bump, although living in Sydney is incredibly expensive and I am beginning to fear that I will never have the money to buy an apartment.

'I'll sit with Juliet,' says Abigail as she runs her hands around her head, making sure that her tightly wound mousy-brown bun has not dared to loosen itself.

My auburn hair is cut into a short bob so I don't need to wear it up.

I reach across the table and pat Juliet's hand, reassuring her that I will be back with the gesture, and then I stand up and leave the dining room. She doesn't meet my eyes, instead concentrating on lifting the sandwich to her mouth again.

'Now let's hurry this up,' I hear Abigail say as I walk away and I have to resist the urge to say anything. Abigail is brusque with patients, jollying them along and keeping them in line. Juliet didn't respond well to her last time she was here and she certainly won't respond now.

Outside the doctor's office, I smooth my uniform, making sure my nametag is straight and tucking my hair behind my ears before I knock.

'Come,' she calls.

Dr Schaffer is in her fifties with fine black hair that she wears loose around her shoulders and full lips. She has been here for just over a week so I have yet to interact with her beyond a greeting in the morning. It is not easy to replace a head psychiatrist in a hospital and I did see a parade of doctors in and out of the unit for a week after Dr Choudry left as the board interviewed candidates. I hope they have made a better decision with Dr Schaffer than they did with Dr Choudry.

'Ah, Lacy, thanks for coming in for a chat. Do sit down.' She indicates a chair on one side of her desk. Although she hasn't changed much about the office since Dr Choudry used it, she has changed some of the furniture, adding a rich green sofa and matching chairs instead of the leather furniture he had. She has also added flowers in vases on a side table and a matching white console on one wall. Today she has carnations in pink and red, lending the space a cheerful air. It's a much more pleasant place to be now.

I sit down, glancing at her desk where she has her computer and a notepad and nothing else, apart from a thick file with the name Juliet Cordell across the front of it. From what some of the other nurses have said I believe she has a husband and children but there are no pictures in the office. No psychiatrist I have ever met has displayed pictures of their families. You never know what will be triggering to a patient. And psychiatrists are also quite paranoid about anyone knowing anything about their personal lives. When I was training, I remember hearing stories of patients who stalked their doctors and nurses, even a dreadful situation where a young psychiatrist was attacked. It's better that patients have no idea if their doctors are even married or not. We are, after all, dealing with the mentally unwell. And sometimes those people are looking for someone to blame if they cannot find a way to feel better. In here, nurses and doctors can become targets.

'Not at all,' I reply to Dr Schaffer with a smile.

'So,' she says, taking off her glasses and putting them down onto the desk in front of her, 'we have quite an unusual situation with Juliet.'

'Yes.'

'We are not a criminal psychiatric facility but it was determined that the best place for her was here because she has been here before.' Dr Schaffer has a low, soothing voice and I can immediately see that patients are going to respond well to her.

'Yes, that's what Abigail said. I really didn't expect her to return. She was here for three months following a suicide attempt and was released around six weeks ago. I was surprised they decided to send her back here as well but perhaps it really is the right place for her. We helped her once. I mean, we tried. I had hoped that we wouldn't see her again.' I cross my legs and rest my hands on my lap.

'Dr Choudry helped her or thought he had, yes, but now the police need to ascertain if she is stable enough and mentally fit enough to be charged.'

I resent the mention of Dr Choudry, as though the psychiatrist is the all-knowing, all-seeing god of this place and the only one able to help, but I think Dr Schaffer might be different. She has, after all, called me in to talk about Juliet. I wonder if she knows the full story of why Dr Choudry left.

'I believe you and Juliet were quite close when she was here,' she says with a smile, letting me know that she does not disapprove of that.

I nod. 'We were. I mean, I think that I get along with all my patients but she did seem to like me.'

'I have her file and I've started reading it. Dr Choudry has a lot of handwritten notes that are somewhat hard to read but I'm getting through them. I wanted to see if you had some insight into her that I could use to help her.'

I nod my head eagerly and feel the warmth of appreciation inside me. I think Dr Schaffer and I are going to get along really well. 'Anything I can do to make her time here easier, I will.'

'The police have given us two weeks to make a determination. She will, of course, not be allowed to spend her sentence here. We are a private facility.'

'What if she's not guilty?' Two weeks is no time at all. It could take her two weeks just to open up to me properly again, just to start talking to me and for her to really listen to me when I speak to her.

Dr Schaffer sighs. 'I understand that you have a relationship with the young woman but from what the police have told me it's pretty cut and dried.'

'But wasn't she found locked in the basement?' I have watched everything I could about what happened over the last couple of days but there are frustratingly few details.

'Bizarrely, the door wasn't actually locked. There was a padlock lying on the floor at the side of the door but it wasn't locked. She could have opened it at any time.' I absorb these details that are not public knowledge, nodding my head.

'But her hands are so bruised, as though she had been banging them against something. Maybe she didn't know the door was unlocked?'

'All she had to do was turn the handle and push the door. They are pretty sure she put herself in there and acted like she couldn't get out. That's not something the press know or anyone else really, except the police and now me and you.' Dr Schaffer stops speaking and picks up her glasses, replacing them on her face. 'I shouldn't have told you that, sorry. I'm not used to dealing with this kind of situation.' Alarm crosses her face and I quickly reassure her.

'I will never say anything to anyone about what we discuss in this office.'

At St Augustine, we treat patients with addiction issues and eating disorders and depression and anxiety. Most of our patients come from wealth and fame and they are able to pay the high fees for private treatment, that remains private despite snooping journalists. We have had more than one celebrity in here. Dr Schaffer was surely not expecting a patient in Juliet's situation in her first week at the hospital or, indeed, ever.

'Her parents were found slumped in chairs in the living room. They couldn't be woken.'

'How horrible,' I say, shaking my head, imagining the police knocking on the front door and then gaining access to the house and discovering Juliet's parents and then her.

'Yes,' agrees the doctor.

'She told me...' I hesitate, not sure if I should tell the psychiatrist what Juliet said. 'She told me Adam did it.'

'The police did say she repeated the name Adam to them as well,' she says, rubbing at the bridge of her nose.

'Do you think he was a friend or a boyfriend?' I sit forward in my chair, eager to hear the answer.

'Do you think it's possible that in the short time since she left here, she met someone who committed this terrible crime?' asks the doctor with a shrug.

I shake my head. 'Probably not. But it's not impossible, is it?'

'No, I suppose nothing is impossible. Although Dr Choudry has written, in his typed notes, which are very few compared to the written ones, that she had a tendency towards embellishment and imaginative stories.'

'I think Dr Choudry didn't...' I don't say any more, aware that I don't know Dr Schaffer at all. I have no idea how she will react to my real opinions about Juliet.

'Didn't?'

I weigh up speaking out versus keeping quiet and decide that the most important thing is that Dr Schaffer knows that Juliet is fragile and in pain. 'I think he didn't listen to her and that some of what she said may have been true.'

Dr Schaffer glances down at the thick file on her desk. 'Hmm.'

'I mean, if she was telling the truth last time, it would explain what happened with her parents. Especially since she was sent back to live with them – not excuse it but maybe help explain it.'

'Perhaps.' She looks at the cream metal filing cabinet in the corner of her office. 'I still have a lot more of the file to get through. His writing is very bad, even for a doctor,' she says with a dry chuckle. 'But I will bear in mind what you've said.'

'I know her quite well, at least I think I do, and I would never have imagined her capable of murder but perhaps being home was just too much for her. I can imagine it would have been quite harrowing to be living with the people you have accused of abuse.'

'People under stress can do some terrible things. But this seems to have been planned quite well, according to the police.'

'It's so extreme.'

'I know, although it's not murder right now, only attempted murder.'

I nod my head, feeling sick to my stomach. 'Have the hospital given any updates?'

'Both her parents are still in comas. It looks unlikely that they will survive. If she says anything to you that you feel could help me establish her reasoning in committing this crime, please come and speak to me.'

'Absolutely, of course I will.' I stand up, and taking advantage of how easy she is to talk to, I ask her the question that's been buzzing around my head for a few weeks. 'I know it may not be my place to ask but do you know exactly why Dr Choudry left?'

Dr Schaffer's face shuts down and she shakes her head.

'It's just that when people leave, we usually have a dinner to say goodbye and... well, Dr Choudry was here one day and gone the next and I...' I am stumbling for an explanation for my question. 'Never mind, it's obviously not important,' I say as I turn to go.

'I don't think it is,' she replies and I feel my face burn. I just want to leave now.

'Oh, and Lacy,' says the doctor when I get to the door.

'Yes, Dr Schaffer?'

'Do be careful. The police believe she attempted to murder

her parents. Whatever is true, we have no idea what she may be capable of.'

'I'm always careful and I like Juliet and I think she likes me. She wouldn't hurt me.'

'I hope not,' she says as I open the door to leave. 'I truly hope not.'

TWENTY-FOUR

Mandy Schaffer

I've finally gotten everything unpacked and put away in my new office. This week I even remembered to bring in flowers, which I always feel adds something positive to the space. When the board hired me, they let me know that I will be dealing with patients suffering from anxiety and depression. Another one of the doctors works with addiction cases and those in the grips of anorexia, which is fine with me. I'm really grateful to have gotten the position since it allows me time with the kids in the evening, something that was rare when I was on call at the public hospital. The whole place looks like a nicely maintained retreat, except for the internal paint colours, which are a bit ghastly. But the rest of it is lovely and the surrounding grounds are particularly beautiful and peaceful. I'm really happy with the change and I look forward to helping my patients.

Unfortunately, I have been thrown a bit of a curveball in the arrival of Juliet Cordell, a young woman who attempted to poison her parents. It seems likely that she will succeed at ending their lives.

She was here before under the treatment of Dr Choudry for a suicide attempt. I have no idea why she was released when it seems that she developed a fixed delusion that she had been abused by her parents but perhaps the cost became a factor. I understand she did not, despite his recommendation, continue treatment when she left here, having only one session with Dr Kelly. I've spoken briefly with Janet Kelly, who told me that Juliet recounted an incident of abuse but when pressed on the details eventually simply lied. 'It was easy to see that she was lying,' she told me. Juliet did not return for a second session so Janet can't say any more than that. I am aware, from blood tests done at the hospital, that she stopped taking her medication, although for how long, I can't be sure.

I am really not clear on how to deal with her and I'm grateful that I have Lacy, who spent a lot of time with her when she was first here. I would like to recommend that Juliet be moved to a criminal psychiatric facility but the board members have all agreed that she should be here. No doubt, the optics of a young woman being released and then attempting to murder both her parents is not ideal. The hospital name has been splashed all over the internet for a few days, even trending on social media with the deplorable hashtag of #nuthouse-fortherich.

Juliet came here after a suicide attempt and left, it seems, in more trouble than when she arrived. Definitely not something that the board wants to have in the public sphere. That's why they have agreed to fund a two-week stay.

News reports are all discussing the hospital, and when I spoke to Jacquie, one of the board members, on the phone, she told me that they are all 'keen to get this nightmare over with'. I'll obviously do my best to help the young woman and figure out if she is able to stand trial but I don't have much hope for her. Hospital staff where she was initially treated after being found describe her as violent and uncooperative. She refused to shower or eat and remained almost catatonic in bed until she was brought here. She was heard whispering, 'Adam will come for me,' over and again, sometimes for hours.

Abigail told me that Lacy managed to get her into a shower so that is, perhaps, an indication that some trust already exists between the two of them, and that this may be to our advantage in determining her state of mind and perhaps the reasoning behind what she is said to have done.

But I am very cautious about exploiting that trust or involving Lacy too much. I don't want her to feel that what happens to Juliet is strictly down to what she may be able to achieve with her. That's not healthy.

I think Raj Choudry's notes will help as soon as I can decipher them. The man really took having a doctor's handwriting too far. And after learning of the reasons why he left this job, I am not sure I can trust anything he says anyway. The staff are, obviously, curious as to why he left but only Abigail and I know and I would like to keep it that way. It will do no one any good to learn the reason why he was asked to leave and the matter is under review now so it's best kept quiet. My predecessor's behaviour is not my focus right now. I need to figure out what happened to this young woman and why she tried to hurt her parents. I look forward to meeting with her soon so that I can do my job in the best way possible.

TWENTY-FIVE

Lacy

The next day, I find Juliet in the dining room having breakfast when I arrive for work. She is sitting alone but at least she's eating. When she was last here, I was on the evening shift, starting at 4 p.m. and ending at midnight. It was a quieter part of the day to work and allowed me to spend extra time with my patients but Abigail decided that I needed to move to days. I feel like sometimes she does things just to irritate me, but if I were to complain, I am sure I would be told that nurses are swapped from shifts all the time and that I am no more special than the next person who wants to work at a time that suits them. I prefer night work because it means my days are free to do as I like, once I have a few hours of sleep, and nights are easier. Patients are mostly asleep.

Now that Juliet has returned, I'm actually grateful to be working during the day so that I can be with her as much as possible.

'The police liaison officer dropped off a suitcase of clothes for you,' I tell her, squeezing her shoulder gently. She is at a table in the corner, with her back to the room, her shoulders hunched and her hair unbrushed, wearing the same green tracksuit she came in.

'Where did they get them from?' she asks, looking up at me. She seems more alert despite the fact that they have started her on her medication again. Hilda was on shift overnight and told me that she slept well so that's a good thing.

'Your house, your bedroom at home.'

'Home.' She nods. 'Home,' she repeats. I watch her face and I can see that her eyes change and it seems like part of her just disappears. 'My parents... are my parents here?' Despairing confusion washes over her face and I feel my heart sink. I would like her to be able to acknowledge what she did and explain why she did it. I believe that would be the best thing for her. But I can see we have a long way to go and I know we don't have a lot of time with her.

She looks around her as though surprised to find herself sitting where she is sitting. Looking back at me, her blue eyes narrow and I can see that somewhere inside her, she knows the answer but also that she doesn't want to admit it. Perhaps she is just struggling with being on her medication again. But she is suddenly more confused than I would expect her to be, more lost. Whatever happened when she was living with her parents has been catastrophic for Juliet's mental wellbeing.

I sit down in the other chair across from her and grasp her hand. 'Your parents are in hospital, Juliet,' I tell her gently as I did yesterday. 'Remember? They're not... well.' It's the best I can manage.

She drops her gaze to her food and I watch as tears fall onto the half-empty plate, mingling with the dry piece of toast and powdered scrambled eggs she has there. The facility has a relatively good menu and she could have chosen yoghurt and fruit, even pancakes, but instead she chose a dish that is tasteless. She is punishing herself. I can see that.

'I didn't want to do it,' she whispers and I find myself holding my breath, afraid to make even the slightest sound.

When she says nothing else, I ask her softly, 'What didn't you want to do, Juliet?'

'I...' she begins and then she looks up at me. 'Lacy,' she says, 'are my parents here? Is it time for me to go home?'

I believe she knows what really happened but it is too awful for her to face. I cannot imagine how she will feel if both parents do not make it, what she might do.

The mind is a wonderful thing, capable of protecting itself from the most terrible experiences in life. It can also turn against you. Looking at the state of her, I can see that Juliet is struggling, really struggling. She was in a fragile state the first time she came here; now she is thin glass, already cracking, and a single touch will shatter her into pieces.

'Shall we go and get you out of this and into some of your own clothes? You'll feel much better.' It is easier to redirect her than to try and answer the question or to tell her, again, that her parents are in hospital because she is suspected of putting them there, because she tried to kill them both. But she failed to.

Nodding, she stands and leaves her plate, following me to her room, where the suitcase has been placed on her bed. I unzip it while she stands watching me, her shoulders rounded and her face a mask of misery.

She seems wholly incapable of murder. But then no one *seems* to be capable of murder. It's not like a person is born with the capability to hurt someone else. Something must happen to them in their childhoods, in their lives to push them to that point.

Even someone who murders another human being has an explanation for why it happened. We all like to tell ourselves we are good people who only want to do good things. We all want to believe that we would only do something terrible if we were pushed to that point and then, surely, the person we hurt deserved it.

The ability to get up every day and exist in this world is mostly a matter of telling yourself the right story, the story that keeps you happy, whether it's true or not.

Do Juliet's parents deserve to die? Who knows. Right now, they are still alive. The police have not told the public exactly what she used to poison her parents. That's something they are keeping quiet.

No one knows the whole truth of what happened. I keep reminding myself of that.

Taking out some black tracksuit pants and a red T-shirt, I show them to Juliet and she nods. 'Do you want me to help you shower?'

'No, no... thank you.'

She disappears into the bathroom and I unpack the rest of her things. There's not much because the case was packed by a policewoman who was instructed to only bring what was absolutely necessary.

Last time she came here, her mother had packed for her and she had added family photographs for Juliet to put up on the desk and look through when she wanted to, photographs to remind Juliet of how much she had to live for, of how much she was loved. I remember going through the photographs with her as she told me where each one was taken. They seemed the perfect record of a beautiful life. I remember staring at a picture of her as a baby, looking at how her mother gazed down at her with such love and feeling envious. I don't have children and I'm not sure that I ever will have. Juliet's parents looked like they loved her very much.

It's not something I would ever admit to but even though she was struggling when she first came here, it seemed to me that she had enjoyed a wonderful life before her accident and that she had every opportunity to enjoy a wonderful life after it.

I thought her spoiled and selfish. I should never do that with a patient.

I looked at that picture of Juliet and her mother every day. I couldn't understand what she had to be upset about or to keep being upset about. The accident that ended her career was terrible but she was still so young, still capable of doing anything she wanted with her life. Her parents were supportive and only wanted her to get better. I understood what had happened to her but part of me thought, *Pull yourself together and get on with it.*

I never said that to her, obviously. And she has her demons, more demons than anyone even knew about. The truth about human beings is that we are all fighting our own battles.

I find that helping others makes it easier to deal with things that are bothering me.

Juliet emerges from the bathroom, clean and dressed, her blonde hair in a neat ponytail.

'That's better, isn't it?'

'Has he come to see me, Lacy?'

I place the empty suitcase at the bottom of the small cupboard and then smooth her bed for her. 'Who?'

'Adam. He said he would come for me no matter what happened but I'm not locked in the basement anymore so he won't know where I am, but maybe the police told him?'

She is holding the green tracksuit and I take it from her, placing it in the laundry basket for cleaning. 'No, no, he hasn't come,' I tell her. Here she is lucid and clear, as though the confusion in the dining room never happened at all.

She sinks down into the chair next to the small desk. 'But he said he would come. He told me he loved me and he would come.' She lifts her legs up, wrapping her arms around her knees and resting her chin there. No concern for her parents, I notice, but she sounds calm and clear and so I take the chance to question her about everything.

'You remember Adam locking you in the basement?' I need to know exactly what she remembers and how much.

She nods.

'Why did he lock you in there?' I sit down on the bed.

She looks at me, glazed confusion in her eyes. 'It was... I don't know.' She shakes her head and buries her face in her knees. It seems I have lost her again but is that the truth? Is this all an act?

'Do you know where he lives?' I ask. 'I can tell the police to go and speak to him.'

Shaking her head, she gets up from the chair and comes to lie down on the bed as I stand up. 'I don't know, I don't remember the address. It was a building near the train station and it had a lift,' she whispers.

I stroke her hair lightly. 'Perhaps have a nap and maybe you'll remember something and then I can tell the police. I'll wake you in time for your session with Dr Schaffer.' I don't know what else to suggest.

'Okay.' She sniffs and obediently closes her eyes. I know Dr Schaffer has prescribed sleeping pills but I also know that last time Juliet stayed here, she only pretended to take them when a nurse was watching her. Instead, she stored them under her mattress for a couple of weeks until they were discovered. We learned to check every night and make sure she took them. I remind myself to check under her mattress in a few days and see if she is doing the same thing.

I leave her room, closing the door quietly behind me.

Dr Schaffer has asked me to check in with her before I deal with any other patients. When I get there, I knock softly to let her know I'm here.

'Ah, Lacy,' she says when I open the door.

'The police brought a suitcase of clothes for Juliet. I was with her now when she showered. She asked me about Adam coming to see her. Apparently, he told her that he would come for her if she stayed locked in the basement.'

Dr Schaffer nods and I can see that I have done the right thing in telling her. I am so glad she appreciates my input.

'So strange. Has she told you any more about him? In our first session, she told me that she can't remember his surname or where he lives. I wondered whether he was even real, but perhaps he does exist and she's protecting him.'

My heart races at the idea that Dr Schaffer believes 'Adam' exists. The way Juliet talks, he could easily be a figment of her imagination.

'She said he lives in a building near a train station,' I tell her, knowing that this is of no value at all.

She pushes her chair away from her desk and stands, going to the window that overlooks the gardens. People are walking around still in T-shirts because the start of autumn has held onto the summer weather. I see a young man deliberately stepping on the fallen leaves as he might have done when he was much younger.

'It seems inconceivable that a young woman like her would do such a thing as trying to kill her parents,' says Dr Schaffer as she continues to stare out of the window.

'I agree,' I reply as I peer at the open notebook on her desk while the doctor's back is turned. It's upside down so I can't make out much but there is a boldly written sentence that stands out: *Call Rajesh again about notes re. Juliet.*

I wonder why Dr Choudry has not returned her call and if it has anything to do with his sudden disappearance. She turns back and I step away from the desk quickly as she moves over to her notebook and shuts it with a sigh.

'Look, Lacy... I'm only telling you this because you are so involved with Juliet but I would ask that you don't repeat it to anyone.'

I nod my head. 'Of course.'

'The police called this morning to tell me that both parents had large quantities of temazepam in their systems. They have waited to let me know because they hoped that Juliet would confess to giving it to them, and then if I told them, it would be an admission of guilt on her part. That's why they were both in comas when paramedics arrived. Juliet had a prescription for sleeping pills that she has filled twice since she left the clinic. That's fifty tablets. Divided in two it wasn't quite enough to kill them unless it had been combined with a lot of alcohol, and while there was some in their systems, it wasn't enough to... God, this is so horrible to say... do the job, I guess. Although it may still be the case that both of them succumb.'

'Do you think they will? I mean, have the doctors said anything more?'

She shakes her head. 'Something the police are keen to know is exactly how she got her parents to take the drugs.'

'Oh.' I have no idea what else to say.

'I think it's looking likely that Juliet planned this very carefully. The fact that she can't seem to really remember what happened – and that when she does, she blames "Adam" – seems to be indicative of some kind of psychotic break or of someone who has thought this through. I don't think we can help her here and I do believe the best thing for her would be a transfer to a criminal psychiatric facility.

'But she's not...' I shake my head. 'Please don't do that. I think she will be better with a bit more time. She has moments of clarity, and when she adjusts to the medication, that may get better. Honestly, I don't think she will survive being locked up with criminals. And they don't know for sure, not really. Someone else could have done it and made her think she was locked in there. Maybe she was given some pills as well.'

The doctor sits down at her desk, picking up a pen and opening her notebook to a fresh page. I know her next patient is due any moment. 'She wasn't. I don't know if she will ever be able to stand trial, so what good are we doing?'

'Maybe if Juliet can... grasp what happened she may have another explanation. She told Dr Choudry her parents were abusive. If she can truly understand what she did, she may have an explanation.'

'I have considered that,' says Dr Schaffer, twirling the pen in her hand, something that I find really distracting. 'If she is guilty of this crime, we want to understand her motives. She's so young and I hate to think of her spending years locked away in a criminal facility. Perhaps we do owe her a little more time, but, Lacy, I have to tell you, I am not hopeful.'

'I understand,' I reply, hoping that Juliet will be able to stay with us as long as possible. The more time she is here, the better.

I go to my locker to get the snack I have packed for myself. We are allowed to eat the food in the dining room but I prefer to bring snacks from home. Looking in the mirror in the morning, I can see that I am gaining weight around the middle, the curse of getting older, so I am trying to cut back on the dining room food, which tends to be quite starchy and high in sugar.

As I grab my Tupperware of celery and cottage cheese from my insulated lunch bag, I glance at the picture I have of my mother.

Good mothers raise good children. Juliet's mother seemed like a good person if photographs are anything to go by. And yet, Juliet has done this terrible thing.

I take a bite of my celery, letting the crunching sound cover the thought.

'She's not well,' I mutter as I chew, reminding myself to be professional.

Before I leave, I lift my hand and stroke the photograph softly, my thumb running over my mother's face.

I wish I could go back and change things but I can't. I shake my head and close my locker door.

I need to get back to work. It's time for me to get Juliet to her next session with Dr Schaffer and I am eager to see if the doctor can find out any new information at all. Even something small may help us figure out what really happened. And that's all anyone wants.

To find out what really happened.

TWENTY-SIX

Lacy

The days have passed more quickly than I would believe as I do my best to keep a close eye on Juliet and work with my other patients. This morning, nearly a week after she arrived, I am running late for work because I didn't sleep well last night and I rush into the locker room to put my things away, grateful that I have clocked in with a minute to spare. I am spending too much time thinking about Juliet and what's going to happen to her. Ruminating on things always affects my sleep and last night, well after midnight and a lot of tossing and turning, I eventually turned the light back on and scrolled through social media for an hour. I follow people on Instagram who I went to school with, even though it hurts to see those I never liked or those who didn't like me living perfect lives. The women all have husbands and children and fill up their pages with perfect holiday photos. In my own life, I haven't been as lucky but it's possible that one day I may be. Anything is possible.

Waking late, I hurried out of my small apartment without breakfast or coffee and that always makes me feel like I haven't started the day right. As I'm slipping my phone into my pocket, I feel the buzz of a notification and I look at the screen. It's a message from the estate agency who manage my apartment as they do many in my high-rise complex. My heart sinks when I see it's a notification of yet another rent rise. My apartment is one bedroom, with one bathroom and a small galley kitchen and no parking space, although there's no way I would be able to afford to run a car anyway. I find myself shocked on a daily basis as to how much things cost and how quickly prices are rising. Life would be easier if I was dating someone who made proper money but I'm not. You can't have everything I suppose. I have gone through periods in my life where I thought that I would never find someone to fall in love with, to create a family with, but I can feel it within my grasp now, although uncertainty is creeping in. Still, one day I hope to put up my own family photos on Instagram for people to glance at as they scroll through on their way to the next picture.

It would be nice to not have to worry about money anymore but that's far into my future and I need to deal with what's happening now. I can't help thinking, as I do every time money crosses my mind, that this isn't how my life should have turned out. I shouldn't be unmarried at thirty-six and living from pay cheque to pay cheque. Shaking my head, I push the thought away because it's never a good idea to go down the path of 'what if'.

As I'm going to leave the locker room, Kendra walks in, her dark hair in a perfect chignon and her pretty face make-up free. Kendra is only twenty-six and she still has the lovely blush of youth on her skin.

'Did you hear?' she asks me, raising her perfectly arched eyebrows.

'What?'

'About Dr Choudry, about why he left,' she says with a smug little smile.

I'm running late as it is and I want to be there for Juliet when she comes out of her session with Dr Schaffer this morning. Dr Schaffer is seeing her every day in an attempt to ascertain her mental competence. But I also want to know what Kendra has to say.

Taking a deep breath, I return her smile. 'Do tell,' I say, knowing that Kendra is a good gossip. If anyone has all the information, it's her. She's been working here for a year and seems to be friendly with everyone, from the gardeners who maintain the grounds to the board members who run the hospital. And if she knows something, she likes to share it with everyone. I don't want to be the last to hear.

Kendra looks around, making sure we are alone in the locker room. 'Well,' she says, 'apparently he was reported to the Australian Medical Association and the Australian Health Practitioner Regulation Agency for sexual misconduct.'

I sink onto a long bench that faces my locker, feeling my face grow hot. 'Do you know who reported him? Was it a nurse or…?'

'Well, these things are anonymous, but from what I hear, it was a nurse on behalf of a patient. He was big into special breathing exercises with his patients.' She winks at me. I'm not quite sure what she means but I get the gist.

'And… you definitely don't know who it was?' I can feel my heart thudding in my chest. I knew there was something odd about Dr Choudry the moment I met him.

Kendra shrugs. 'Like I said, it's anonymous.'

'But someone must know who reported it, and how did you find out anyway?'

Kendra is standing next to her locker and she steps towards me, leans down and whispers in my ear, 'I went out with Jacquie's son, Damien, last night. He's not for me but we had a good time. He had lots to say about the hospital. Lots.'

My mouth feels dry. Jacquie Wheeler is one of the board

members who administers the hospital. The last time I saw her was at the Christmas dinner for the staff last year. Her son came as well since he's working as a psychiatric registrar in one of our public hospitals. I think Jacquie wants Damien to be an integral part of running this private hospital eventually so she's getting him ready for that role.

'When did you meet him?' I ask her.

Kendra shrugs and goes back to her locker, opening it and pulling out a muesli bar from her bag, which she unwraps and bites into. 'At the Christmas party,' she says with her mouth full, 'but then we matched on Tinder a few weeks ago and we've been chatting. He's cuteish, tall with blue eyes, but he's really, really into himself... and I am the most important person in any relationship.' She laughs.

'I'm sure that's... unethical,' I tell her as I stand up.

Kendra waves her hand at me. 'It doesn't matter. I told him this morning that we're better as friends and blah, blah but at least I found out about the esteemed Dr Choudry, so worth it. Apparently, he was reported about three months ago but the wheels of bureaucracy grind really slowly in this hospital.'

'They do, very slowly for doctors but not for us nurses.' I go to leave the locker room as I think about a nurse who worked here last year, a woman named Estelle who got into an altercation with a patient and swung out to defend herself, hitting the woman she was fighting with and breaking her nose. Estelle was gone the next day. The rules for doctors are different, it seems. Dr Choudry was allowed to keep working until the board was forced to make a decision. I wonder if another patient came forward or something like that.

'I wonder who the patient was,' she says as I open the door to leave the locker room.

'Well,' I say, deliberately keeping my tone casual as though I really don't care at all, 'tell me if you find out.'

As I hurry towards Dr Schaffer's office, I remember Dr

Choudry waving away my concerns about patients, telling me that he knows more than anyone and refusing to listen to Juliet when she told him she had been harmed by her parents as a child. He shouldn't have done that. I wonder what will happen to him now. He may never be able to practise again, which won't be a bad thing. I don't think he's a very good psychiatrist.

Checking my watch as I get to Dr Schaffer's office, I am grateful to see that Juliet's session would have just ended. I stand quietly outside, my eyes on my white shoes that are looking a bit scuffed. I catch my breath as I let the news about Dr Choudry turn over in my mind.

'Lacy,' I hear and I look up to see Abigail and a man I haven't seen before coming towards me down the hallway. They stop in front of Dr Schaffer's office.

'What are you doing here?' she asks me, or rather demands of me.

I glance at the man, who is tall and thin and wearing a lanyard around his neck. I notice a spot of something red on his blue tie, probably a drop of tomato sauce but I can't help thinking it looks like blood.

'I thought I would take Juliet back to her room or to breakfast, just give her some support. I know she's finding the sessions quite difficult,' I tell Abigail.

'I'm sure there are other things you could be doing.' She throws her shoulders back, asserting her authority as the man looks down at his phone, completely uninterested in our exchange.

I look at the man standing next to Abigail again and she sighs, realising that she will have to introduce us or she risks being downright rude.

'This is Detective Inspector McDougal,' Abigail says, her voice going up a tone, which is what happens when she talks to the doctors and board members as well. In my head I call it her 'smarmy' voice. I'm pretty sure it helped her get the job of unit manager.

'Oh,' I reply.

'He has asked to speak to Juliet under the supervision of Dr Schaffer, so you can go and get on with seeing to other patients. I'll stay with Juliet and get her where she needs to go when we're done.' She offers me a smug smile, impressed by her own importance.

I step back, knowing that I have no choice in the matter. I'm not sure Juliet is ready to be questioned about anything at all.

Abigail knocks on the office door and then opens it, going inside with the detective following her. I know I should leave but I wait for a moment, irritated to have been dismissed, once again, by Abigail. I really am having the worst morning. I should be in there. I really want to know what Juliet is saying and if she is telling them what happened, if she is even able to tell them what happened.

And then I hear Juliet shout, 'No... no, I won't, I won't.'

I lift my hand to open the door to go inside but then stop myself. Abigail would disapprove of me interfering. I turn around, determined to get on with my morning.

As I'm walking away, the door opens and I turn back to see Abigail. She steps out into the hall, her mouth stuck in a disapproving frown. 'She'll only talk to the detective if you're there.' She sighs. I know that it irks her that a patient has asked for me.

'I'm happy to help,' I say, letting my voice rise up a little in imitation of her smarmy tone.

And then, concealing my smile at her annoyance, I follow her into the office to see Juliet on the sofa, while the detective sits in an armchair near the doctor's desk. I sit down next to Juliet and she reaches out and grabs my hand, squeezing hard.

'I'm here, Juliet,' I whisper to her, 'I'm here now.'

TWENTY-SEVEN

Lacy

Juliet turns to look at me, bewilderment on her face. 'He says my parents are in comas, that they might die.' Her eyes are bright with tears and her nose is running. I grab a tissue from the box on the coffee table in front of the sofa and hand it to her and she wipes her nose.

'We talked about that, remember?' I squeeze her hand back, knowing that sometimes, a physical sensation keeps a patient present in a situation, even when they want to disassociate. I'm not sure if this is what Juliet is doing when it comes to what happened in that house, but I give it a try.

'He says they think I tried to kill them, that I poisoned them with sleeping pills, but I didn't do that. I wouldn't do that. Adam was just going to talk to them, that's what he said.'

She lets go of my hand and then looks down at her own hands. Her cuticles are ragged and I can see dried blood on at least five of her fingers. She must have had a very difficult night. I don't know why the detective has told her all this. It seems to me to be a very stupid thing to do with a mentally fragile person. But perhaps that's why he wanted to do it in front of Dr Schaffer.

I reach out and take her hand again as I nod. 'The police are trying to figure out what happened. Do you think you can help them? Can you tell them what you remember?' I can feel Abigail's frustration at having to call me in here and what I would really like is to be able to get some information from Juliet the way that not one other person can. I would like Dr Schaffer to appreciate all I am doing to help.

Juliet looks around the room and then down at her hands again. I know that she is finding it upsetting to be the focus of so much scrutiny.

'Adam did it.' She nods her head. 'It must have been him. He knew they were bad and he wanted to help me. He must have given them the drugs. Maybe he... put them in the cocktails.'

The detective, who has a long face and drooping green eyes, clears his throat. 'What cocktails, Juliet?'

I remember Dr Schaffer telling me there was some alcohol in her parents' systems.

'I don't like cocktails and neither do my parents but Adam came over and he brought the bottles and he said he'd been on a course...' She shakes her head.

'And tell me, Juliet, did Adam have a cocktail as well? Did you?' the detective asks and Juliet nods.

'I did. He did. But there weren't any pills in our cocktails. He only put them in my parents' drinks. Adam is in computers. He's not a barman... but he did it. I know he did it but he was trying to help me because he loves me and they were bad people.'

'The thing is, Juliet,' says the detective slowly as he leans forward, 'there were only three glasses that had been used. They were rinsed and next to the sink. We have tested them and we found traces of alcohol and sleeping pills in two of them. We have even tested the glasses in the cabinet and found nothing. Only three glasses were used.'

He sits back after dropping this little nugget of information.

'Adam was there, he brought the bottles,' Juliet snaps, and I can see that she's getting angry. But also that she seems to be here and cognisant of what she's saying.

The detective sighs. 'We did find bottles in the liquor cabinet, but there are no fingerprints on them that we can use.'

'Adam's not a barman,' Juliet says, her gaze going to the window.

The detective sighs again and I can see that he's finding this tiring. 'The trouble is we have no information on "Adam"' – he uses his fingers to air quote around the name – 'at all. If you could tell us where he lives, a surname, where he works, anything at all might help.'

Juliet ignores him and looks at me, pleading with me to understand. 'They were bad people, you know they were bad people, Lacy, don't you?' Tears spill onto her cheeks; her desperation to have someone believe her, to have someone on her side, is heartbreaking. But I have to admit that some part of me wants to shake her as well. *You had everything and look what you've done with it.* It's not fair of me because her childhood will always haunt her. Whatever happened has led to her hurting her parents and, seemingly, blaming someone who doesn't exist. It's a wonder she didn't try to take her own life again.

'Juliet, we need you to focus for a bit if you can,' says Dr Schaffer. 'Can you tell the detective anything else about Adam?'

Juliet lets go of my hand and sits forward, dropping her head into her hands, blocking all of us out, blocking everything out.

We sit in silence. The detective looks at Dr Schaffer and she whispers, 'Give her some time.' He sits back in his chair, his irritation obvious.

'Adam was in IT,' says Juliet finally, lifting her head. 'It was something with computers but I forgot where he said he worked. He was only living near the station because his company rented him the apartment for a year. We walked to his apartment from outside the bar I went to... the Butcher's Beer Garden,' she says, a smile appearing on her face. 'I remember it. I had a vodka and then we walked for twenty minutes. Adam came to get me because I was sad.'

The detective writes this information down.

'The Uber picked me up around the corner when I went home.'

The detective clears his throat. 'You don't have the Uber app on your phone Juliet. We checked.'

She blinks and I can see her dismissing this piece of information. 'Adam is from Melbourne and he was... he was going to take me with him when he went back, he was going to... we just needed...'

'Needed?' the detective prompts and Juliet sits up and back, crossing her arms, and I see something flicker across her face, a look that tells me she is worried she has said too much. I am more interested in the fact that she is *aware* she may have said too much.

'What did you and Adam need, Juliet?' asks Dr Schaffer.

'Money?' suggests the detective, and Juliet glances at him quickly and then looks away.

'We only needed each other,' she says, staring out of the window.

'Okay,' says the detective. 'How many times did you go to his apartment?'

'Once and then he was... he said he would come for me. If you tell him where I am, he'll come for me.' She nods as she speaks.

'But we can't find him,' explains the detective, speaking slowly as though he is talking to a child. 'We don't know anything about him and' – he takes a breath and I can see that he's working up to something – 'and you were the one who called us, remember? You called the police so that we would come and help your parents.'

A light sweat breaks out on my forehead. She called them? I had assumed a neighbour called the police for some reason. The information that Juliet made the call has not been on any of the news reports.

Juliet shakes her head. 'No, I didn't,' she insists. I look at Dr Schaffer but her face is impassive and I think that means she has known this bit of information but has chosen not to share it. If Juliet had her phone, why didn't she just call for help when she found herself locked in the basement?

'I didn't have my phone,' says Juliet.

'We found it just outside the basement door, next to the padlock, Juliet. They were together on the floor. Do you remember me telling you that when you were in the hospital?'

Juliet shakes her head. 'I didn't, I didn't,' she mutters.

Shifting in his chair, the detective takes out his mobile phone and we all wait as he flicks through screens and then he touches something and a voice fills the room.

'Police, accident, emergency?' a man says.

'It's an emergency. My parents hurt me. They hurt me and they should pay for what they've done.'

I feel my breath catch in my throat. It's Juliet's voice.

'Okay,' replies the man she has connected with. 'Can you tell me how old you are?'

'They don't deserve to live,' Juliet replies. She sounds very young but it's definitely her voice.

'I'm tracing your phone, sweetheart. Can you tell me your name?'

'They hurt me and they need to pay.'

'Okay, sweetheart, can you tell me where you live…?'

When the call ends, all of us sit in silence for a moment before the detective begins to speak again.

'Juliet, we know you placed that call. We have your phone and we've looked at your records in details. The only people you have been in contact with in the last month are the police on this call and your mother. There's no one called Adam in your phone, in your records or in your messages.'

Juliet stares at him, her face expressionless.

Dr Schaffer is trying to keep her face still, but I can tell she is shocked, too.

What will Juliet do now?

TWENTY-EIGHT

Lacy

Juliet's eyes widen, her lips tremble, and she begins rocking, hugging herself, muttering, 'No, no, no.' And then she bursts into tears, howling with despair.

The detective moves back in his chair, seemingly afraid of her behaviour and I quickly stand, looking over at Dr Schaffer who says loudly, 'I think it would be best if Juliet took a break,' over the noise Juliet is making.

I touch her elbow and then pull her arm, forcing her to stand up. Once we are at the door she calms down a little, gulping and sniffing.

Out in the hallway with the office door closed behind us, she moves away from me and takes deep breaths, her tears drying quickly. I hold out my hand to her as her eyes dart around as though she is seeking someone. 'Come on, Juliet, we can get you something to eat, maybe some biscuits?' I suggest.

'Lacy,' she says, all traces of her distress suddenly gone and sounding as though she has only just seen me. She grabs my hand.

We walk to the day room together, where I watch Juliet choose two chocolate biscuits with intense concentration, biting down on her lip and looking over the whole plate carefully.

'Ready?' I ask when she has them on a plate, and she nods.

She can get back to her room without me but I follow her there anyway.

'Perhaps have a rest?' I suggest when she is sitting on her bed, clutching the plate as though she has no idea what to do with it.

'Adam put the pills in the drinks,' she mutters to herself. I decide to ignore the remark. There will be no benefit to my telling her the same things the detective just told her.

I turn to leave and she says, 'Do you know what else Adam did?'

I stop by the door to her room and turn to face her. 'What?'

'He killed Benji.' She picks up a biscuit and smiles as she takes a big bite.

'He killed Benji,' I repeat.

'Dead, killed him dead,' she says and then she giggles.

In shock, I stare at Juliet as she munches through the chocolate biscuit and then picks up the second one from the plate, finishing it in two bites as though she is starving. I am silent as I watch her and I think that over her chewing, I can hear her humming as she stares out of the window in her room.

'He killed Benji,' I finally say again, and she turns to me, looking a bit shocked to see me there, and then she nods her head.

'What...?' I begin but she puts the empty plate down on her side table and curls up on her bed.

'I'm tired,' she says.

'I know, but maybe you can tell me about Benji,' I try. 'I would like to hear more about Benji.'

I already know who Benji is, of course. When she was here the first time, after she had recovered physically and when her mood seemed to be stabilised from the medication, she talked about Benji a lot. Her anger at the young man who failed to catch her, leading to her hurting her knee, was palpable sometimes, floating in the air around her as she talked about him. I never mentioned her obvious hatred for the young man to Dr Choudry because I thought it was not something he needed to know and he wouldn't have appreciated my input anyway, but back then she told me she wished Benji was dead many, many times.

I didn't think she meant it. I believed it was a way for her to express her anger.

'I'm tired,' she repeats. She has her back to me and I can see that her body is tense. She wants me to leave and I know that she will say nothing more now.

'I'll see you at lunch,' I tell her but she doesn't reply and I leave her room, shutting the door softly behind me.

I have other patients to check on and I know I need to stop by the front desk and talk to Kendra about exactly what needs to be done.

Last time Juliet was here, her mother called every day and her parents came to every family session, seeking to help their precious daughter, but now there is no one to call and no one to care how she is doing.

Her comment about Benji bothers me. It feels like something has shifted in Juliet. Now a situation that I thought I understood completely has changed. I can't believe she actually called the police. I never would have expected that. Why did she call them and stay locked in the basement? If her phone was outside and away from her, how did she call them? How? That's what I would like to know.

I thought I knew Juliet after spending so much time with her last time she was here but what if I'm wrong about her? What if she is not the sweet, damaged young woman I think she is but instead is something much more sinister?

When Juliet was first here and she struggled with sleep, I would take her a cup of tea and sit by her bed while she talked. One of the reasons why I prefer the night shift is because there are fewer people around, fewer people to check up on me and what I'm doing. I had more freedom to spend time with Juliet then.

She would sip her tea and grow sleepy, but she kept talking and I would listen and let her know that I believed what she was saying, that I understood her pain. 'If I'm feeling sad or worried or upset about anything, I have a small collection of worry dolls I talk to. They're small dolls that are given to children at night in Guatemala and it's said that if the children whisper their worries to the dolls, the worries disappear overnight. You can whisper your worries to me, Juliet.'

'Sometimes I don't want to talk,' Juliet told me and so that's when I talked until she was able to close her eyes.

I know that her hatred for Benji was deep and wide.

'He joined another company, you know,' I remember her telling me. She explained that Benji left the company they had both once been dancers for and went somewhere else.

'He's a very good dancer,' she said. 'They gave him the lead role in his first ballet with them.'

I could see in the way she screwed up her face when she talked about this that she could taste the bitterness she felt over Benji's good fortune.

She juxtaposed that with her own life of living in a small apartment and having, as she put it, a 'shitty' job. 'Every morning when I got out of bed and put my foot on the floor, my knee would send a burning pain up my leg so I was reminded every single day of what I'd lost,' she told me one night.

'That must have been very hard for you,' I said.

'It made me want to die,' she replied, looking right at me, her blue eyes wide in the dim room where only a bedside light was on. 'And he just got to keep living his life.'

'But you can't let that be the end of your story, Juliet. You're still so young.' I had been sitting in a chair by her bed, and the door to her room was slightly open. I hoped that if anyone needed me, I would hear them, but I knew that I had to stay with her.

'He should have been arrested,' she said.

'But he said it was an accident.' By then Juliet had been in the hospital for three weeks already and I had heard what Benji had done many times.

'He lied. And now my career is over.'

'I'm sure there are many wonderful years ahead of you. You just need to find something else to do, and one day, you may dance again. Perhaps you can even teach?'

'You sound like my mother. When I went into the operation, she told me that when I came out, I would be able to go back to my career, that I would dance again.'

'She was trying to make you feel better,' I told her. Juliet had finished her tea and I could see that she was more relaxed. I hoped she would sleep.

'She lied,' she said, her voice dreamily soft.

'Maybe you need to talk to her about that, in your family session. Perhaps you can ask your mother why she lied. I mean, has she ever lied about anything else?'

Juliet's body stiffened and I wondered why but then she relaxed again and I didn't want to push her when she was supposed to be going to sleep. 'I'm sure she was just trying to make you feel better,' I said.

Her eyes closed and I could see that she was sinking into sleep. 'Talk to me,' she whispered and so I did. I sat with her until I was sure she was fast asleep.

I spent many nights with her like that, just trying to get her to see that she still had a future, and then when she began telling me about her childhood, I tried to listen with an open mind. Some of the things she said were very hard to hear.

. . .

After several hours with other patients, it's time for my lunch, and even though I have packed myself a salad wrap, I feel the need for something more substantial.

I go to the dining room and grab myself a bowl of the pumpkin soup and a grilled cheese sandwich with a chocolate doughnut for dessert. I will regret the calories later but now I'm starving for sugar, fat and salt, for the feeling of being full and satisfied.

I take my tray to the balcony, where I know I won't be disturbed.

Taking my phone out of my pocket, I google 'Benji, ballet dancer, death'.

I haven't seen anything on the news about him in the last few months but then I rarely watch the news. I'm sure nothing has happened to the young man but I need to check.

Google rewards me, or punishes me, with the first article that comes up.

AUSTRALIAN BALLET STAR KILLED IN HIT AND RUN

My body shivers as a cool wind blows around me and I read the article.

This is not what I expected, not what I expected at all.

TWENTY-NINE

Mandy Schaffer

I find I am struggling with this situation. Juliet veers wildly between knowing what happened and not knowing what happened and I cannot help the feeling that I am being manipulated at the hands of a clever sociopath. Her tears turn on and off and occasionally I get a glimpse behind the façade to an angry young woman. I know that she was deeply distressed over the end of her career and that's what led to her suicide attempt. But the allegations of abuse against her parents seem to have come out of nowhere.

She keeps mentioning 'Adam'. At first, I was inclined to believe he existed and that he had taken part in Juliet somehow convincing or forcing her parents to ingest enough temazepam to send them into comas, despite how outlandish this seems. But speaking to the detective has made me even more confused.

'We have been canvassing the area,' he told me after Lacy left with a very distraught Juliet, 'and there is a coffee shop close to where Juliet lived with her parents.'

He explained that he had gone in to see if anyone had ever

seen Juliet with anyone else but no one had, although the owner vaguely recognised her. 'There is a waitress who is away overseas who may be more help but we have to wait for her to get back,' the detective told me, and then he took a card out of his pocket and showed it to me, placing it on my desk.

It's a business card from a collection of business cards on the café's counter, something I see everywhere, and the more I studied it, the more bizarre it seemed. Juliet has described Adam to me as tall with brown hair and beautiful brown eyes and she told me he is in computers, cybersecurity.

The business card is for a man named Adam VanDerBeek, with the words, **_Adam VanDerBeek, your resident computer geek._** There is a cartoon drawing of a handsome man with brown eyes and brown hair, holding a computer.

I thought the detective was showing me the card to tell me they had found the mysterious Adam but he informed me that he had contacted the man only to find that he is actually a forty-five-year-old who lives with his husband in a high-rise apartment building close to where Juliet lives, which is, coincidentally, close to a train station. He has never seen nor heard of Juliet; she talks about a romantic relationship with him and that's obviously not the case here.

I realise that if she did frequent the coffee shop, the business card is something she would have seen often as she was waiting for a coffee or paying her bill.

'So, she saw this and, somehow, created this man?' I asked the detective.

'It a theory we're working on,' he told me.

I am good at my job. But am I good enough to deal with someone like Juliet? To deal with her level of delusion and manipulation?

The detective will get back to me when he knows more and I am also hoping that Raj returns my call. He is proving really difficult to pin down although I am aware he is in the middle of disputing the allegations against him. It's odd that he's been accused of sexual misconduct for the first time in his career and that no one else has come forward despite enquiries being made.

And what's even more odd is who reported him, which is a little titbit I'm sure Jacquie Wheeler never meant to drop when we caught up for a coffee today.

She wanted to check in and see how things are going now with Juliet.

I'm sure she didn't mean to bring it up but when I was telling her what the detective told me about the situation with Juliet, she shook her head and said, 'As if we don't have enough to deal with.'

And then she told me about who had made allegations against Raj. What's more concerning is that he didn't even try and defend himself. He just resigned and told the board he would fight the allegations alone.

'That is really strange,' I told her and she agreed with me.

I have never met Raj but I have googled him, and from everything I have read he is a respected and compassionate psychiatrist. And yet this report has been made.

Is it true, and if it is, what does it mean for his patients? Especially the very vulnerable ones like Juliet?

Did anything that happened in their sessions lead to what has happened with this young woman once she left the hospital?

I have so many questions and I can't help feeling that I will never get the answers to any of them. In a short time, this young woman will be removed from my care and I worry I will have done absolutely nothing to help her.

That's if she even wants my help. Or if she even deserves it.

THIRTY

With my eyes glued to the article, I bite into the grilled cheese, feeling the grease coat my tongue as I chew.

> *Police are calling for witnesses to a hit-and-run accident that occurred late on Saturday night or in the early hours of Sunday morning on Talbot Road. A jogger, who has asked not to be identified, noticed the body by the side of the road at 6 a.m. and notified police. The man is believed to have died sometime between the hours of 11 p.m. on Saturday night and 3 a.m. on Sunday morning. The body has been identified as that of Benjamin Marsh, a lead dancer with the New Australian Dancers company.*
>
> *The death of the promising young dancer has left the ballet community in shock. Speaking about his sudden death, Evelyn Origin, director of the company, said, 'We have lost a beautiful dancer and a beautiful soul. The world of ballet is poorer for his passing and I hope that whoever committed this callous act will soon be caught and brought to justice. He*

was only at the beginning of his career and I believe he would have gone on to be one of the best male dancers in the world.'

A spokesperson for the family said that his parents are too grief-stricken to talk publicly but that the death of their son will haunt them forever. 'He was dearly loved by all those around him,' she said. Police are asking for any witnesses who may have been in the area at the time to come forward with any information that could be connected to the crime.

The bite of grilled cheese lodges in my throat and I have to grab my can of Diet Coke and take a huge gulp to get it to move down.

Even in the cold wind, I feel my body grow warm. The article is from two weeks ago and is accompanied by a picture of the young man. He is standing on one leg, up on his toes, the other leg extended behind him. His perfect dancer's body is dressed in grey tights and a brocade waistcoat with a white shirt; his hair is slicked back and there is a wide smile on his face. I can see the joy he feels in the moment.

Juliet has been here for a little over a week. She was living with her parents when this happened, free to come and go as she pleased. It could all be a coincidence but then why did she tell me that Adam killed Benji? Why would she say such a thing?

I try to imagine Juliet behind the wheel of a car, chasing down the man who she believes ended her career on purpose. How would she have found him and known where he was? I experience a surge of anger at Juliet because I hate feeling like this, like I might have been wrong about someone, like I might be wrong about a lot of things.

The ping of a message on my phone makes me glance at the screen and I can see that my lunch hour ended five minutes ago.

I need to talk to you, reads the message. I stare down at the words and then I shake my head and sigh, but I don't reply. I have enough to deal with right now, more than enough.

I stand and hastily shove the last bite of grilled cheese into my mouth. I will have to save the doughnut for later.

As I'm returning my plates to the kitchen staff, Abigail walks into the dining room and sees me, marching over to me, a clown-like frown on her face. 'There you are. Your lunch hour is over and there's lots to do. We're running very behind today.'

Resisting the urge to snap at her, I decide to apologise instead. 'I'm so sorry, Abigail. I had a… bit of a family crisis. I was just sorting things out.'

'Oh,' she says, immediately changing her tone, 'I'm sorry, is everything okay? Is it your parents or your… husband?'

Abigail and I have worked together for four years, and in that time, I have learned all about her husband and her two perfect children, a son and a daughter who are both the smartest in their classes and the most popular children in their years at school, according to her at least. Her locker is festooned with pictures of them winning awards, both academic and sporting, and she never stops going on about them. I have also heard about her holidays and her home renovations, despite the fact that we are not friendly at all. She doesn't really care who is listening to her, as long as someone is. She, however, knows nothing at all about my life outside this hospital.

I have no reason to share that I live in a one-bedroom apartment and that I spend a lot of time alone. At least I did until six months ago.

I think about the text I just received: *I need to talk to you*. It can't be good. That phrase is never good in a relationship but I'm not going to tell Abigail one thing about my private life. I should have been more careful obviously. I am not the kind of person who gets a happily ever after. Everything that I have ever had in my life, I've had to take. I put myself through university working part-time jobs and living in a share house, even sharing a room with another girl. I have worked hard to become who I am and I have had precious little help from anyone.

'My mother,' I say because I know she's not going to accept me not giving her some information. 'She's having some health struggles, but I think I can deal with everything else after work. I'll see to those patients immediately,' I add, resisting the urge to mockingly salute her.

'Great and if you... need any time off, please do let me know,' she says and then she leaves the dining room.

My mother is dead but Abigail doesn't know that and she will never need to know that.

I dream of one day not having to get up in the morning and come here. I suppose I could find another job but all nursing jobs are more or less the same.

I don't believe I will have to work for much longer – at least, that was my hope. I am still young enough to have a child, to create the kind of family I have always dreamed of. And I still hope to be able to do that. Perhaps I will not have a husband by my side when I do but I can accept that.

I need to talk to you. The text is going to repeat in my mind for the rest of the day but I cannot let it affect my work. Inside me, my stomach is churning. The grilled cheese was obviously a bad idea on a day when I can feel that everything I had hoped and planned for my life may be in jeopardy. We will talk; we will definitely talk because I have a lot to say.

I leave the dining room and go to the front desk to get my list of patients to deal with this afternoon.

Juliet is leaning over the front desk, her face flushed red and her jaw clenched. Kendra has her hands up as if to stop her from talking.

'What's going on?' I ask, hurrying over.

Kendra offers me a weary smile. 'Juliet wants to call her parents. I explained that she can't do that right now.'

Kendra is trying to get Juliet to calm down. There's no point in her telling Juliet what we have been telling her for days. Her parents are still unresponsive and may never wake up.

'Lacy,' snaps Juliet, standing up straight and clenching her fists. 'Why can't I call my mother? I want to go home. I don't want to be here.'

Kendra looks at me, her green eyes widening as she silently pleads for my help.

'I tell you what, why don't you come with me now and we can discuss a good time to call your mother,' I tell Juliet, holding out my hand. This seems to calm her down because her hands relax and her shoulders drop a little.

'Come on,' I say, 'I can take you back to your room. Or we could go to the craft room. I know you love painting.'

'Painting,' says Juliet and then she looks around her. 'Lacy,' she says, as though she has only just seen me.

'Yes,' I reply, 'come on, we're going to do some painting.'

Juliet nods and takes my hand, although she seems bewildered at where she finds herself.

I cannot help but think that if this is an act, it's a very good act. I will have to tell Dr Schaffer about my conversation with Juliet and what she said about Benji. Would she have been capable of hurting the young man? It's possible. Juliet swings wildly from one type of behaviour to another and I can't quite get at the truth. Perhaps this is a game she is playing but I am smart enough to figure this out. At least I hope I am.

She shouldn't be here. I should never have seen Juliet again. But life doesn't always go according to plan. I know that better than most people.

Together we walk along the corridor to the craft room, where we have a psychologist, Gloria, who specialises in art as therapy. She's an older woman with long grey hair that hangs in a plait down her back and she has endless reserves of patience for everyone at the hospital.

When I open the door to the room, I'm grateful to see only

two other people, both working with clay. It will mean that Gloria can give Juliet some extra attention.

'Juliet would like to do some painting,' I tell Gloria, who nods and smiles.

'Welcome, Juliet. It's lovely to see you today. Why don't you grab an apron and I'll set up an easel for you.'

Juliet does as she has been told; the angry, confused young woman from only moments ago has disappeared and she is docile and compliant.

I help her on with the apron and decide to give talking about Benji another try, now that she is calm. What I would like to believe is that the young man was killed by someone else and Juliet just read it and it became part of her memories. And somehow, she then decided that Adam was responsible for Benji's death.

Memory is a fragile thing and can easily be manipulated. That's why Dr Choudry never believed any of the things Juliet was saying and I do understand that. It's easy enough to make someone accept a situation as a memory. Some psychologists did an experiment about it once. They took a group of young adults and discussed four childhood memories with them, inserting a false one into the mix. They were told that their parents had disclosed these memories. The false memory was of the young adult getting lost as a child, in a shopping centre. It had never happened to any of them. But once they heard the three true memories, they simply accepted the fourth one as true. All of them suddenly recalled being lost in a shopping centre.

But perhaps Dr Choudry's scepticism was more about who Juliet was, a young woman. Despite the advances women have made in the world, I have noticed that the medical system is still biased against the testimony of women and children. Dr Choudry saw a depressed young woman and took the testimony of her parents over hers. Women have always been judged as unreliable when it comes to their own bodies and minds. No matter how many advances have been made in the field of medicine, women are still judged by many as simply being hysterical.

I thought Dr Choudry was judging Juliet because she was a woman and because she was young and because she had made a terrible judgement call in attempting to take her own life. But what if he was right about her? What if she was even more unwell than even Dr Choudry knew or understood? Than even I understood?

We sent her home. And perhaps she should not have been allowed to go home. That's how it looks now, as though the hospital made a mistake that resulted in a terrible tragedy.

I lead Juliet over to the easel and Gloria hands her a paintbrush and a palette and then one of the other patients calls her. 'I'll be back in only moments, Juliet. Have a think about what you would like to paint today.' Juliet nods her head and stands, staring obediently at the white paper pinned to the easel, the dry paintbrush in her hand.

'Juliet,' I say softly but she doesn't look at me, instead staring at the paper and biting down on her lip. 'How did you feel when Benji died?' I ask her, keeping my tone soft and neutral.

She turns away from the easel and smiles at me, her eyes lighting up and her whole face changing.

'Fabulous,' she says and then she giggles. 'He got what he deserved. Adam said so and Adam knows everything.'

'But weren't you upset, even a little?' I ask.

She nods her head and then brushes a hand across her face and I realise that tears have appeared. 'I would never have hurt Benji,' she says. 'I hated him but I would never have hurt him. Adam hurt him and then he locked me in the basement. And then he gave my parents... He made them drink...' She falls silent.

'Right, my love,' says Gloria, returning. 'What are we going to paint? How about the ocean? I love to watch the waves, don't you?'

I move away from Juliet and leave the craft room, nausea rising inside me. When I first met Juliet, I really wanted to help her and understand her and then the more I knew about her and her life, the closer we became.

When she left the hospital, I was certain I knew exactly what she was going to do, how things in her life would play out, but now I'm questioning everything I know and think.

Because what if I'm entirely wrong about not just Juliet but about everything?

THIRTY-ONE

Lacy

The next day, I arrive early and manage to get through a lot of work while I know that Juliet is busy with breakfast. I don't want anyone to point out that I am not achieving everything I need to because of the time I am spending with Juliet.

As I am coming out of a patient's room after helping her with bathing and dressing, Abigail comes marching up to me.

'Lacy,' she says, 'I need a word.' It's a command that I can't refuse so I nod and follow her into an adjacent empty room.

She closes the door behind us, which is unusual, and at first, I assume that she is going to brief me on a new patient who will shortly be arriving but instead she says, 'We have a problem.' Her mouth settles into a thin line of disapproval and I feel sweat begin to collect under my arms. *Don't panic*, I remind myself because I know that panicking never achieves anything.

I don't say anything, letting the silence between us extend as she stares at me. She is waiting for me to bumble into the conversation with questions but I'm not going to do that.

'Some medication is missing,' she says.

I nod my head and narrow my eyes. 'Oh, that's not good,' I say. Medication missing is not a problem. It is a catastrophe. We are in a hospital where many of our patients experience suicidal ideation and the medication is checked every day. Whenever it is dispensed, it is logged and accounted for. I don't ask which medication because she will tell me soon enough.

'Yes,' agrees Abigail. 'Apparently two vials of temazepam were tampered with and similar pills substituted. Kendra only noticed because a couple of patients who usually respond well to the sleeping pills had very bad nights.'

How clever of Kendra, I think but don't say.

I am suddenly very glad not to be nursing unit manager.

'So, what do we do now?' I ask Abigail.

'Well, first, Lacy,' she says, my name coming out of her mouth as though she is tasting the acidic sting of a fresh lemon, 'I wanted to ask you if you knew anything about it.'

'Of course not, Abigail,' I respond sweetly. 'But I will be happy to help you get to the bottom of it. I assume you've begun searching all patients' rooms?'

'Yes, and if you could take the other side of the corridor for me that would be good.' She sighs. Abigail was hoping for a confession, for an easy solution to her problem. She is probably confronting every nurse on the floor like this.

'Absolutely,' I tell her.

We're not going to find anything. Anyone who goes to the trouble of stealing pills that are stored in such a secure way is not going to leave them where they can be found. Of that, I am sure.

I move off but Abigail stops me. 'Sorry, Lacy, first I need to take a look in your locker. I'm sure you understand.' She smiles, only half her mouth moving.

'Now?' I ask, stupidly, anxiety squeezing my lungs so I am forced to take a deep breath.

'It will only take a moment and then I can cross you off the list.' She reaches into the pocket of her scrubs and produces a pencil and a printed-out list to show me. I can see that a number of the staff have already had their names crossed off. Why haven't I heard about this yet?

'Sure,' I say, adding a dash of enthusiasm to irritate her.

'After you.' She indicates with her hand and I walk quickly to the locker room, where I fumble with the lock for a moment before getting it open, cursing my shaking hands.

'If you could step back,' says Abigail when I have the locker open, and I do, holding my breath and feeling naked as she goes through my things, quickly lifting and sorting through everything.

'Well, of course I don't expect to find anything in our staff lockers,' she says when she's done, although I can hear a distinct touch of disappointment in her tone.

'I'm sure none of the staff would take medication meant for patients,' I reply, stepping forward to close my locker door, but as I do, she stops me, holding the door open and gazing at the picture of the mother and the baby there.

'Is that your mother?' she asks.

'Yes,' I say.

'Strange,' she murmurs. 'I'm sure I've seen that picture before.'

'It's been in my locker for a while,' I say.

'I don't think I've ever seen it in your locker but it is so familiar,' she says.

'I'm sure a lot of mother and baby pictures look alike,' I say, clenching my fist to remind my body to hold itself steady.

'I'm sure they do,' she replies and then she steps away from my locker and shakes her head.

'You'll get on with the room searches now. And please do not discuss this with either staff or patients before I have gotten to the bottom of it.'

'I won't,' I answer her, 'just need to use the bathroom.'

Abigail nods her head and leaves the locker room, and I run for the bathroom and throw up my breakfast, leaving me with a hollow empty feeling.

THIRTY-TWO

Mandy Schaffer

My mind is spinning today with everything I have learned. Abigail was waiting for me when I got in this morning, which is very unusual, and she told me that she needed to speak to me urgently.

It appears that an amount of medication is missing and it has only just been noticed. There are procedures in place for this sort of thing, of course. At this time, Abigail has no idea who to suspect but she is very worried and is making sure that all the nurses search patients' rooms.

Right after she left to get on with the urgent task of finding the missing medication, Detective Inspector McDougal called. Apparently a more thorough search of Juliet's home has revealed a stash of pills inside her mattress. She had actually cut a pocket inside the mattress and stuffed them all in there and that's why it went unnoticed the first time the house was searched.

'There were more than fifty pills, both the sleeping pills and the anti-anxiety medication, so based on the amount in a single prescription, we can assume that nothing has been used,' he told me, meaning that the police now have no idea where she would have gotten the pills from to poison her parents. I instantly connected the two... but Juliet had been out of the hospital for weeks before her parents were given the pills. There is no way the missing pills would not have been discovered in that time.

But I put it to the detective that perhaps Juliet is telling the truth and that someone else was involved, someone who brought the pills with them and may have locked her in the basement and come back a couple of days later to use her phone, or perhaps even used AI to make it seem like Juliet was the one calling the police. Heaven knows anything is possible these days but the detective didn't seem to agree with that. 'Juliet is still our only suspect,' he told me. 'I bet you're fond of those true crime podcasts,' he said and I knew he was laughing at me. I felt myself flush because that's true.

'In my experience, the simplest explanation is usually the right one,' he told me.

But the police aren't always correct about everything.

I wish Raj would return my call. I've left several messages already. News on the grapevine is that he will be allowed to keep his licence because there is not enough evidence against him but I haven't had that confirmed, which makes me wonder why the nurse who reported him felt the need to say something on behalf of a patient.

I am sure I will never find out which patient accused Raj of sexual misconduct, and anyway, there are other things to concentrate on.

Juliet's time here is coming to an end soon enough. Her parents are still in comas and gravely ill. And I am no closer to the truth about what happened. I have even examined the idea of one of her parents committing a murder-suicide but I cannot find any reason, from what I know of the family situation, for that to occur. Both parents were healthy and strong and her father was still working.

The young man, Adam, who Juliet keeps mentioning, is nowhere to be found. It is beginning to seem very likely that Juliet made him up and yet... I cannot help wondering about him.

When Juliet and I speak, her memories of everything they did together seem to ground her in the present. It is the only time in the sessions when she seems to be fully with me despite the fact that she is still adjusting to the medication. If Adam is a product of her imagination, he is extremely vivid. Perhaps he is another part of her personality, one that has been tasked with vengeance against her parents. But this seems absurd to me.

Maybe she does actually have an accomplice, one who has perhaps washed his hands of her and walked away. I have asked the staff who come into contact with Juliet to allow the fantasy – if that's what it is – of this young man to persist in the hope that it will allow her to communicate some of her reasoning behind what she did and also explain exactly how she did it. That is a strategy the detective and I have agreed on. Despite his questioning of my theories, he does accept that as a psychiatrist, I know best how to get the most information from Juliet.

But honestly the questions surrounding this young woman seem impossible to answer.

THIRTY-THREE

Lacy

Searching the patients' rooms for the missing medication takes me the rest of the day and causes chaos on the ward with everyone objecting to the intrusion. It's made worse by Abigail wanting us to refrain from telling any of the patients why we are searching their rooms. Many of the patients threaten legal action at having their rights violated, but when they admit themselves to the hospital, they do sign waivers so that we are able to conduct searches of their rooms if we feel they may be in danger of hurting themselves.

I am grateful to go home at the end of my shift, during which no medication has been located and Abigail has informed all the staff that outside investigators will arrive soon to see if they can figure out what happened.

On my way out, I am waylaid by Kendra, who is leaving at the same time as I am.

'This is a bit of a screw-up,' she says companionably as we walk out together and head towards the train station, trailed by a whole lot of other people who have also just ended their shifts.

'Obviously, it's something that could lose Abigail her job.' I am very aware of the people around us and I know that this same conversation is going on behind me.

'Yeah,' she agrees, pulling her phone out of her backpack and opening the screen. 'I wonder if they'll ever find it.'

People begin to peel off in other directions and soon, it's just me and Kendra. I wish she would leave me alone. I need some time to think and destress from the day.

'If she does lose her job, you would be next in line,' she says.

'And what of it?' I ask her as we wait for the light to turn green to allow us to cross the road and walk the block to the train station.

'Well, you hate her.' She laughs. 'And you hated Dr Choudry.'

We have crossed over the road now but I stop and turn to her, aware that this is all meant to provoke me into talking so that Kendra can feed her ever-growing addiction to gossip. 'I have no idea what you mean.'

She shrugs. 'I'm just saying that it would be a boost for you.' Her green eyes twinkle mischievously.

I'm so irritated by her behaviour that I want to scream. 'This is not a joke, Kendra,' I say and turn away from her, stomping down the street.

When I am finally on the train, I get a message: *Are we seeing each other tonight? We need to talk.* I respond with just one word. Last night I told him I had a migraine, an excuse I find useful when I need it. But tonight, I can't be bothered with anything other than a negative.

NO.

I have a feeling I know why he needs to talk. He's fallen for someone else, slept with someone else, cheated when he was supposed to be loyal to me and only me. This is not the first time that's happened to me. I've been dating for decades and it never gets any easier and now I am angry with myself for trusting him at all, for letting him into my life and planning a future for us. I don't want to talk to him until things at work are sorted out.

I need to be alone to think about things. What once seemed simple is now a lot more complex. Having outside inspectors in the hospital will be an intrusion and I have no desire to answer what I am sure will be an exhaustive list of questions. At least my charting is impeccable, so I don't have to worry about that.

And I am more than capable of pushing the inspectors in the direction I think they should go in. I wonder if it is really possible that Abigail could lose her job, and as I stare out of the window on the train, I decide that it is. What Kendra said is true: I would be next in line unless they bring in someone from outside. But do I even want the job now? It feels like a lot less time with patients and a lot of administration and putting out of metaphorical fires.

One thing is for sure: I am running out of time with Juliet. I need many more weeks with her before I get to the truth of what happened to Benji and her parents, and most importantly, I need her to acknowledge exactly what her part was in all of it. That's crucial. She needs to know exactly what she did and admit it. Things need to speed up.

Tomorrow, I will push her more than I have been doing. Tomorrow, I will get her to accept that Adam doesn't exist even though Dr Schaffer doesn't want us to do that. Doctors don't always know what's best for a patient, and Dr Schaffer has had very little time with Juliet, despite their daily sessions.

Juliet needs to accept reality now. And then that will make everything easier.

THIRTY-FOUR

Mandy Schaffer

It's after midnight and I have just put down the phone from Raj Choudry, who is in a fairly bad way. Because the investigation is still ongoing, he has no idea who reported him for sexual misconduct. I thought about telling him what Jacquie said but almost immediately dismissed the idea because this is not a situation I care to involve myself in. I am sure I would lose this job for telling him who reported him. It seems that the situation is close to a resolution now anyway. The unnamed patient involved has been interviewed and denied anything happening at all but the fact that he was reported is enough to do the damage. It's optics. He may be cleared completely but the report will follow his career forever.

I am sure Raj will be exonerated and I do feel deeply sorry for him. But he does sound more than a little paranoid. Perhaps I would be as well but he ended our conversation with the words, 'Watch your back over there. I don't think anyone can be trusted at St Augustine.'

I have been very careful with all my patients because of the allegations, so I am, in a sense, watching my back.

But it is quite a confronting thing to be told to do. We're a hospital dedicated to mental health. How can we run on suspicion and fear?

I felt terrible asking him about his notes on Juliet after that part of the conversation but he changed the subject himself, asking me why I had called. I had only left messages asking him to call me, not told him why I needed to speak to him.

'I'm afraid I just can't read your notes... and I was really hoping that they would give me some more insight into her,' I told him.

He got really upset about the fact that she was back in our hospital. He had not heard or seen anything about it on the news, although it's been less than two weeks since it happened and I know he has been embroiled in his own troubles.

'She shouldn't be there,' he told me.

I explained about her just being with us until I was able to determine if she is capable of standing trial.

'Look,' he interrupted me, 'I'll send you my notes. I'll type them up tonight.'

'Oh, you don't need to start now, it's so late,' I protested but he spoke over me and I could hear the concern and anger in his voice.

'I can't believe I've let this happen. I was going to talk to the board about this. But I never really knew if I had anything. And then the allegations...' he said.

'I understand,' I told him.

'I'll send you my notes,' he said again and abruptly hung up.

I have no idea what is going on and I am surprised when an email pings into my inbox from him shortly after. But the email doesn't contain his notes, just one line.

Juliet isn't safe at St Augustine.

THIRTY-FIVE

Lacy

Once I am home from the hospital, I take a long, hot shower, washing away the day and everything I am worrying about.

I keep a bottle of whisky in a cabinet in my small living room and I pour myself a generous amount. I can only have one drink because I need to be at the hospital bright and early tomorrow. I don't like what's going on. I need to figure out a way to take control of this situation.

When my buzzer rings, I know who it is. I rarely get visitors and I know he wanted to come over tonight, to talk.

I told him I didn't want to see him. So I ignore the irritating, high-pitched whine of sound. But he is relentless and so, eventually, I put down my glass on the coffee table and let him into the building. I live on the seventh floor and I wait a minute before opening my front door. Hopefully I will be able to send him on his way again as soon as possible.

'Nathan,' I say when I see him, 'I thought I told you I didn't want to see you tonight. I've had a difficult day.'

'I don't care,' he says.

There is something of the petulant child about him sometimes. I know that he resents that I make more money than he does but he has made the choice to stay in his dead-end job in the bowels of the hospital, running the laundry where the machines are on an endless twenty-four-hour cycle of washing and drying linen and clothing. The only reason I even knew that he existed was because he catches the same train I do to get to work.

We progressed from smiling at each other to waving at each other to walking into work together in the morning and then from there, we began seeing each other. Am I in love with him? Sometimes I think I am... but perhaps I am just frightened of being alone forever, of never having the children I want, of never creating the family that I so desperately desire. I was worried when I got his text a couple of days ago, concerned that he wanted to end things but I have been going through it in my mind, separating myself in preparation, distancing myself from him in the way that I have learned to do. If it's over, perhaps that will be for the best.

No one at the hospital knows that we are dating, that we have been together for six months. When I am honest with myself, I admit that this is because I am embarrassed about what he does. I once dreamed of marrying a doctor or another nurse or someone else with a university degree but Nathan is kind and only wants to please me. He's not pleasing me now. He has always been inordinately grateful to be with me and I like that.

He is easy to talk to and I've told him everything about me. I think it's the first time I've ever done that. I have always held something back with the men I date.

We have been together since our first official date and everything was going well... until it suddenly changed.

'Look...' I sigh, 'I don't have the energy for this. I'll call you tomorrow.'

He shakes his head and then runs his hands through his

chestnut hair and I realise that he looks tired, worn down, pale. He works most nights but has some, like tonight, off, which at least means we have had some time together since I moved to the day shift. It's difficult to navigate a relationship on two different schedules and perhaps that's why he's pulling back, why he wants to talk to me. I'm not ready for this to end but at the same time I am angry with him for not being able to just do as I asked. I am still in this and at the same time, I am pulling away as well.

I can feel my dream of a house in the suburbs disappearing.

'I can't do this anymore,' he says, jamming his hands in his pockets.

Biting down on my lip, I wonder how hard I should work to keep him with me. I am no stranger to the end of a relationship. I think I've gotten pretty good at just moving on. The trick is to always hold something back although I had hoped that Nathan would be different, so I haven't been as careful as I should have been. Now I am angry for allowing myself to become more invested in a man than I usually do.

I don't want to lose him. Or, at least, I don't want to lose him right now.

'Things will change soon,' I say soothingly, stroking his arm.

He pulls away. 'No, Lacy. I don't think this is working for me and it was probably a mistake. I wanted to tell you in person, but I'm done and I think you should stop... This is not good.' He means to be firm, to tell me what to do, but I watch his eyes flick around and then I can see he decides against trying to make me see his point of view.

He steps back and turns but I try to keep him here, moving to touch him, stroking his arm and chest and then moving down, even though we are standing in my doorway. I need to keep him engaged, at least until I am ready for him to go on his merry way. But he doesn't even look at me, instead jerking away, out of my reach.

And now I know for sure, in the way that all women know. He's switched his loyalties.

'You've cheated,' I say, spitting the words into the air.

'No... no,' he mumbles but he can't look at me. 'I just... this is not for me, I'm sorry,' he says and then he's gone.

I am left alone in the apartment, which is what I wanted for tonight at least. But now I know I will be alone forever.

I will never trust another man. What's the point?

I do not cry. I will not cry. Will he simply forget about me now, about everything we shared and dreamed of?

Perhaps that would even be for the best. He knows too much about me.

I down the whisky and then I allow myself another one, despite having had no dinner, hoping to fall asleep quickly. I need this day to be over.

Arriving at work the next morning, I am jittery with caffeine after waking at 5 a.m. with a pounding head. I avoid talking to anyone beyond a morning greeting. I make my way straight to Juliet's room, determined to get her to acknowledge what she has done, what the truth is, to at least achieve something with my life this week.

She is sitting in the chair, facing the window, watching a pair of pink galahs snack on some sweet gumballs that are dropped by the liquid amber trees throughout autumn.

'Good morning, Juliet,' I say, and I can hear that my tone is brusque but I have lost patience with this young woman and everything to do with her. I was such a help to Juliet when she first came here. And she needs to help *me* now. She needs to remember and acknowledge the truth. Then everything will be fine. I assure myself that I only want to *help* Juliet, that I am thinking only of her and my career. Maybe Abigail loses her job and I am rewarded for helping with Juliet. I will make a good manager and the increase in pay may allow me to begin saving extra money. I want to have a child and it seems that I will not have anyone to have one with. But I can do it alone.

'What if Adam never comes?' she asks me, turning from the window to look at me with her large blue eyes.

It's time to force her to acknowledge reality, the terrible, harsh reality that no one will tell her.

Maybe if she believes that she has created this person out of thin air to be the instrument of her revenge, it will help her prepare a proper defence. She needs all the help she can get or she will be thrown into a hospital and she may never leave. I don't want that for her. I want her to face what she has done, to face who she is. There have to be consequences for hurting people.

I take a deep breath. 'Listen, Juliet, the police have looked into this. They have searched everywhere and they cannot find a man named Adam that matches your description. They went to the apartment that you said you went to and it's got a family in it, a mother and two children. They can't find Adam, no one can.'

I have made that up. The police have not found Adam's apartment because it doesn't exist, not in any real sense.

'What? That's not right, Lacy,' she says, her voice wobbling with tears soon to be shed. 'He exists, you told me you believed me, just like all the other times. Please tell me you believe me, Lacy, you're the only one who does.' She gets up and comes towards me, grabbing at the top of my blue scrubs, clutching the material desperately.

I am going to be firm with her. I will not allow her to remain in this fantasy. I pull her off me and push her towards her bed. 'Listen to me,' I say as I sit her down on the bed. 'You need to acknowledge what's going on here. There is no Adam. He was someone you made up and I don't blame you; no one will blame you because you needed to make him up. You needed him to help you because you were treated so badly, because your parents refused to admit the things they had done.'

'No.' She shakes her head. 'No, no, no. The police are lying, you're lying, you're all lying. I did not make him up. He came to my house and he... he locked me in the... It was him and I didn't make him up. He loves me and he will come for me, he promised, he promised.' Her voice rises to a shriek and she stands, walking around the room. She stops by her desk, muttering, 'He will come for me, he will come for me.' She grabs the plastic jug of water from the desk and lifts it high above her head, bringing it down with enough force to smash it on the floor.

'He promised!' she yells as the water runs everywhere. She pulls at her hair. 'He promised, he promised!' she screams and then she starts to run for the door.

I catch her quickly. 'He doesn't exist, Juliet,' I hiss, 'you made him up. And you did that so you could kill your parents. You poisoned them, Juliet, and now they are dead and you will be in prison for the rest of your life.'

'No, no, that's not true.' She struggles as I hold her, kicking out and trying to scratch at me with her non-existent nails. 'He was just going to talk to them. He wanted them to confess. He was just going to talk to them.'

'They're dead, Juliet. You killed them.'

Her body stills with this awful realisation and I let her go.

'No, no, no,' she repeats, her voice rising with each repetition. She begins hitting herself, scratching at her arms, drawing blood, and I grab her, forcing her back to the bed as she kicks and screams, 'No!' She is stronger than I thought she would be and we struggle together for a moment until I can hit the emergency button on the wall. In an instant two other nurses are in her room, Kendra and Sonia. Kendra grabs her as she struggles, lashing out at everyone. She and I struggle to get Juliet to the bed and Sonia runs for a sedative. Kendra and I hold her down as Sonia administers the injection and within moments her body grows limp and her eyes blink slowly.

'I didn't...' she says.

'Shh,' I tell her, 'it's okay, it's all going to be okay.'

Her eyes close and she is asleep.

'What happened?' asks Kendra, her hair mussed as she pants.

'I have no idea,' I reply. 'We were talking about what she wanted to have for lunch and suddenly she just went...' I shake my head. 'Poor girl.'

'If you ask me, the sooner she's out of here, the better,' says Sonia and she leaves the room with Kendra.

And now I am alone with Juliet, who is sleeping the drugged sleep of a person in a fragile mental state, a person with something to hide, a person who has done something terrible.

I sit down on the bed. I lean forward and whisper in her ear, 'Now why did you have to do that, Juliet? Why on earth did you do any of it?'

THIRTY-SIX

Mandy Schaffer

I am sitting here, sick to my stomach, and I know that I need to move, that I need to go and get Abigail, call the police, do something, but right now, I can't seem to do anything except type this as I try to process my thoughts.

It's just after lunch and this morning we had an incident on the ward with Juliet throwing a fit out of nowhere. Since the day she arrived, she has been docile and quiet, and yet today she became violent. I have been unable to believe this frail young woman could hurt anyone, but today she showed that her anger makes her strong and that she is capable of injuring people. It took three nurses to subdue her. Lacy was with her at the time and says that the behaviour appeared out of nowhere and for no reason.

But there is always a reason. I am against sedating patients unless it's absolutely necessary but Kendra and Sonia have both indicated that Juliet's behaviour was unmanageable. I called the detective and left a message, telling him that she needs to leave this hospital. We are not equipped to deal with her. And after what Raj emailed me, it's best if she's gone.

While I was waiting for Lacy's report into the incident, I decided to sit down and do some work before my next patient came in.

That's when another email from Raj popped up, in which he had typed out many of his notes from his sessions with Juliet.

At the top was a paragraph in bold writing, and after reading it through twice, I still can't believe what it says.

I really need to figure out what's going on here.

And why.

THIRTY-SEVEN

Lacy

Juliet's behaviour yesterday was disconcerting for all involved but pretty much what I expected. I did not expect to hear from Abigail shortly afterwards that Dr. Schaffer was going to have Juliet sent away earlier than she would have been. 'We cannot have violent patients at the St Augustine,' she told me.

She leaves tomorrow and so this morning, I know what I need to do. Nathan has not returned my calls or text messages. Our relationship is well and truly over. I am glad he works nights and that no one knew about us. I will simply erase him from my mind and I hope he does the same about me. I should never have trusted him and I am worried that he may do something foolish.

Instead of focusing on him, I make the decision when I wake up to focus on Juliet and what she needs.

But as I arrive at work and place my bag and lunch into my locker, Abigail comes into the locker room.

'Dr Schaffer wants a quick chat,' she says, her mouth pursed in its usual frown.

'Can it wait until my lunch break? I have quite a lot to get on with,' I reply casually, making sure that I maintain a relaxed posture as I close the locker. In my peripheral vision, I see that the picture I usually have there is gone. It must have fallen down but I can't look for it now.

'No.' The reply is clipped and short, leaving no room for argument. Now I know that I need to be worried, on guard. Something is going on.

I consider telling Abigail that I feel sick but I know she won't believe me. I do feel sick. Something is wrong. Something has happened. But I can't go home. I need to speak to Juliet again.

Abigail indicates that I should walk in front of her as we leave the locker room, and for a moment, I feel like a prisoner being escorted to her execution. Is that what this is? I only needed one more day.

'How is Juliet this morning?' I ask but Abigail doesn't reply and so we walk in silence until we get to Dr Schaffer's office. Panic roils inside me.

Dr Schaffer's office door is closed and I lift my hand to knock.

'Don't bother, she's expecting you,' says Abigail, and I open the door with a trembling hand. She's seated behind her desk, her eyes on her computer screen, but she looks up when I come in.

'Lacy, good.' She stands and comes around the desk and then she indicates that I should sit down. Her usual warm manner is gone. Instead, I can read some anger in her stony expression. And now I am very, very worried.

Abigail sits in an armchair and Dr Schaffer takes the chair next to her desk and I have no choice but to sit on the sofa, where I feel myself sink into the soft cushions. I have to look up to meet Dr Schaffer's gaze.

'I know Juliet is due to be moved tomorrow. I'm sorry that I haven't been able to help more. I do think that it would be better if we had more time and I know that yesterday she was very distressed and that's really come out of nowhere...' I am babbling but both women are quiet, inspecting me as though I am a curiosity. Embracing silence seems like the best option so I lean forward and put my hands on my lap, sitting up straight.

'That's fine,' says Dr Schaffer. 'I actually wanted to have a chat about you.'

Shifting on the cushion that is suddenly uncomfortable, I wait in silence to hear what she's going to say.

'Abigail said that you have a picture in your locker that belongs to Juliet. Apparently, it's a picture of her with her mother.'

'I... That's... Why would I have that?' My heart thrums in my chest. 'I mean, it's me and my mother...'

'Yes, that's what Abigail said you told her but here's the thing, Lacy. It's not.'

'I recognised that picture, Lacy,' says Abigail. 'Juliet used to look at it all the time when she was last here. It's her and her mother.'

Dr Schaffer stands and goes around to her desk, opening a drawer and taking something out. When she returns to her seat, I see she is holding the picture. It hadn't fallen down. It was taken, stolen from me.

'How did you...?' I stand up, deciding on offence instead of defence. 'How on earth did you get that? It's illegal to go through someone's private things. That was in my locker.' My face burns as fury twists inside me.

'Abigail has the right to go through staff lockers.'

'No, she doesn't,' I protest. But I'm wrong, I know I am.

'Sit down, Lacy.' The words are a command and I have never heard a tone that low, that threatening from the psychiatrist. My body obeys without me thinking about it.

Dr Schaffer looks down at the picture and then she shows

me the back. *Susan and Juliet* 2004 is written on the back of the photo, but I know that already. I've studied that photo for months now. I know everything about it. I know that it's taken in a garden and that behind Susan, white jasmine covers a timber trellis. I know that she is sitting at a round table where lunch is laid out, a large bowl filled with green salad and a heap of barbecued meat on a platter. I know that Susan is gazing adoringly at baby Juliet, who is wrapped in a light pink blanket, her eyes shut, her little body relaxed.

'You're right, it is of Juliet and her mother,' I say, hating how high my voice has gone. 'I don't know why... I said it was my mother... I guess I didn't want to have to explain it to Abigail. But I found it when I was cleaning out her room after she left. I was going to give it back to her, mail it to her or something, but I kept forgetting and then when she came back here, I realised that I hadn't and... I was worried it would make her feel worse, especially after what she did.' I hate this feeling. I don't know what to say and my words stumble and trip.

Both women stare at me. Abigail's mouth twitches into an almost smile but quickly settles into its usual frown. Dr Schaffer's dark eyes search my face. I can see that neither of them believes my explanation.

'It was a mistake,' I try again.

I clench my fists, hating Abigail with every fibre of my being. *Interfering bitch.*

'I haven't done anything wrong.' The silence from these two is starting to make me crazy and the urge to leap out of this chair and run, just leave and never return, overwhelms me.

'Having the picture, keeping it when it did not belong to you, is something that I find very troubling, Lacy,' says Dr Schaffer, 'especially since you were so close to her when she was here for three months. We will be conducting a thorough investigation into your relationship with her.'

'I've only ever tried to help her. She came here after a

suicide attempt and she left able to function in the world and that wasn't thanks to Dr Choudry,' I spit.

Dr Schaffer shakes her head as though she cannot believe what I've just said. 'She tried to kill her parents, Lacy.'

'Maybe they were bad people. They abused her, you know.' I find my eyes filling with tears and I hate myself for my lack of control.

The doctor leans forward. 'I managed to get hold of Dr Choudry. He typed up his notes on Juliet for me. I want to read you something, Lacy, if you will let me.'

The only thing I want to do is get out of here but I have no option but to nod.

She studies me for a moment and then, looking down at her phone, she clears her throat lightly and begins to read.

I have become concerned about the relationship between one of our nurses, Lacy, and Juliet. It seems to me that they are spending far too much time together and that some kind of co-dependent relationship may have developed. In my last session with Juliet, she was detailing an incident of abuse in which her mother pushed her down the stairs, and when I questioned the details, she stopped speaking and then whispered, 'Lacy says it happened on a Tuesday,' as though reminding herself of what to say.

I asked her what she meant by that and she denied saying it at all. When Juliet arrived here, her anxiety and depression stemmed from her disappointment over the end of her career. I believed that her depression was situational and could be managed with antidepressants and a great deal of therapy.

Allegations of abuse only began to surface a few weeks after she arrived. I am hesitant to write this down but could it be possible that Lacy is not just encouraging Juliet to remember her abuse but may in fact be planting memories of abuse? It's such a bizarre idea that I can't think how to address it. The concept of the repressed traumatic memory is largely discredited and was in fact responsible for a pandemic of allegations of abuse that occurred in the 1980s, but I have never actually seen someone attempt to implant false memories.

In an effort to find out exactly what is going on, I have taken Lacy aside and told her of the incident but she seemed as confused as I was by Juliet's words.

She categorically stated that she has never had an actual discussion with Juliet about her mother pushing her down the stairs and informed me that they rarely speak about what Juliet is accusing her parents of. But is that the truth? Lacy works nights and is largely unsupervised at this time because we have less staff on.

Juliet denies the words and in subsequent sessions, when I have mentioned what she said, she has appeared mystified, as though I have made up what I heard. I have had a chat with Abigail, who has now been promoted to nursing unit manager on my suggestion, but she is not able to give me any more information. I have told Abigail that I believe Lacy and Juliet spend far too much time together but Abigail tells me that Lacy seems that way with many of her patients. 'She has some kind of a saviour complex, if you ask me,' is what Abigail said. Again, I cannot verify this. When I first arrived here, I did explain to Lacy that I thought it best for her not to attempt to engage with me over patient treatment, which I know she took badly.

Juliet will leave soon. We are getting somewhere. At her last session she admitted that she had, perhaps, made up some of her memories, which I took as a positive sign. Her parents are keen for her to be released and to be able to get on with her life. I believe that some separation from Lacy will do her good. I have suggested to Abigail that Lacy is switched to days so that more people are able to see her interact with Juliet.

A ringing in my ears stops me from hearing any more, and I sit forward and place my hands on my head, trying to make it stop. When I look at Dr Schaffer, there is a look of judgemental sympathy on her face and I want to get up and punch her until she bleeds. *What do I say? How can I explain? How do I get out of here?*

I need more time with Juliet. I need to be able to finish what I started. I sit up and throw my shoulders back, summoning all my strength.

'Dr Choudry hated me and he's just making up rubbish because he was embarrassed that I helped Juliet more than he did.' My voice wobbles a little as I struggle to control myself. 'He thought he was so clever with all his stupid breathing exercises but he's just an old pervert. I know he touched his patients inappropriately… I know he did and I had to… tell someone and that's why he dislikes me so much…' I trail off and I have a vison of myself standing in a hole with a shovel, digging deeper and deeper when what I need to do is get out.

Abigail and Dr Schaffer exchange a look.

'I think it would be best if, once we're done here, you leave for today,' says Dr Schaffer gently. 'We need to investigate this more thoroughly. I'm sure you understand that we do not want you anywhere near Juliet again.'

'But I need to see her…' I begin.

Abigail stands and looms over me. 'Lacy, there are many things about this situation that are very troubling. When Dr Choudry first came to me with his concerns, I couldn't verify what he was saying one way or the other, and then Juliet left soon after that and she did seem better. I thought it was an isolated incident and we would not see her again but now I must bear some guilt for not looking into this more.'

'He was making things up. He hated me because the patients loved me more than they loved him.'

Dr Schaffer frowns and stands up and I can see I've made another mistake. I want to pull at my own hair, causing myself enough pain to make my stupid words stop spilling out of my mouth.

'We are not here to be loved, Lacy. I am willing to listen if you have an explanation for your attachment to this young woman but you must see that this is not appropriate behaviour.'

In her hand her phone buzzes and, still staring at me, she answers it.

'Oh, yes, thank you for returning my call,' she says, her voice taking on a more official tone. Instead of saying anything else she simply listens, nodding her head, and I don't quite understand why she is so rudely taking a phone call until I realise from the way she keeps looking at me that it must be about me.

'I should go,' I say, standing up. 'I'm not feeling very well.'

'Thank you,' says Dr Schaffer to the person on the phone. 'We'll see you soon.'

I walk towards the door slowly, hoping that they do not stop me, that they will let me go.

'Lacy,' says Dr Schaffer, an edge to her voice, 'please sit down. We have to finish our conversation.'

'No, I...' I keep moving but Abigail touches me on the shoulder to stop me. 'It would be best if you sit down, Lacy.' And for the first time since I met her, Abigail looks like she feels sorry for me and that is almost more than I can bear.

My legs grow weak. I don't know what to do. I need to see Juliet again. I need to. But I slink back to the sofa instead. If I leave, I will never be allowed back into this hospital. And I cannot leave without finishing what I started.

THIRTY-EIGHT

The child, the girl, grows up and the memories recede far into the past. Only when she is angry or sad does she pull them out and examine them, and if she ever discusses them with her parents, they appear mystified by what she is saying. If she talks about them too much, her parents suggest therapy and drugs, and she knows that they will silence her any way they can.

She keeps quiet, concentrating on studying, on getting out of the house, getting away.

Her dream is to become a nurse, to be the one who can stop the pain in others the way nurses have done for her all her life. At eighteen, she leaves, struggling on very little money because she will not take a cent from her parents. But she manages to get through university and become a nurse. She does not speak to her parents for more than a decade. She does not acknowledge their existence until one day, she receives a message from her father at the hospital where she is working. He has tracked her down.

Your mother is dying.

He adds the details of the hospice so that she will know

where to go. She does not want to see her mother but she needs to try, one last time, to get her to admit what she did.

She enters her mother's hospital room slowly on soft nurse's feet. Her father is sitting by the bed, a tall man diminished by age, stooped over with sparse white hair. And she remembers that she was born when he was over forty as was her mother. Perhaps they were too tired to raise a child, to love a child, but that is no excuse.

'Lacy,' says her father, when he sees her.

'I can't stay long,' she says.

He nods his understanding and he gets up from his chair. 'She's in and out.'

Lacy nods.

'I'll leave the two of you together. I'll go get a coffee,' he says and he leaves the room. He does not touch her, does not offer a hug; in fact, he barely even looks at her and that suits her fine.

She doesn't want to sit in the same chair he was sitting in so she drags a plastic chair from its position against the wall and sits on the other side of the bed, her gaze going to the ghost-pale, gaunt woman in the bed. She is wearing a dark grey turban and Lacy knows that underneath, she will be bald. Chemotherapy is harsh on the body and takes a greater toll the older you are. Inside her, a tiny spark of joy fizzes at the woman's suffering.

Sensing her presence, her mother opens her eyes and turns to her. 'Lacy, you came.'

'You're dying. I came because you're dying. I came to tell you—'

Her mother waves her hand. 'Spare me,' she says, her voice dry and cracked. Nurse Lacy would offer water, would offer ice chips, would offer a cool cloth to soothe a brow. Lacy, the daughter, does none of this. She holds onto the plastic arms of the chair, clutching her anger so that she does not leap up and claw at her mother's translucent skin.

'I wanted you to have some pictures,' her mother whispers, 'there, in that box.'

Lacy turns to see a box on a table, a shoebox.

'I don't...' she starts to say but then she stops, wondering what the pictures will show, wondering if she will be able to see the pain and terror on her face or if, somehow, the two-dimensional version of Lacy the child will not reflect the truth. There were always lots of pictures in her house and she has seen them all. Why does her mother want her to look at these? Does she wish to carry Lacy's fabricated childhood all the way to the grave? Is she expecting her daughter to look through the pictures and decide that her childhood was a happy one? It's ridiculous but her mother is dying and this is the last time she will see her. What harm could the pictures do after all the other harms that have been done?

She gets up and picks up the box and then returns to her seat, taking off the lid and flicking through the collection.

There is nothing unusual in the pictures. There she is as a smiling baby, as a happy toddler, an excited pre-schooler clutching a pink lunchbox, a shy five-year-old starting school. The pictures go on and on. Only in two of them can she tell that something else was going on in her house, something other than a normal childhood. In both she is wearing a plaster cast on some part of her body. And then she can see it in her eyes, can read what she knows happened.

'Why did you hurt me?' she asks as she lifts her gaze from the pictures to see her mother watching her. The child who was hurt is still trapped inside her, still waiting for an explanation.

'I never... never hurt you. I loved you. There was always something... something wrong with you.' Her mother's words are gasps as her lungs try for air. 'You cried so much when you were... a baby. You were not... good like other children. You tortured me... hated me... just tortured me.' She wheezes and coughs. 'You were supposed to be my dream... real... realised... but you were a night... a nightmare.' There is more coughing, the woman's body convulsing in the bed with the force of it.

Lacy doesn't ask if she needs help, doesn't call a nurse. Instead, she keeps going through the pictures until she has reached the bottom of the box and she pulls out the last picture.

It's of a woman, a very young woman, and a baby.

They are in a hospital bed, the woman's legs trapped under tightly tucked sheets, the baby wrapped in a pink, blue and yellow striped blanket.

'Who's this?' she asks her mother, showing her the photo, but her mother just closes her eyes.

Lacy stares down at the young woman, wondering who she could be. Her parents are only children, just as she is, or at least, that's what they've always told her. She has no other relatives because her grandparents are dead on both sides.

She sits back in the chair and stares down at the picture, wondering who the young woman is. It's an old picture, slightly degraded, so the young woman's face is unclear. Is this her mother? Is this her mother with another baby? Does she have a sister? Did she have a sister? The woman in the picture does not resemble her mother; in fact, she looks to be a teenager still – so who is she?

Her father returns to the room. 'Who's this?' she asks him and he looks at the picture. 'Where did you get that?'

'At the bottom of the box. Who is it?'

'No one, it's no one, just put it back.'

'No,' says Lacy, standing up and dropping the box on the bed. 'I'm keeping this one.'

'It's not yours to keep,' says her father as his eyes dart from side to side, refusing to land on her face.

'It is now,' she says.

He steps towards her, his hand out to take the picture but she pushes past him and he falls backwards, against a wall.

'You were always a problem,' he says. 'Always!' he yells.

She doesn't answer him, doesn't even stay to listen as he begins to say something else.

She leaves with the picture clutched in her hand, determined to find out who the young woman is and who the baby she is holding is. The idea that there is someone out there related to her, possibly related to her, an aunt or a cousin, someone, anyone who could tell her why her parents were so awful, what made them evil, is a hope she clings to.

When her mother dies, she does not go to the funeral. She asks her father once more, in a text message, who the girl in the photograph is but he never replies and she never asks again.

She puts her parents behind her, even as she uploads the image and searches for it all over the internet. Two years pass and the picture is just something she looks at now and again as she continues to treat all the broken people and move on with her life.

And then she meets a man and falls in love and they are everything to each other. They both come from nothing, although he has love for his parents, a love that she is jealous of. They promise each other they will work hard together, struggle together to build a life. It will all be fine and one day they will have a happy family home. She believes that she will have the life she has always craved.

'We'll never have enough money,' they say to each other when they look at the price of houses in Sydney but they keep hoping.

And then one day, Lacy has a new patient, a damaged young woman who comes with a collection of beautiful photographs, memories of a loving childhood. They have been packed by her mother in the hope that they will keep her tethered to the world so that she will not try to take her life again.

Lacy sits with the young woman, going through the photographs, trying to control her envy until she gets to one particular photograph of the young woman.

'Who's that?' she asks her.

'Me and my mum, just after I was born,' says the young woman.

A coincidence, a shifting moment in time, something that should never have happened except for two people coming together by chance and an old photograph being shared.

'Me and my mum,' the young woman has said. 'Me and my mum.'

And Lacy's whole world falls apart.

THIRTY-NINE

Lacy

The three of us sit in a widening gulf of silence in Dr Schaffer's office.

A sharp pain begins behind my eye, causing me to wince, but neither one of them asks me what's wrong.

The cream-coloured internal phone on Dr Schaffer's desk rings and she stands and goes to answer it.

I hear someone shouting and then Dr Schaffer says, 'Yes, yes, okay, I'm coming.'

'What is it?' asks Abigail, standing up.

'Two of our patients are fighting in the dining room,' says Dr Schaffer, her exasperation at this development obvious.

Abigail says, 'We're short-staffed, I'd better go and help.'

'I'll come with you,' says Dr Schaffer and they both go to leave, forgetting, in their panic, that I am sitting there. I should offer to help but would they want me to? I have no idea.

At the door, Dr Schaffer stops and turns to me. 'Lacy, Detective McDougal is coming to speak to you, just to see if there is anything more you know. Please wait here.' That's not why he's coming to speak to me and I know it.

She is saying it like I am here of my own free will, like I'm just going to wait to have a little chat with the detective, but I'm not stupid. I need to leave now. The doctor hovers at the door for a moment, as if questioning whether or not she should leave. But then a scream floats through the air. And I am so grateful the fight has started. It will help.

'If you wish to continue being employed by St Augustine, you won't move,' says Dr Schaffer, darting off.

I was going to play this one way and now I think I will have to shift things. But I certainly won't stay here unless they lock me in.

And they wouldn't do that. I nod quickly and sit back against the sofa pillows as though I mean to stay right here like a good little girl.

I hear more shouting. It must be chaos in the dining room. Fights are rare but they do happen, and when they do, they tend to fold in whoever is around. Chaos is attracted to chaos and there are probably a few patients now that need to be separated. Some of them will need to be sedated.

I wait until I hear the click of the door closing and then I get up and go over to it, leaning my ear up against the pale timber. With my eyes closed, I will my headache to disappear and I concentrate hard to hear the sound of footsteps walking or running away.

When I know they are gone, I turn back to Dr Schaffer's desk and grab the photo of Juliet and her mother. In the pocket of my scrubs, I have the photo I took from my dying mother, the photo that told a different story of my life, the story I could never find until I met Juliet.

I take it out and put the two photos together, as I have done many times.

Susan in 2004 looks just like Susan in 1989, as though the

years have not passed at all. In the first picture she is obviously a teenager, fifteen, maybe sixteen, and her hair is long but the distinctive shape of her face, the bright blue of her eyes, the way she is holding the child are easily recognisable. Except in the photo from 1989, she is not happy, not gazing down with love but instead looks frightened. I only noticed the difference when both pictures were together.

It took me some time to find the truth, to trace it all back with the help of a website that finds information on closed adoptions. And once I knew it, my rage was all-consuming. It was so unfair, so horribly unfair. The life I craved was the life I should have lived. Another child lived the life I was supposed to live. And I hated that child for it. I hated my birth mother, my real mother, for it as well.

I couldn't sleep at night because of the fury that raced around my body.

When I told Nathan, he told me to introduce myself to Juliet's parents. To tell Susan, Juliet's mother, that she was *my* mother too. That I knew the truth.

'Maybe they're nice people. Maybe she always wanted to meet you.'

That is the one great difference between me and Nathan. He has hope for people. His parents are sweet and kind and loved him and so he thinks the world is generally a nice place, except for the fact that he never has enough money – he is consumed by that, by the fact that he wasn't able to afford university. He talked about money a lot, more than most people, and that's why I thought he would help me. I promised him a future with lots of money.

But Nathan was weak. Too weak to do what needed to be done. He panicked and failed but I won't fail.

My parents were not just abusive. They were gaslighting monsters and they weren't even my real parents. Juliet had the life I should have had. She had the money, the privilege, the love that should have been mine. And she didn't even appreciate it.

I had a plan for today. It involved pills I have stolen. There are two more vials of temazepam that contain substituted pills as Abigail will soon find out. They were all for Juliet. Last time we had to watch her take her sleeping pills and this time, she has been watched as well, but it's possible that she has found a way to only look like she is taking them, possible that she has been hiding them instead. That's what I hoped everyone would assume. She threw a fit yesterday. It would not have been too much of a stretch to believe that she took her own life today, especially once she realised that 'Adam' didn't exist.

Now the plan is ruined. But maybe I can still get what I want.

Folding both photographs up, deliberately creasing them over Susan's face, and shoving them in my pocket, I open the office door. There is no one in the corridor and I can hear yelling and the clatter of breaking dishes coming from the dining room. I hope Juliet is not there, that she is in her room.

Mementos become very important to patients in this hospital when they are away from their families and the outside world. Most come with pictures of loved ones to remind them of why they are fighting to heal themselves. In the last few days, I have been moving them around, placing pictures belonging to one patient into the drawers of another. It's difficult to get enough time with Juliet during the day. I needed the other staff to be distracted and I have been waiting for an argument to break out, for two patients to accuse each other of theft. It may not have happened when I was here and then I would have had to find another way. But as it turns out, luck has gone my way, for probably the very first time in my life. The timing is perfect.

Next to Juliet's room, there is a supply cupboard, filled with everything that might be needed for general first aid. Nothing in the cupboard is dangerous because even though it's locked, patients can be very clever about getting access to things, but at the bottom, behind a box of crepe bandages, I have hidden a small silver scalpel.

I bought it with my own money last week and placed it there just in case. I will not have the time to give her any more pills. This is my insurance policy.

In the other pocket of my scrubs is the key to the cupboard that Abigail did not think to take from me. I make my way over to the cupboard quickly, unlocking it as I glance around me, panicked that someone may come along. But I am quick, and with the scalpel in my hand, I open the door to Juliet's room.

She is, as I had hoped, asleep. The sedative they gave her yesterday would have made her really groggy and the apple juice I left for her by her bed would have made it worse. I added three pills to it but I knew I needed to do more today. I didn't want her found and helped last night. I can see by the empty glass that she has drunk it all.

I'm pleased. One more thing has gone my way. I wanted to have one more day to feed her many glasses of apple juice, but now I have run out of time and so the scalpel will have to open up old wounds.

Her parents were supposed to die and then Juliet was supposed to die and then there I would be holding out my hand with my DNA test and my sad story for anyone who was interested.

'It won't work,' Nathan said.

'We will have millions if it does,' I said. And that's why he helped. He loved me. I think he loved me but he still failed and now he is done with me.

It wasn't actually the money I wanted. I wanted Juliet to know what I had felt like growing up, what I had gone through. So I gave her my childhood at night, whispered the stories as she dozed in her bed after a doctored cup of chamomile tea, told her over and again that her parents were abusive. I told her my troubles, gave her the pain of my past, and when she was filled with my stories, I knew she just needed a small push in the right direction to make the woman who gave me away to people who abused me pay for her crimes.

Susan should never have given me up. She should never have allowed me to be raised by monsters.

And if she had no other choice, she should have left the adoption open so that I would be able to find her and claim the life that was mine.

I wanted Susan to suffer along with her daughter. And I know she must have suffered. Juliet would tell me at night about making her mother cry in family sessions.

'If she hurt you, she deserves it,' I comforted her. 'It's her own fault.'

And now Susan is in a coma, and after this, I will make sure she doesn't wake up. I can still hear shouting from the dining room as I close the door behind me and I am grateful that the sound is now muffled.

With the scalpel gripped tightly in my hand, I walk slowly towards Juliet.

'Hello, Juliet,' I say to her sleeping form. 'It's your sister.'

FORTY

Lacy

Sitting down on the bed, I take one of her hands in mine and run my finger across the raised scar on her wrist. It will be so quick. And she is so deeply asleep, she won't even feel it. I may have overdone it with the pills but it's hard to know exactly how much is needed. Her parents had too little because they only got through one drink.

A beautiful and perfect plan fell apart because I needed help from a man, from a man I loved, or thought I did. I planted the seeds while Juliet was in hospital. Nathan needed to make sure the flower of hate grew in Juliet. And then he needed to finish what I started. But he failed.

The room is bright with autumn light from a beautiful blue-sky day, and I think, as I stare down at her with her blonde hair across the pillow, that she looks just like Sleeping Beauty. But no prince will come along to wake her. I thought I found my prince in Nathan. He was willing to do so much for me, even to turn himself into someone else, but I know he got queasy in the end about what we were doing. He didn't give them enough.

He should pay for that. But I can't think about him now.

I touch the scalpel to her skin, and I take a breath. The shouting from the dining room disappears as I concentrate on exactly what I'm doing.

I press down, just enough to test if she will wake up or not, but she doesn't stir and then I press a little harder and a drop of blood appears. Juliet moans, her eyelids struggling and failing to open. I push harder and more blood appears. I need to be quicker about this or I will be caught here. It's going to leave a lot of mess. But it will be a mess that I don't have to clean up.

As I push down harder, I think about why I became a nurse. I wanted to be the one to take away pain but here I am administering it; perhaps this will take away the greatest pain of all. It will take away my pain.

'Lacy, stop,' I hear and I startle, turning my head to the voice, even as I keep the scalpel against her skin.

Nathan is standing in the room. I didn't even hear the door open. But he is here.

'Nathan?' I say, wondering if perhaps I have imagined him here. But he is here and I know it's because he has come to help me.

'You changed your mind,' I say, feeling delight inside me at his love and loyalty, but he shakes his head.

And it is then that I see he is not alone.

Abigail is here as well, standing behind him. Dr Schaffer is next to him and the detective with the long face is here too. They are all watching me. The detective has his hand by his side as though he is holding on to something. When did they all get here? How did I not notice?

I was concentrating, lost, wrapped up in this all being over, at finally freeing myself from the awfulness that I grew up with.

'Please don't do anything, Lacy,' says Nathan. 'Just put it down and we can talk.'

'You don't want to do this, remember,' I say softly. I look at him and admire his brown eyes and his brown curls, the same way Juliet admired them, I'm sure, when he was Adam. He has kind eyes and I liked when they were focused on me but I think he didn't just play with Juliet, didn't just do what I told him to do. I think he might have fallen for her because who wouldn't? She is a fragile princess and everyone loves a fragile princess.

'I don't want to… no. I don't want you to do it either. We were very wrong,' he says and he takes a step towards me. 'I sent the police to her house to help her and her parents. I couldn't… I went back and unlocked the door like you said to but then she was crying and asking to be let out and her parents were… I just couldn't do it, Lacy.' He takes another step towards me.

'Don't,' I say, pressing down a little harder, and more blood appears. Juliet moans again and shifts in the bed.

I move the scalpel to her throat so that they know not to try anything. 'Don't come near us.'

Dr Schaffer raises her hands. 'Now please, Lacy, please, you don't want to do anything stupid. You don't want to hurt Juliet. She hasn't done anything wrong.'

'She did everything wrong!' I shriek, hating how hysterical I sound. 'She had everything, everything that I should have had, and she didn't appreciate it.' I am ashamed that tears appear. I haven't cried in a very long time. I taught myself not to cry, not to show fear or pain. I taught myself to be strong but I am feeling so weak now. It's all gone wrong.

'I don't think that's true. Nathan has told us everything. I know that you have suffered and that's not fair but Juliet is not responsible for that suffering. I think she is a struggling young woman and she had no idea that you were related to her. She would like to meet you, I'm sure. She would welcome a sister.'

'No, she wouldn't. She is spoiled and ungrateful.' I push the scalpel against Juliet's throat. I'm glad that she is not awake to stare at me with those pathetic large blue eyes. A stripe of blood appears by her throat, dark red and bright against her pale neck.

'She has no idea what struggle is,' I whisper.

'I need you to put down the scalpel, Lacy,' says the detective softly. 'Put it down now and everything will be okay.' He comes towards me and I can see that he is holding his gun now, and that he is pointing it at me.

Shaking my head, I sniff, embarrassed about my tears. 'Nothing will be okay. 'Everyone was supposed to think she killed her parents and then killed herself. She had found out so many terrible things in the hospital after all. People who try suicide are often known to try again and succeed. And then it all would have been mine. Do you understand? I planned it all. I had the pills prescribed for myself over months and all Nathan had to do was use them properly. She was never supposed to come back to this place. She was supposed to be dead.' I take a deep breath and sit up straight knowing that my plan was good and right. 'But when she came back, I adjusted, I rethought everything, and I knew that if she killed herself, things would still go my way.'

'But that can't happen now,' says the detective. 'It can't happen and you know that because we are all watching. If she dies, it will be your fault and you don't want that. You're a nurse. You help people.' His voice is even and calm and I think about what he's saying. He's right. I do help people.

I move the scalpel away from Juliet's neck and grab a tissue, dabbing at the blood. I am a nurse after all.

'I don't help people who don't deserve it,' I whisper as I move the scalpel back to within cutting distance. Necks are so soft, so easy to slice through. She could be dead in moments but now all these people are here and I am hesitant to do this in front of all of them. People struggle with the sight of blood.

'You need to leave, all of you. You need to leave or I will kill her.' I take a deep breath, keeping myself calm. Getting upset never does any good. Mostly it just causes more pain. I learned that growing up.

'Lacy,' I hear Nathan say. 'It's over, just put it down.'

'No, no, I can't do that, she deserves to die, you know that. Just like her mother. They deserve to die.'

'I know.'

'She's such a whiny bitch. Imagine getting depressed because you couldn't be a dancer anymore.' I snort. 'I never had the chance to do that, Nathan. My mother broke my ankle when I was ten and it never healed properly.' I stare down at Juliet's white neck as I speak. I need to concentrate.

'I know.'

'I was raised by monsters.'

'You were but Juliet's mum didn't know that. She thought giving you up for adoption was the best thing to do.'

'I don't believe that,' I say and I feel calm, as though I am floating. 'Why are you here, Nathan? I don't want you to get into trouble.' I turn my head to see him. He is standing so close that I can smell his aftershave. I love the smell, the tingling freshness of it.

'I went to the police this morning,' he says. 'I... told them everything, everything we had planned, everything you did. Everything I did. We couldn't... It wasn't right. Juliet is not a bad person, Lacy. None of this is her fault and her parents aren't bad people either. What we did was wrong, very wrong, and I... just couldn't do it anymore. You've tried to drive her crazy and we... we got caught up in the idea of the money but it's not right. I'm sorry.' His beautiful brown eyes have filled with tears. He is weak. I should have seen that but I loved him and I thought he loved me.

I feel his betrayal as though the scalpel is slicing into my heart.

'I need to do this,' I say, pressing the scalpel into her neck and watching as scarlet blood dribbles out.

I push harder as I sense the detective moving closer. 'I will kill her,' I whisper and he stops moving but I'm going to kill her anyway.

All three of them were supposed to die, Juliet and her parents. It was all supposed to be over in one night and then he messed it all up. I thought my chance was over, once he failed. I never expected them to send her back here but they did. And I took that as a sign. I need to do this. I should do this. It's the right thing.

My hand is sweating and I grip the scalpel harder as it slips. I push down again and she opens her eyes, big and blue, sad little girl eyes.

'Lacy,' she whispers.

I am shocked at her voice and I sit back a little. And it is then that the detective comes for me.

Grabbing the hand holding the scalpel, he twists my arm behind my back until it hurts and I drop the scalpel, hearing myself whimper.

I feel my body go limp and I let him wrench my other arm behind me as well, feel plastic tighten around my wrists.

He hauls me up off the bed. 'It will be okay,' he says but that's not the truth. He is lying to me just like my parents did, just like Nathan did when he said he wanted to help me. Everyone who is supposed to love me lies to me. The detective doesn't love me but why shouldn't he do the same thing?

The room erupts in noise and confusion, shouting and rushing as the detective pushes me out in front of him, removing me from Juliet.

I am forced to walk down the corridor, my face burning with humiliation as I am judged by the patients who I treated yesterday, by the nurses I work with, by Martha with her noisy tea trolley.

And I feel, as the detective and I emerge into the cool autumn air, that my parents, the people who raised me, have won. They have destroyed me because they have made me destroy myself in my quest for the life I was supposed to live.

They have won because they never loved me and, truly, no one ever has.

FORTY-ONE

Juliet

She is stuck somewhere dark, and she can't get out. And there is
pain on her wrist, and then by her neck. Her eyes are glued shut
but the pain is pulling them open. Light appears and she sees
Lacy. But she doesn't look like Lacy. 'Lacy,' she says and then
the darkness pulls her back again.

She sinks down and thinks she can see her mother and
father at the kitchen table. They are sitting together, a plate of
chocolate muffins in front of them, and Juliet is so happy to see
them.

'I'm sorry,' she tells them. 'I was wrong and I'm sorry.' But
they don't look at her. They just sit, staring at nothing. 'I'm
sorry,' she shouts and she moves to touch them but something is
holding her back. She can't get to them.

Her body is being touched. She can hear voices and
shouting and then someone is shaking her. Rough hands are
pulling her out of the darkness. 'Juliet, Juliet, wake up,
wake up.'

Her heavy eyelids struggle to open. She wants to shake off the hands, to block her ears, but she can't.

Forcing her body to find the strength she needs, she opens her mouth. 'Stop,' she breathes, 'just stop.' And then she manages to open her eyes, squinting in the light.

Dr Schaffer is looking down at her. 'Thank God,' she says.

Juliet wants to be asleep again, cannot be awake now because Lacy told her that Adam doesn't exist. He doesn't exist. She made him up and she was the one who killed her parents.

Her parents are dead. Did she want them dead? No, no, no.

'Listen to me, Juliet,' says the doctor, shaking her, 'try to stay awake, you need to try and wake up. I'm going to use cold water on you.'

A freezing-cold square of towelling touches her face, shocking her into taking a deep breath, and she struggles to get it off her face.

'Good, good,' says the doctor, 'you're going to be okay. I think you'll be fine.'

'My parents are dead,' Juliet cries, the words coming straight from her broken heart. 'I want to die.'

'No, Juliet… no, stay with me.'

But she can't stay. She needs to get back to the kitchen so she can talk to her parents. She needs them to understand that she is sorry. The darkness is pulling at her, dragging her down again. It is too strong. It cannot be fought with cold or voices. She wants to be in the darkness because she can also see some light. There is light and she knows if she can get to it, her parents will be there waiting for her and she can tell them that she didn't want them to die. She didn't.

'Will she be okay?' she hears a man ask. 'Will she be okay?'

She recognises the voice. It's Adam. He said he would come and he did. He has come for her. He promised and he kept his promise. It's too late but he kept his promise.

He came for her.

EPILOGUE
THREE MONTHS LATER

Juliet

Juliet opens her eyes in the dark of the winter morning. Turning on her side, she glances at the clock on her bedside table: 5.55.

She's accepted this time now. Looking it up on the web one day, she read that it's an angel number that signifies change, transformation and growth. She's not sure she believes in angels but she's also not sure she doesn't believe in them.

Because an angel must have been watching over her and her parents during the very worst time of their lives. It all could have ended very differently. And it nearly did.

Getting out of bed, she shivers in the cold air as she dresses quickly for her walk.

On the floor, snuggled up under his blanket, Oscar opens one eye and then uncurls himself, stretching luxuriously the way he always does, making her smile as she leans down and rubs his belly.

'Walk time,' says Juliet as she stands and ties her hair back. The goldendoodle shakes his caramel-coloured head, standing and stretching again.

Downstairs in the kitchen, her mother is waiting, warmly dressed and ready.

'How long have you been up?' Juliet asks and her mother smiles.

'A while.' Her mother doesn't sleep much anymore, not since she woke from her coma. She woke first to be told her husband had suffered a minor heart attack. She hovers over him now, watching him in a way that irritates him, but at least he is here to be irritated.

'I'm...' Juliet begins, an apology forming.

'Don't do that,' her mother says before Juliet can even allow the heavy burden of guilt to pounce on her. Because her mother knows that the guilt Juliet feels over what happened is always just behind her, waiting for her to drop her guard.

'I'll get his harness on him; give yourself a moment to let it all go,' says her mother and Juliet nods. When her mother has left the kitchen, Juliet sits down on a chair and touches the timber table with her hands, holding herself here in the present.

It's better to sit here for a moment alone than to talk to her mother because her mother is dealing with her own demons as she comes to terms with the fact that Lacy was the baby she gave up for adoption at sixteen. 'Her parents insisted on a closed adoption and I thought they had been thoroughly checked out. I thought they were good people,' she said, her voice heavy with horror when she found out. She has repeated this many times since.

Lacy's biological father was someone she had a brief relationship with who then disappeared the moment she told him she was pregnant. Through the police, she has sent the name to Lacy, just a name and a brief description of who the man is. He may not even be alive anymore. The world changes in an instant and the future is never certain.

'I knew I couldn't take care of a child and I was fortunate to have parents who supported my decision to have the baby and give it up for adoption. I thought I was doing the right thing. I hoped to give a couple a chance to be a family. I was told they were lovely people,' her mother has explained.

'Why didn't you ever tell me about her?' Juliet asked, only once.

'I don't know. It felt like a mistake that I made and I didn't want it to affect the rest of my life. I should have told you. I should have looked for her but... it was so traumatic that I just... wanted to leave it in the past.'

Juliet believes it is her mother's right to want that, to have wanted that.

The irony is that if Lacy had told Juliet the truth, both she and her parents would have welcomed Lacy into their family. It would not have made up for her horrible childhood but they would have, perhaps, been able to show her some of the love she deeply desired.

Although it seems that Lacy was far too damaged for a hopeful future. Juliet keeps remembering the night Lacy told her about the worry dolls that children are given in Guatemala. Lacy said she would be Juliet's worry doll but it was the other way around as Lacy sat next to her bed and whispered all her terrible memories into Juliet's head, unburdening herself of her past. But that wasn't enough for Lacy and so she had to convince Juliet that the memories were hers.

Part of what Juliet is struggling with is that she was weak enough to allow this to happen.

'Not weak, but suffering and feeling alone,' Juliet whispers in the quiet kitchen. 'But that's the past. It's over.'

Her mother and father didn't die. They were not given enough alcohol combined with temazepam to cause their deaths.

Juliet doesn't know if this was because Adam who is really

Nathan gave them less than Lacy instructed or because they only managed one drink before they were both asleep. She likes to think it was because he didn't give them enough on purpose and that he never gave her any because he felt something for her. He did call the police so they would all be found, which Juliet will never stop being grateful for.

'Perhaps if they had a higher tolerance for alcohol, they would have ingested a great deal more. As it was, the first cocktail was strong and they were both asleep by the time "Adam" had locked you in your basement. He couldn't get them to drink any more and then he panicked and left and only came back a couple of days later to open the padlock and use your phone to call the police,' Detective McDougal explained when Juliet was finally awake enough to understand. 'He had recorded every conversation the two of you had ever had and he managed to put together a voice call for emergency services. He has said that he felt terrible after he locked you in. Eventually he couldn't live with it and came to us to confess.'

Adam/Nathan understood that what he was doing was very wrong.

Neither Juliet nor her parents were supposed to live.

And then, Lacy would have gone to the authorities and proved that she was the only relative still living. 'Police will think it's a murder-suicide,' she told Nathan. 'Her parents were abusive and she was sent home to live with them again. Anyone could have seen what would happen.'

But then Adam/Nathan couldn't go through with giving Juliet the drugged drink. Guilt or love? Juliet will never know.

Lacy believed that she would inherit everything. Would it have worked? Maybe, but maybe not.

It was more important to Lacy that all three of them were dead and that they had all suffered on their way to that death. Something inside Lacy is very broken and beyond repair.

Juliet knows that she was supposed to lose everything, even

her life, and it stuns her now to think that she tried to do that to herself, that there was a time when she could not see her way out of her dark depression over the loss of her career.

She did not lose her parents although she did lose many months of her life, her belief in the medical system and her ability to trust people. She has lost faith in herself and her memories.

It has been difficult, on the bad days, to remind herself that she was ill and being manipulated by someone she has come to think of as truly evil.

Despite this, she also has moments of overwhelming sympathy for Lacy. The X-rays she saw of a broken wrist, ankle, ribs and fingers actually do exist, except they are Lacy's X-rays. Lacy's childhood was a confusing and terrible time and Juliet knows that it fundamentally changed the way Lacy sees the world.

Benji died in a hit and run but that was pure coincidence. He had been on his way to see her when he was hit by a car. But his death did prompt Adam/Nathan to begin questioning what he was doing and why he was doing it. He assumed Lacy was responsible although he still went ahead with some of the plan.

Lacy's lawyer is trying to get her declared mentally unfit to stand trial. Adam/Nathan has admitted his guilt, and the help he has given the police will be taken into consideration at his sentencing later in the year. Lacy was the one who reported Dr Choudry for sexual misconduct with another patient in an effort to get rid of him because she knew he was suspicious of her. She needed Dr Choudry out of the way because he was going to get her fired.

Juliet has testified to everything Adam/Nathan did, but she was able to do it via a computer link, sitting in Dr Schaffer's office, and she hopes she will be able to do the same when it comes to Lacy. She doesn't trust herself to see Adam/Nathan again. She has no idea how she will react.

And that's why she hasn't opened the letter he sent. It came from prison, the return address shocking to see. She gave it to her mother to keep, not wanting to throw it out and not wanting to read it. Not yet. Will she ever be ready? She's not sure.

But now, she needs to find a way forward in her life. She is on medication and she will be seeing Dr Schaffer every week for as long as she needs to. There is always a way forward. It's hard, sometimes almost impossible, but there is a way forward out of the darkness.

Her world is a different place now. And a lonely place. How will she ever love someone, trust someone? It feels impossible but she is, as Dr Schaffer keeps reminding her, only twenty-two. Her birthday was quiet, just her and her parents, but her present of Oscar is the best thing she's ever received. The little dog makes her smile more times a day than she can believe. And sometimes, he will listen to her talk, cocking his head to one side as she tells him everything she is thinking and feeling and then he will lick her face if she cries.

'A terrible thing happened to you, Juliet,' Dr Schaffer told her only yesterday at her appointment, 'but you're still here, and your parents survived and they have forgiven you. Don't give up now. Live your life the best way you can.'

She knows she has to find a way to exist in the world, a way to live her life. One thing she does have is her parents' help and support. 'Take your time, get on your feet again,' her father says when they talk about her future.

In the first weeks after they woke up, Juliet apologised to her parents so many times that eventually they asked her to stop.

They know how she feels. And it was not her fault. 'It wasn't my fault,' she whispers as she stands and goes to pull on her jacket against the early-morning chill.

Later today she is meeting with her old ballet teacher, Lizette, who contacted her last week to ask if she would consider teaching a class of seven-year-olds. Teaching has never appealed to her before but she remembered walking into her first class with her mother and how that felt and so she has agreed to meet with Lizette and discuss it, just discuss it.

Outside, the first slivers of light are beginning to appear and Oscar is bouncing with energy.

'Okay?' asks her mother.

'Okay,' says Juliet.

'We love you,' her mother says softly as they begin to walk.

'I know,' says Juliet because she does know.

They love her and they always have.

Dear Juliet,

I don't know if you will ever read this but I hope you do. There's so much I want to say to you, to explain, but I know that you might not want to hear it.

I never wanted things to go so far.

You have to understand that I was in awe when Lacy started speaking to me. She's a nurse, someone capable, efficient and educated, someone who helps people. I thought she would always ignore the guy who only worked in the laundry. And when she started speaking to me and eventually agreed to a date, I was over the moon. I really loved her. I knew that I would do anything for her.

When she told me about her childhood, I was so angry for her. I wanted to make it better and that's why I agreed to the plan. And for the money. I'm not going to lie and say that didn't have something to do with it.

Before I met you, I thought you were what she described, a spoiled, entitled brat who didn't deserve anything she had.

But you're not like that. Getting to know you showed me who you really are.

It was so hard to play pretend with you even as I really fell for you. I had to stay out of sight and never be seen with you. I even gave the waitress at the café money to tell you that you hadn't paid and that you were alone. I told her it was a prank for TikTok and that you would find it funny. I felt really awful about that. I felt awful about a lot of things but I had to do what Lacy told me to because I was afraid I would lose her. But then things changed and I realised that maybe... maybe she wasn't the woman for me. Maybe it was you and that's why I didn't put the pills in your drink. It's why I told you I was sorry when I came back and why I eventually went to the police and confessed.

You were supposed to die but I thought if I could get your parents to give us a whole lot of money, Lacy would be happy to leave you alone. But that wasn't enough for her.

I couldn't hurt you the way she needed me to and I know that made her angry. I know I ruined her plan.

I did love her but when I saw what she was capable of, when she explained what she was going to do once you came back to the hospital, I felt like I didn't know her at all. She was going to make sure that neither you nor your parents survived after I supposedly messed things up and I knew I had to help you, to save you.

I'm glad we stopped Lacy from hurting you. I'm glad I helped save you.

I hope that you will forgive me, forgive me for everything, and that one day, when I'm free again, you'll let me take you out, just the two of us, on a real date as Nathan and Juliet.

Because the thing is, Juliet, I love you and I have a feeling I always will.

Love, Nathan (Adam)

Lacy

Being a nurse gives you a certain status here. The other women come to me when they are feeling unwell or when they have hurt themselves.

I have yet to share why I am here. All I have said when asked the question directly is, 'Difficulties with my family.' Whoever I say this to asks nothing further. Instead, they nod their understanding of just how complicated family relationships can be.

If they have seen the few news reports on what happened, they don't mention it. People are discreet in here, in the same way we were discreet at the St Augustine.

I think I will be here for many years and there is, strangely, a kind of relief in that. My lawyer did not succeed in having me declared crazy. But then, I am not crazy.

I was trying to *help* Juliet finish the job she had done so poorly.

I will not get married. I will not have children. I will emerge from prison older and wiser and perhaps, just perhaps, better at getting what I want. That's the hope I am holding on to now.

I understand that no one will come to visit me and no one cares I am here.

But I won't let them forget about me. I want them to think of me always, to remember, and to worry about what happens one day when I am no longer locked away.

And so today I am writing letters. Some people might say that one repeated sentence cannot be considered a proper letter, but I wanted to make my message clear. I have covered three separate pages. One for my father, one for my biological mother and one for Juliet. None of this was my fault. They need to know that. Everything that happened is because of them. Because of their abuse, their negligence, their stupidity.

I have covered each page with a message, a reminder, something for them to think about. Just one question.

What have you done?
What have you done?
What have you done?

Hello,

I would like to thank you for taking the time to read *What Have You Done?* If you enjoyed this novel and want to keep up to date with all my latest releases, just sign up at the following link. Your email address will never be shared and you can unsubscribe at any time.

www.bookouture.com/nicole-trope

This was a complicated cast of characters to write about.

I felt deeply sorry for Juliet who was a fragile young woman, easily manipulated. Ballet was her life and I am sure it would be very difficult to lose your future in an instant.

And I felt sympathy for Lacy, an abused child whose anger at discovering the truth about herself turned her into an abuser.

But I felt mostly for Juliet's parents. A grown child who is making accusations of abuse would be a terrible thing to have to endure.

Juliet's parents were innocent but continued to try and love and support her. Lacy's parents were guilty and continued to lie to her until the end. No parent is perfect but no child is either.

I believe that Juliet will be happy as a ballet teacher and that she will move forward with her life and find a way to trust someone new so that she can eventually have the happy ending. I think she will open Nathan's letter one day, far into the future and by then, she will be able to simply shake her head, finding what she went through to be a surreal nightmarish memory and nothing more.

Lacy will never be happy because she will always be consumed by the past and by what she should have had. I see her clinging to that forever.

As always, I will be so grateful if you leave a review for the novel, especially if you loved the book and can avoid those pesky spoilers.

I love hearing from my readers – you can get in touch on social media. I try to reply to each message I receive.

Thanks again for reading,

Nicole x

 facebook.com/NicoleTrope

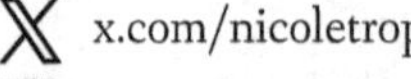 x.com/nicoletrope

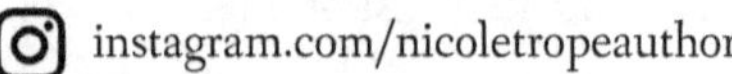 instagram.com/nicoletropeauthor

ACKNOWLEDGEMENTS

My first thank you, as usual, goes to Ellen Gleeson for helping me whip this story into shape.

I would also like to thank Jess Readett for publicity.

Thanks to DeAndra Lupu for the copy edit, Liz Hatherell for the proofread and Mandy Kullar for making sure everything is just right.

Thanks to the whole team at Bookouture, including Jenny Geras, Peta Nightingale, Richard King, Alba Proko, Ruth Tross and everyone else involved in producing my audio books and selling rights, and spreading the word on my novels.

Thanks to my mother, Hilary, for once again reading this novel twice.

Thanks also to David, Mikhayla, Isabella, Jacob and Jax.

And thank you to those who read, review and blog about my work and contact me on social media to let me know you loved the book. I love hearing your stories and reasons why you have connected with a novel.

Every review is appreciated and I do read them all.

PUBLISHING TEAM

Turning a manuscript into a book requires the efforts of many people. The publishing team at Bookouture would like to acknowledge everyone who contributed to this publication.

Audio
Alba Proko
Sinead O'Connor
Melissa Tran

Commercial
Lauren Morrissette
Hannah Richmond
Imogen Allport

Cover design
Head Design Ltd

Data and analysis
Mark Alder
Mohamed Bussuri

Editorial
Ellen Gleeson
Nadia Michael

Copyeditor
DeAndra Lupu

Proofreader
Liz Hatherell

Marketing
Alex Crow
Melanie Price
Occy Carr
Cíara Rosney
Martyna Młynarska

Operations and distribution
Marina Valles
Stephanie Straub
Joe Morris

Production
Hannah Snetsinger
Mandy Kullar
Nadia Michael
Charlotte Hegley

Publicity
Kim Nash
Noelle Holten
Jess Readett
Sarah Hardy

Rights and contracts
Peta Nightingale
Richard King
Saidah Graham

Dear Reader,

We'd love your attention for one more page to tell you about the crisis in children's reading, and what we can all do.

Studies have shown that reading for fun is the **single biggest predictor of a child's future life chances** – more than family circumstance, parents' educational background or income. It improves academic results, mental health, wealth, communication skills, ambition and happiness.

The number of children reading for fun is in rapid decline. Young people have a lot of competition for their time, and a worryingly high number do not have a single book at home.

Hachette works extensively with schools, libraries and literacy charities, but here are some ways we can all raise more readers:

- Reading to children for just 10 minutes a day makes a difference
- Don't give up if children aren't regular readers – there will be books for them!

- Visit bookshops and libraries to get recommendations
- Encourage them to listen to audiobooks
- Support school libraries
- Give books as gifts

There's a lot more information about how to encourage children to read on our websites: **www.RaisingReaders.co.uk** and **www.JoinRaisingReaders.com**.

Thank you for reading.